STILETTOS
&
STARDUST

First published in 2019 in the United States
by Straight on till Morningside Prints

Cover Design by Sarah Anderson of No Synonym Book Covers

ISBN 978-0998794594

Straight on till Morningside Prints
11923 NE Sumner St., STE 709378
Portland, OR 97220

www.DLPitchford.com

A GENDER SWAPPED CINDERELLA STORY

STILETTOS & STARDUST

TRUE LOVE'S WISH

BOOK 1

D. L. PITCHFORD

BOOKS BY D. L. PITCHFORD

TRUE LOVE'S WISH SERIES
Stilettos & Stardust
Roses & Revelry
Spindles & Spelunking

BILLIE DIXON SERIES
If We Had No Winter
The Longer We Dwell
Who We Might've Been
Every Time We Fall

ANTHOLOGIES
Dreams of Darkness

FOR ALL YOUNG SCIENTISTS IN THE MAKING

We need your brains, your determination, and your heart in the years to come.

CHAPTER 1

NOAH

THE PLAQUE AT THE BASE OF THE SAPLING SAYS, *IN MEMORY of Dr. Genevieve Barton, National Hero.* The city placed it here in the city park less than a week after it happened. Less than a week after you went away.

For good, this time.

The little memorial service was a big deal for Tourmaline, but I suppose having an astronaut who's gone on three NASA missions is monumental for a tiny town in Maine.

A light dusting of snow coats the faded grass, and I settle on the wooden bench nearest the tree. The cold permeates my jeans, but it doesn't bother me.

Nothing bothers me anymore.

"Hey, Mom..."

I've come here every day for the past five weeks, since the day they installed the plaque and this poor white ash sapling. But I'm the only one.

Dad hasn't visited you since the memorial service.

"They posted it this afternoon." I lean back against the bench and tug my phone from inside my coat. "Let's look at it together."

Two months ago, after a month-long series of emails deliberating the matter, I finally submitted my online application to Archer Collins University, the best science and engineering college on the East Coast. Maybe in all of the U.S.

Today is December 20th—the day the Admissions Office posts acceptance information to the potential students' accounts.

The page loads slowly—hundreds of prospective students are probably checking their results—and I wait before scrolling down.

Mr. Noah Barton,

Congratulations! You have been accepted to the esteemed Archer Collins University—

The rest doesn't really matter, does it?

My eyes dart back to the plaque under the tree, and I turn off my screen. "That's it, then. I got accepted." My foot taps the frozen ground, and I unlock my phone again to scan the rest of the page.

Everything is simple and straightforward: Here in my Archer Collins account, I will receive notifications about financial assistance and fill out the roommate survey. They invite me to revisit the school, and my ACT and SAT scores, along with my GPA, mean I can apply for their Trustee Scholarship.

But it's hard to be excited.

Attending Archer Collins has been my dream since fifth grade, when you took me to the Josiah Archer – sponsored space exhibit in Portland. You showed off astrolabes and telescopes, space suits and satellite images, and even a 3D model of the International Space Station. You told me all about your latest mission—where you worked and slept—using that model.

Two months ago, the acceptance to Archer Collins would've been the most exciting thing to happen to me.

Now, I don't know if I want to attend.

I tug my coat tighter. Temps turned uncharacteristically cold mid-November. Now that it's December, the high is only in the teens. We'll have more snow and ice after sunset. We may even have a white Christmas.

"You were supposed to be home for the holidays this year, Mom."

Instead, your sapling looks particularly sad: only four feet tall with five main branches and no leaves.

Not that you being away for special events is irregular. Most of my childhood was spent waiting for you to come home. Between ASCAN training, mission training, working as a flight controller, assisting with engineering, and the months spent on the ISS, family came second.

"I know holidays were never important to you, but you promised." My voice cracks. "You're not supposed to break your promises, Mom."

The snow is thicker when I arrive home. The storm that wasn't supposed to arrive till close to midnight is already dropping flakes. The sun hasn't even set yet.

But worst of all, there's a black sedan in the driveway.

I park my bike in the garage and close the garage door before heading inside the house. Shoes, slick with snow and grime, stay in the mudroom, and I pad through the house in a pair of well-worn, cotton socks. The hardwood floor feels warm after being outside.

Voices stream from the kitchen, and I hover by the doorway, out of sight.

"How was your flight?" Dad's voice is a deep baritone—as deep and thick as you'd expect from a man of his stature. "Didn't expect you till tomorrow."

"Yeah, well…"

That's Cliff, home from college for the holidays. I'm impressed he bothered. Last year, he went to Hawaii with one of his girlfriends.

Yes, one of. He usually has a few women in tow.

"Booked the flight six months ago. How's the string bean doing? He up in his room on his computer again?"

His words almost make me wonder if he cares.

"I—" Dad falters. "He wasn't here when I got home."

Cliff snorts. "Oh, does he finally have a social life? That'd be a first."

I slump against the wall.

He has a point. The closest thing to a friend I've ever had was Mom.

For a long minute, Dad doesn't say anything. "Ethan has leave this holiday. He and Meredith are getting in tonight, staying through New Year's."

"Nice." Cliff moves with the conversation without hesitation. "So everyone's gonna be together this year."

Not everyone.

But neither of them will say that.

We were all supposed to spend Christmas and New Year's together. During the day, we would celebrate, and at night, Mom and I would climb onto the roof and she'd tell me about her months away while we looked through her telescope.

"Any idea where you want to eat dinner? All five of us can go out once Ethan and Meredith get in."

Cliff chuckles. "We celebrating something?"

"It's not every day I get my three boys together anymore."

The last time Ethan and Cliff came home was right after the accident, but they didn't stay long. They both had important things to do—football games to play, a Marine Raiders assessment prep course to complete. Apparently, our mother dying wasn't a good enough reason to stay.

"I could go for a good lobster roll." Cliff's tone is non-committal. "The seafood in Oklahoma leaves something to be desired."

Dad's laughter echoes through the kitchen, and there's shuffling—someone walking. "We can go to Pearl's. I'll get ready. Ethan should be here in the next thirty minutes."

I step back into the dark pantry before Dad passes on his way upstairs, but Cliff stays in the kitchen.

Hesitant, I linger in the silent pantry, not wanting to draw attention to myself. After a moment, I edge forward and poke my head out.

"Why're you hiding, String Bean?"

I jump, clutching the door frame for support, and turn. "Ethan?" I clear my throat. "I wasn't hiding."

In the hallway, Ethan stands, thick blue coat unzipped and spread open, hands slung in his front pockets, his tanned olive forehead crinkled with curiosity. "You were hanging out in the pantry with no light on for…no reason?"

I cross my arms. "I have a reason, thanks."

"And it is?"

"None of your business."

Ethan snorts. "Sure you have a reason, kid." He tugs me against his side and drags me into the kitchen. "Come on, String Bean. I want a beer."

When we enter, Cliff looks up, thick dark-brown hair plastered to his forehead, and grins. "There you two are. What took you so damn long?"

I slink out of Ethan's grip, and he doesn't notice.

Instead, he crosses the room to punch Cliff in the arm, then yank him into a half hug. A man-hug.

"A beer sounds like a great idea," Cliff says when they separate. He opens the fridge and pulls out a couple cans. "You want one, String Bean?"

My nose twists up into a sneer. "I'm seventeen. In what world would I be drinking alcohol?"

Cliff snorts as he hands Ethan the second can. "True."

"But that has nothing to do with your age," Ethan adds. "I drank my first beer at fifteen, little bro. You're the anomaly."

Cliff doesn't bother holding back his laughter. "That's the damn truth."

Honestly, I'm impressed Ethan knows the word *anomaly*.

I look away. "As far as I'm concerned, not requiring alcohol to have a good time is a good thing."

But Cliff sends me a derisive smirk. "I can definitely have a good time without alcohol, don't you worry about that."

I cringe. "I don't need to know about your personal life."

Ethan pops the tab on the cheap beer and takes a long gulp. "Right, wouldn't want to upset the virgin."

"You probably get off plenty with that stupid microscope anyway."

I scoff. "Cliff, it's a telescope—for looking at faraway things in space." I turn to sift through the cabinets—we may be going out for dinner, but I need to occupy my hands, a distraction. "Microscopes are for looking at tiny things up close."

"Like your dick," Ethan says through his laughter.

Cliff too laughs.

Unbelievable.

Only six weeks after the accident, and they're carrying on as if nothing changed. Doesn't matter that our mother is gone. All that matters is making stupid penis jokes and getting drunk. They're exactly the same.

Does her death even bother them? Do they miss her?

My stomach convulses, and I snap the cupboard shut. I've already lost my appetite, and we haven't left for dinner.

"Oh, hey, man…" Cliff cocks his head. "Where's Meredith? She settling in?"

Ethan sets his beer on the island. "Nah, she's not coming."

"Damn, really?" Then, Cliff snorts. "Well, at least I won't have to listen to you humping at 2 a.m." He waggles his eyebrows at me.

But Ethan's face is grim.

"Everything alright?" I inch closer. "Did you two break up?"

He shakes his head. "Don't get emotional on me, String Bean. It's not a big deal. I'd rather have a few beers tonight if it's all the same to you."

"Whatever." I nudge between them to reach the hallway. "I'm gonna get ready."

On my way upstairs, I pass Dad, now in gray slacks and a Polo shirt. I hurry past him to the second floor and the safety of my bedroom.

I can't stand to be in the same room as them for another minute. Not right now.

Dinner's going to be fun.

CHAPTER 2

EDEN

"You will not believe this!" I slap my hands on the table, and on the opposite side, Tinsley, her shoulder-length blond hair pulled into a high ponytail, looks up with wide eyes, mouth agape. "I got the notification from Archer Collins. Archer freaking Collins, Tins, can you believe it?"

Tinsley rolls her green eyes and pops her gum. "Of course I believe it, Edie. I was sitting next to you when you filled out the application. It's hardly news that an Ivy League college will respond to their prospective students."

I collapse onto the chair. "Don't ruin this for me, Tinsley. It's a big deal."

"Yes, but screaming in the library goes against everything you believe in, Edie."

I bite my lip and glance around; several people glare back. "Sorry."

Tinsley leans across the table. "Have you read it?"

I hold back my laughter. "Of course. I was refreshing my screen every two seconds until the page updated."

She snickers. "What's the verdict then?"

Excitement bubbles under the surface, and I barely manage to contain myself. "I got in. This is the best science school on the East Coast, and I got in!"

Tinsley grins.

"I mean, of course, I got in. I'm top of our class, Senior Class President, I've been a finalist in the last three regional STEM fairs, I have a 4.12 GPA, a 32 on my ACT, a 1510 on my SATs, and my IQ is 137."

"Plus all the hours you spent organizing our school's disaster relief after Hurricane Vito...as a freshman," Tinsley adds.

"Is that impressive?" I can't hide my grin. "I did everything I could to get accepted short of convincing Mama to send me to prep school—"

"Speaking of your mother—" She levels me with a serious gaze. "Have you told her about this?"

All excitement dissipates. "Not yet. I don't...I don't know where to begin. Do you know what the first thing she'll say is?"

Tinsley tilts her head from side to side, lips quirked to the side. "'Archer Collins is an expensive place to find a husband'?" A devious smile tugs at her lavender-painted lips.

I roll my eyes.

"You applied without telling her you want to go there, Edie." Tinsley blows another bubble, and the *pop* is loud. "Your mom expects you to go to a small private school and drop out when you find a serious boyfriend. She's going to flip when you tell her about Archer Collins."

My stomach drops.

While Tinsley has a particularly snarky way with words, she's not wrong. Mama encourages me to do well, but she never cared about my academic achievements—grades and intelligence aren't important to her. Which is her prerogative.

I just wish she realized how much they matter to me.

"I'll figure that out when I get there," I finally say, but determination courses through my blood. "Besides, she can't complain about the money—look at this!" I unlock my phone and shove it into Tinsley's hands.

"'The Trustee Scholarship,'" she reads.

"Exactly!" I scoot in my chair. I can't hold still. "It's this amazing opportunity. I qualify to apply for it because of my ACT and SAT scores. I could win up to thirty thousand dollars in annual scholarship money. That's incredible!"

Her eyes flit across the screen, lavender lips pursed. "How do you apply?"

"There's a weekend sometime in February where I go to this banquet to chat with current students and alumni. I stay in the dorms with a sponsor student for Friday and Saturday night, and on Saturday, I have a forty-five-minute interview with a couple faculty members."

Tinsley raises an eyebrow. "So you have to tell your mom before February."

I wince.

Yes. I have a deadline now.

"What if she says you can't go?"

"I don't know." My voice quivers—it's a serious concern. If I can't make it to the Trustee Weekend, I can't get the scholarship. "I'll figure it out."

Tinsley nods and holds her tongue. She knows as well as I do how difficult that conversation will be.

Mama won't want me to go, and I have yet to figure out how to convince her. I'm not sure I can. In the past, Papa would vouch for me, but he's unable to now.

Tinsley taps her acrylic nails, a fluorescent plum to match her lipstick, on the tabletop. "Speaking of permission, have you asked about New Year's Eve?"

I close my eyes. "I can't go."

"Because it's a boy-girl sleepover?" She scoffs. "You're such a goody-two-shoes. You didn't have to tell her that, Edie."

To be fair, Mama would flip about boys at a sleepover, but she'd say no long before I got to that part of the explanation.

"We're going to the Bartons' party that night, Tinsley. She won't let me out of it since I missed the memorial." I lean back, trying to relax, but I'm as irritated as Tinsley. The last thing I want to do is waste an entire night at a social event I couldn't care less about.

"They're still having their party?"

"Every year."

She shakes her head. "It hasn't been that long since, you know, Mrs. Barton died."

"Doctor," I correct. "She was a doctor. Why does everyone forget that just because she was married?"

Tinsley rolls her eyes. "Either way, it seems awfully early to have a huge celebration when she only died like six weeks ago."

I inhale sharply.

Everyone remembers the date. The whole world watched on October 30th as the Space Shuttle *Endurance* tore apart upon reentry. Not long before the shuttle broke atmo, an oxygen tank in the service module exploded. Metal shards damaged the heat shield, igniting the pressurized gas and destabilizing the capsule to the point it tumbled and ripped apart.

It's been almost seven weeks, and they're still picking up debris and body parts spread across Texas. It was heartbreaking, especially since Dr. Barton was a renowned citizen of little Tourmaline, an expert in her field, an idol for young female scientists like myself.

"I wasn't expecting it either, but Mama insisted we pay our respects."

"You mean you and Noah might actually be nice to each other?" Tinsley's mouth gapes open mockingly. "Is that possible?"

My lips twist into a sneer. "I'll be nice if he is."

"He missed all his classes. He didn't complete his finals. Is he going to be at the party? Hell, is he going to complete his senior year?"

I hadn't considered that.

Despite the melancholy situation, I can't imagine Noah Barton not graduating on time. We've fought for top of our class since we were kids. He's been my rival at the New England STEM Fair in Portland for the last seven years and at the local fairs in couple years before that. We've both gotten into the final round since freshman year, but he's placed higher than me two out of three times.

It's been strange without him in class, and I can't imagine competing in the STEM fair without him there too. We get under each other's skin, but the competition keeps me vigilant.

"Of course he'll graduate with us. Noah couldn't live with himself if he didn't graduate on time. You know he already applied to colleges. Deferring would be admitting defeat."

Tinsley swallows, and her lavender lips settle in a straight line. "Deferring because your mother died isn't admitting defeat, Edie. You shouldn't be so…insensitive about other people's feelings."

I freeze.

It's rare I don't know what to say. I always have an answer for everything, a solution to every problem. Even if I'm flying by the seat of my pants.

People have called me bullheaded, bossy, aggressive, but Tinsley always accepts me for who I am. She insists I shouldn't let others' harsh words bring me down. Even when she criticizes me, she's friendly and encouraging.

Technically, calling me "insensitive" is one of the nicest ways to say I'm being rude. Careless. Heartless.

My eyes drift around the library.

We come here often—not because Tinsley finds it interesting but because it's one of the few places my mother approves of. Even if Mama doesn't care about academics, she'd rather I focus on those than get into trouble. The library is my sanctuary. It's one of our regular hang-out spots, but it's also where I come to reflect and be alone.

I wish I were alone now.

"I'm sorry, Edie." Her voice is quiet, but in the silence, it's loud enough. "I didn't mean—"

"You did." I heave a sigh. "Sometimes, I forget not

everyone reacts the way I do. Maybe even Noah Barton needs more time to grieve. I don't know."

Tinsley offers me a sad smile, but it holds no comfort.

"I guess I'll have to be nice if he's there." I shrug, trying to adopt a relaxed tone. "First time for everything, right?"

CHAPTER 3

NOAH

Inside the oven, the crescent rolls rise slowly. They should start to brown in a couple minutes.

Christmas morning has never been a big deal to us. Dad attends the Christmas service at church. As kids, we'd go with him, but I never cared. Now, he only thinks Christmas is important since both Ethan and Cliff made time in their busy schedules. Ethan took leave specifically for the holidays, and unless things change drastically once he's a Raider, he only gets thirty days off a year.

The pan sizzles when I pour in the bowl of scrambled eggs.

I don't cook much, but I have more experience than anyone else in the house. Dad buys freezer meals and shoves them in the oven for dinner. If we have a sit-down dinner.

"How's it going?"

When I glance over, Ethan leans against the fridge.

"Food should be ready in five."

"Need any help?" He joins me by the stove. "I'm not completely helpless, you know." He says it like a joke—he could kill me in seconds, after all—but it's not particularly funny.

"Nah." I nudge the eggs around the pan so they don't brown.

Ethan snags the nearby plates and grabs clumps of hot bacon with his bare fingers. "I can divvy everything up." Hopefully, he washed his hands.

The eggs are bright yellow now with flecks of black pepper throughout, and I lean down to check on the crescent rolls, finally starting to brown. The oven beeps obnoxiously as I turn off the heat—I silence the timer. When I pull the rolls out after dividing the eggs, they're perfectly golden brown.

"Dad's back, right?" I glance over my shoulder.

Ethan nods absentmindedly as he drops the paper towel, glistening with bacon grease, into the trash under the sink. "Yeah, he and Cliff are watching the Christmas Day Parade." He washes his hands in cold water and wipes on a fresh towel.

I frown. "I guess we're eating in the living room, then."

We distribute the crescent rolls and carry the plates out.

In the living room, I settle on the armchair, and Ethan takes the open spot at the end of the couch. Much like Monday night football, I am completely out of place. They devour their food without dragging their attention from the screen; I pick at my plate's content.

If this is what we're doing for Christmas, why am I here? I'd be better off in my room.

By the time I finish, everyone else has been done for a while. I gather the empty plates and head for the kitchen.

There's no point in staying. No point in striking up a conversation. They're watching a parade that was taped a month ago, and we're not talking.

Like I'd be interested if we were.

I rinse the plates and utensils and slip them into the dishwasher. It's not half full yet—we can run it after lunch. But if all they're going to do is watch a dumb parade, I'll be in my room.

I dry my hands on a towel, glancing around to make sure I haven't missed anything. The pans can be hand-washed later, no big deal.

"You going somewhere?" Ethan again.

"Upstairs."

He cocks a thick eyebrow, lips pursed—unamused. "That's not in the spirit of Christmas."

I give a noncommittal shrug. "Does it matter?"

"Don't you want to hang out with us, String Bean? We haven't been together since—"

"Since Mom died, I know."

Ethan assesses me, and I squirm under his stern gaze. Still, he doesn't speak.

I scoff. "Figures. You don't care." I march past him, but his strong hand latches onto my arm.

"Why do you say that?"

I shoot him a quick glare. "You have to ask, Ethan? The three of you only care about food, beer, and a stupid parade. You haven't brought her up since you got here… three days ago."

He doesn't meet my gaze. "What's there to say?"

I grit my teeth.

If he thinks there's no point talking about what happened, if he has nothing to say about Mom, I can't change his mind. His reaction—their reaction—to her death is to carry on as if nothing changed, to pretend it didn't happen. But she's still dead.

"Come back to the living room, Noah."

I tug away, and he releases me. "I'm tired."

He doesn't often call me by my name. Ever since I was little, I've always been "String Bean" or "little bro" or some other infantalizing term.

"You can read a book or something while we watch the parade. We're supposed to spend Christmas as a family."

Are we a family now that Mom's gone?

I trudge down the hallway. "Maybe in a little while."

A hard knock sounds on my door, but I barely lift my head as it squeaks open. "Noah, what are you doing in here?" Dad's firm voice booms through my small bedroom. His dark-brown eyes narrow at the sight of me.

Why?

Because all I'm doing is lying on my bed in the dark. The latest Stephen Hawking lays next to me, but I haven't even cracked the spine in my few attempts to read it. It was the last book Mom gave me before she went on her final mission. I haven't been able to finish reading it.

Dad flips on the light as he steps inside. "Why is it so dark in here? Are you sleeping the day away again?"

I purse my lips.

No, I wasn't asleep.

I wish I'd been asleep.

There have been so many days where I lie in my bed, waiting for sleep to come because sleep is one of the few opportunities to escape my thoughts. I expected the accident to haunt my dreams, but sleep is one of my few reprieves.

The sleepless nights are the real torture.

"Noah—"

"What, Dad?"

His jaw clenches, fingers tighten into a fist. "Come downstairs. We're going to open presents." He doesn't give me a chance to argue before marching out.

What presents?

Like every year, the beautifully wrapped boxes under the tree are for show. We rarely exchange gifts during the holidays. Our Christmas decorations were painstakingly applied for the sake of other people.

When I unlock my phone, I still have the Archer Collins student homepage up—focused on the Trustee Scholarship. I bite my lip. "Hey, Dad?"

In the distance, the footsteps pause, then return, and he pokes his head through my doorway. "What?"

"Can I ask you something? Something important?"

Dad frowns. "What's going on?"

I brandish the phone toward him, but he doesn't come closer. "I got accepted to Archer Collins. There's this great opportunity in February to apply for a huge scholarship, but I have to go there for the weekend—"

"When in February?"

My stomach clenches—could we actually make this work? "It's the second weekend."

He shakes his head, his voice heavy. "Noah, I have work. I can't take you all the way to Pennsylvania because you decided you need to go there for the weekend on a whim."

My breath quivers. "It could cover a large portion of my tuition, Dad. I really want to go here."

He crosses his arms. "There are plenty of excellent schools nearby—including ones that don't cost an arm and a leg because it's in the Ivy League. We cannot afford to pay for you to attend Archer Collins."

"Cliff is going to one of the best football schools in the U.S."

"He got a full ride. Don't demean your brother's talents because you're having a difficult time."

"But Dad, this scholarship could pay for me to go to Archer Collins. Please, this is important to me." I hesitate. "It's where Mom went to college."

He swallows, shifting his gaze away, and the sound is thick in the otherwise quiet room. "I'm going to a conference that weekend, and you're not traipsing across the country by yourself. This discussion is over. Come downstairs."

I drop my phone on the bed as he walks away.

CHAPTER 4

EDEN

MAMA ALWAYS TRIES TO SPEND MORE TIME AT HOME during winter break to give me some semblance of routine. Between all my projects and her job, we don't see each other often, especially with all the hours I've put in at Kresge Laboratories.

I pause in the kitchen doorway as she runs the bread knife through a baguette. "You making dinner, Mama?"

"Bánh mì," she tosses over her shoulder while slathering the inside with mayo. "You're hungry, right?"

Sure enough, the ingredients are spread across the counter: sliced ham, head cheese, liver pâté, pickled carrots and white radish, cucumber, jalapeños, and freshly minced cilantro.

"Of course."

Like most days, I lost track of time. I've been holed away in my room researching microorganisms for this year's New England STEM Fair. I can research on my laptop, but to be eligible for the fair, projects like mine must be completed in a lab. Luckily, when I contacted one of Papa's old contacts at the lab, Dr. Emily Hook pulled a few strings to let me use their facilities. She's the only person I've talked to about the project—it's important and, as such, needs kept confidential. Not to mention, Mama wouldn't know or care what I'm talking about.

"Grab plates, Thien."

A soft smile graces my lips. Mama is the only person who calls me by my Vietnamese name regularly—she reverts to English in public—though Papa switched between the two masterfully.

While I pull a couple plates from the cupboard, she adds the fillings with impressive speed, then slices the long baguette in half.

We eat at the dining room table in silence.

Mama has never been a talker. She dedicates herself wholly to the task at hand and rarely sees fit to distract herself with idle chatter. I can understand that—it's so much easier to concentrate on polyethylene degradation without Tinsley talking my ear off—but sometimes, I wonder if I know my mother at all. If she knows me at all.

I set the sandwich down and swallow, gathering my courage. "Um, can we talk about New Year's Eve?"

Her head jerks upward, her dark-brown eyes focusing on me, assessing me.

Under most circumstances, I will happily take on a role of authority. I've managed and organized my fellow students for years. In first grade, I demanded the school system provide healthier and more ethnically diverse food options, citing my own issues with dairy as an example of why their reliance on Western food is disadvantageous for an increasingly large group, and many students joined my campaign—enough that the school system changed their menu. Papa being the mayor might've helped too.

My mother is a different matter.

After a long pause, Mama nods.

"Tinsley is hosting a sleepover that night." I inhale slowly, keeping my voice steady. "I know we have plans to attend the Bartons' party, but would it be a problem for me to miss this one year?"

Her lips twist into a scowl. It's a lost cause. "Thien, you've made a commitment."

"Of course, Mama." I pick up my bánh mì again, ready to move on.

"I do want to talk to you about New Year's Eve. One of your father's friends has a son attending Archer Collins University in Bethlehem, Pennsylvania. He's twenty-two, pre-law, and about to receive his Bachelor's degree and start law school."

What does this have to do with New Year's Eve?

"His family will be at the Bartons' charity party. We want to introduce you."

I frown. "Introduce me?"

"Colton is eager to meet you. He's smart, conscientious, good family. He'll make good money as a corporate lawyer."

"He's attending Archer Collins?"

She nods.

"I'd love to meet him."

It would be nice to talk to someone attending my college of choice. I can get a better feel for the school, how classes are run, what the professors are like—maybe even having this Colton character endorse me could be beneficial, though I doubt he has much sway on the community.

But I doubt the fact that he attends Archer Collins is why Mama wants to introduce us.

When my parents married, Mama was only eighteen, though my father is eleven years her senior. Not long later, he stepped down as the U.S. Ambassador to Vietnam, and they moved to America. Mama was twenty-one when she got pregnant. The thought of attending college was never an option for her.

For me, it's the opposite.

Marriage—no, a relationship—isn't on my radar. There is far too much I want to do with my life, too many places I want to travel, discoveries I want to make, experiences I want to have.

How in the world can I tell her that?

"Good," is all she says before returning to her sandwich. Silence resumes.

Upstairs, my hands tremble while locating Tinsley in my contacts. I need to talk with her.

Tinsley answers on the second ring. "What up, girl?" In the background, Katy Perry belts out her latest ballad.

I heave a sigh of relief. "Thank god." My voice is hoarser than expected.

"What's going on, Edie?"

Now that the moment is here, I hesitate.

My mother wasn't absolutely clear, and the last thing I

want is for Tinsley to jump the gun, as she is wont to do. But I can't keep this to myself.

"I think Mama secured me a date for New Year's Eve." The words tumble out with unprecedented force, and I wait to make sure I spoke coherently.

Tinsley scoffs. "Wait, she got you a date?"

Okay, coherent enough.

"He's twenty-two."

"What? How does she not find the idea of a twenty-two-year-old screwing her seventeen-year-old daughter incredibly creepy?"

I bite my lip. "Papa's eleven years older than her. She doesn't find it strange."

On the other end of the line, Tinsley's bed squeaks, and she turns down her music. "Okay, fine, but that doesn't mean you should marry off your daughter the moment she comes of age. What the actual fuck?"

A shaky sigh escapes my mouth. "I know, I know."

"What are you going to do?"

My options are slim. Mama has expectations, and as much as I want my freedom, I hate to disappoint her.

"Hope one date will satisfy her?" I stretch across my mattress, but I'm still tense. "The guy attends Archer Collins, so I can ask him about classes and campus. This could actually be a great opportunity."

Tinsley snickers. "Look at you, making the best of a messed-up situation. I don't know how you do it."

I do it because I don't have another choice.

Somehow, I have to convince Mama to let me attend Archer Collins—plus the Trustee Scholarship weekend in February. If that means putting up with an uncomfortable date, I'll do it.

"What if you wind up liking this guy?" Tinsley's voice bubbles with amusement. "Wouldn't that be crazy? To like a guy your mother sets you up with. That's unheard of."

I laugh, though I'm not sure it's funny. "That would certainly be interesting."

He must be intelligent—or at least have immaculate test scores—to get into Archer Collins. But pre-law? That doesn't bode well for his integrity and rationale.

Either way, I'll find out on New Year's Eve.

CHAPTER 5

NOAH

DAD'S DRESSED IN A TUX WHEN I REACH THE BOTTOM of the stairs. It's nearly eight o'clock—the start of his annual charity party—but Ethan and Cliff are upstairs, getting dressed.

And me?

I'm wearing a T-shirt and flannel pajama pants. This party is the last thing I'm interested in.

Dad's eyes darken when he catches sight of me. "Why aren't you dressed? This is an important night."

I'm not sure what's so important about this night—providing a food bank with the funds to keep its doors open or keeping up appearances. Being a commercial real estate developer in a small town means he's on all the time, and half the guests are his clients.

To be fair, he doesn't know how to turn off.

"Dad, can we talk about February again?"

How can I focus on a stupid party—even one benefiting a local charity—with this on my mind? How can I care?

Dad checks himself in the mirror at the base of the stairs and straightens his gold bow tie. "We don't have time to repeat this conversation, Noah. You need to go upstairs and get dressed. Guests will be here any moment."

"I know, Dad." I clasp my hands behind my back in concentration. "This will only take a minute."

"No, you need to spend every minute putting on a suit—at least a dress shirt for god's sake." He shoots me a glare through the mirror. "You're well aware of how important this event is. You cannot mess this up for our family because you want to go to the most expensive school on the East Coast. Get dressed."

"At least let me say—"

He spins on me, brown eyes narrowed into slits. "Noah, we do not have time for you to throw a tantrum right now."

This is hardly a tantrum, but there's no point arguing about semantics. I clench my teeth and jut out my chin. "Can we talk after the party?"

The doorbell rings.

"You can certainly talk." Dad marches toward the door. "That doesn't mean I'll listen. Go get dressed."

The dismissal is final.

I bite back my retort and trudge up the stairs.

That doesn't mean I'll get dressed.

I lean toward the monitor, my fingers tapping rhythmically on the desk. I have three months to perfect this software, to impress the judges at the New England STEM Fair this April. I can't do that if my math is wrong.

The music throbs downstairs as the song transitions.

My eyes narrow. The last thing I need to think about is Dad's idiotic party.

Even still, my attention drifts toward the clock at the bottom right of the screen. It's almost ten thirty. The party has been in full swing for maybe an hour.

Thump!

I nearly jump out of my seat.

What was that?

Slowly, I rise from my swivel chair and crack my door. That was decidedly closer than any revelries downstairs.

Outside, the hallway is dark. The music is louder now—classically styled party music—but it doesn't account for that particular noise.

What does account for it?

That would be Ethan with his lips suctioned to a girl in a shimmering silver dress.

"Jesus, Ethan, didn't you and Meredith just break up?"

They pull apart, and the girl—whoever she is—blushes a fierce red before stumbling backward. She's down the hallway and out of sight in record time.

Ethan shoots me a glare. "Wow, you're a hit with the ladies."

I turn on my heels back to my room, but he follows me inside and leans by the light switch, arms crossed. "So this is where you're hiding."

"I'm not hiding." I drop onto my chair and throw myself back into my computations.

"What're you working on?"

My jaw clenches in irritation. "My project for the STEM fair."

Ethan chuckles. "When are you ever going to grow up? You do that stupid thing every year, and you never win."

"I've been a finalist the last three years, thanks."

He scoffs. "You only placed fifth last year. At least, the year before that you got to the international one—even if you only won a measly five hundred bucks."

To be fair, I'm impressed he remembers. He spent most of my past STEM fairs flirting with other guests and visitors. If he made it.

"I'm not going to justify that with a response."

"Of course you aren't." He clears his throat. "Why are you hiding anyway?"

"Not hiding."

"Did you and Dad have another fight?"

For someone completely idiotic and ridiculous and insanely busy, he's good at hitting the nail on the head.

"We don't fight."

Ethan pushes away from the wall. "Then you shouldn't have any problem coming downstairs, right? Let's get you dressed. Lots of people to entertain, you know. We're hosts."

There's an insult in there somewhere about him and that girl in the hallway, but I have no patience to come up with it.

He flips through my closet and pulls out a shirt and vest. "Wear something nice for a change. Anything's better than shirts with jokes no one understands."

"I'm not the only person who gets jokes about the Fermi Paradox."

Instead of responding, he rolls me closer to the bed by the back of my chair. "Time to get dressed, Noah. You need to make an appearance."

I slowly assess the clothing he laid out: a blue dress shirt, a gray vest, and a pair of dark-blue jeans. I wasn't expecting jeans, but it's a nice incentive to dress up.

He glares, impatient.

"Ugh, fine."

Like every year, Dad hired a local decorating company—one he conveniently helped build from the ground up—to deck the halls in the colors of the New Year. Gold, black, and silver adorn the walls, tables, and light fixtures.

He went all out for tonight. More than normal.

Ethan, his arm hooked firmly around my shoulders, drags me down the stairs with a devious grin. "Let's get you a drink, String Bean. Lots of champagne to be had. Dad won't notice." He steers us toward the drink station, where Cliff is standing with a fancy bottle of beer in hand. "See, Cliff's already had three beers—nobody's said a thing."

I roll my eyes. "A drink is the last thing I want right now."

Although, to be fair, attending this party is the last thing I want.

Dad's New Year's Eve party is usually a hit, especially when there's a gambling room set up in the basement, where all proceeds benefit his annual charity of choice. But this year, we have double the guests, and I doubt this many people want to support our local food bank.

Everyone wants to creep on the family without a mother.

I stand beside Ethan and Cliff, hands deep in my pockets, while Ethan tries to push a flute of champagne my way.

The party is lively, but most people who look our way slow down enough to shoot us sad looks. Dad wants this party to demonstrate to the community that we are strong, ready to move forward, but this is only an opportunity for people to gawk. No one cares; it's schadenfreude.

An older woman in a gold evening gown, her lips in a tight smile, steps forward and clasps my hands. "Noah, you poor dear. How are you holding up?"

She's familiar, but I don't recall her name. Have we ever been introduced?

I clear my throat. "I'm fine, thanks."

Of course, it doesn't end there. It never does.

"I was so sad to hear about your mother, dear." Her eyes flit to Ethan and Cliff, and she sends them a sympathetic smile. "All three of you without a mother—how awful."

Ethan offers her a tight smile. "Yup, awful." His words are dismissive and short.

She squeezes my hands one last time. "Let me know if there's anything I can do to help."

"Right," I say as she retreats into the crowd.

Moments later, she's chatting and grinning with her companions. She cares so much.

I turn toward the buffet. My hands quiver as I fill a cup with punch.

Pull yourself together, dammit.

My eyes study the room again. The guests are mostly

Dad's contacts—people I only meet at these annual events—plus our neighbors and a few people from school. Kelsey Valentine, who lives across the street, fiddles with her yellow-painted nails as her dad marches her into the living room. At least I'm not the only person who doesn't want to be here.

"Thank god I have a drink," Cliff murmurs.

Ethan nods. "It's been like that all evening."

"The hot girls are a nice reprieve too." Cliff waggles his eyebrows with a grin.

All I can do is roll my eyes. "You're disgusting."

But the two of them laugh.

"You only say that because you couldn't get a date to save your life." Cliff laughs at his little joke. "I'd love to see you actually flirt with one of these people."

I purse my lips. Obviously, engaging in this conversation is making it worse.

"Like her…" Ethan's words are quiet, almost distant.

"Damn," Cliff adds.

And I let my curiosity get the better of me.

On the other side of the large room, a girl my age stands, her shiny thick hair pulled into a tight ballerina bun. The black locks shimmer under the twinkling holiday lights, as does the tight, iridescent-white dress that ends well above her knees. Despite the cold, the dress is sleeveless—though with a high neck—and all she wears otherwise is a long beaded necklace and painful-looking stilettos.

I can see why my brothers might find her attractive.

"Is that little Eden Prince?" Ethan takes a long drink from his beer bottle. "When did she get hot?"

If only I didn't know her.

"Seriously." Cliff's nod is emphatic.

I roll my eyes. "She's seventeen. Don't be a creep."

Cliff merely shrugs. "Seventeen's legal."

I pull a face—quickly followed by their laughter. "Legal doesn't make it not creepy. And Eden Prince would never be remotely interested in you."

In the distance, Eden looks tense while her mom and a guy I don't recognize chat amicably. She stiffens, freezes, when the guy slides his arm around her waist and guides her away.

"Besides," I add, "looks like she's already on a date." My brow furrows, my lips tighten, as Eden inches away from his grasp and his grip only tightens.

With a little smirk, Ethan turns his gaze on me. "Do I detect a hint of jealousy, String Bean? You like her or something?"

I blanch. "That's not possible. Have you met her? She's conceited, pigheaded, and completely insane."

"Okay, but you still want to tap that, right?" Cliff shrugs. "I'd do her. She's fine."

Unease settles in my stomach. "You can't say stuff like that," I say quietly. "Even if she were pretty, it wouldn't matter."

Eden and her "date" sit at a nearby table. He scoots his chair closer, but she blocks his advancement by crossing her legs

Ethan snickers. "Right, sure."

To be fair, she didn't have legs that long or smooth during the formative years of our acquaintanceship. Or the particularly nice curve that traces from her back to her round butt. Or you know, boobs.

Because we were seven.

"She's hated me since the third grade when I beat her stupid biogas project." I turn my attention elsewhere—anywhere else. "She thinks I'm a threat. As if I'd want to be class president or that anal. I definitely don't have a thing for her."

Cliff takes another sip. "Well, it's not like you have anything to offer her anyway. Not like us."

I snort. "What could you two offer someone like Eden?"

"I'm going to play pro ball," he reminds me. "Scouts are coming to my next game, you know." He nods toward Ethan. "And this badass, who already fights for our country, is training to become a Marine Raider—the elite of the elite. You can't compare to that."

"She wouldn't go for either of you." I sip the fruity punch. "She has good taste."

It's Ethan's turn to snort. "You think awfully highly of her for someone you consider annoying."

"She is annoying."

"Then it wouldn't matter if I talk to her." Ethan finishes his beer and sets it on the edge of the buffet. "Looks like she could use a little assistance getting rid of her current annoyance."

My mouth drops open as he walks away. "Wait a minute. This isn't a game. Leave her alone."

Being Ethan, he doesn't listen.

CHAPTER 6

EDEN

WHEN WE'RE ALONE—WELL, AS ALONE AS YOU CAN BE IN a crowded house—Colton turns to me with a soft smile, his palm still on the small of my back. "You want to grab a drink?" He nods toward the buffet, but I hesitate.

Noah Barton and his older brothers are hanging out by the buffet tables. The last thing I want to do is show up on his radar. The evening will go much more smoothly if we do not cross paths.

"Champagne or something?" Colton suggests.

I frown—he knows I'm underage—and clear my throat. "Do you mind if I ask you a few questions?"

He cocks an eyebrow, then nods. "Sure, I'd love to get to know you." Instead of the buffet, he leads us to a small table and sits close enough our knees brush.

I cross one leg over the other, all business. "Mama says you attend Archer Collins, right?"

"Yeah, great college. Have you thought about where you'll attend?"

How can he possibly sum up the experience of attending an Ivy League school as a "great college"? Where are his priorities?

I brush his question aside with a swish of my hand. "You're studying pre-law? What are the professors like? Your thoughts on the general education classes?"

Colton quirks his mouth to the side, brow furrowed. "That's not important. What are your plans after you graduate? Interested in a job or something else?"

Irritation tugs my lips into a scowl. I don't want to get to know the guy—I want as much information about Archer Collins from an actual student as possible. Is that too much to ask for?

He stretches out an arm to squeeze my tights-covered thigh, just below the hem of my shimmering dress. "I want to talk about you, Eden."

I shift my seat backward. "There isn't much to say about me." My words are clipped, short.

Colton chuckles. "That can't be true."

Under normal circumstances, I wouldn't hold back, but I don't have a choice. I have to play nice.

"Excuse me…"

Relief surges through my body as I turn toward the new speaker—only to be stunned by the sight of the oldest Barton brother. Ethan, I think.

He quirks a smile. "Eden Prince, I haven't seen you since you were twelve." He offers me his hand. "Do you remember me?"

"You're Noah's brother." Despite my best efforts,

vehemence sneaks into my words, and my eyes dart toward Noah in the distance—he put minimal effort into his appearance tonight. "Can I help you?"

He snickers. "You could introduce me to your friend here." He inclines his head toward Colton, and a smirk settles on his lips. "So I'm not being a rude bastard when I tell him I need to borrow you."

Colton narrows his eyes but offers his hand. "Colton Danvers."

"Ethan Barton. Is this your first Barton party?"

They shake, releasing quickly.

"Yeah," Colton says with a shrug. "My parents have come to these charity events the past couple years, but I'm usually away at Archer Collins. I had a good reason to come home this year." He shoots a smile in my direction.

"Right." Ethan looks unimpressed. "Anyway, I need to steal Eden. We'll catch you later." He snatches up my hand and drags me from my seat.

The moment we're in a separate room, I tear away and put a safe distance between us. "What the hell is your problem?"

Ethan studies me in amusement. "I believe the words you're looking for are 'thank you.'"

I scoff. "Please. You did nothing but try to get me alone. How are you less creepy than that guy out there?"

"Isn't he a little old for you?"

"Aren't you a little invasive and annoying?"

Ethan only laughs and pulls a beer out of his pocket—where the hell are my pockets with room for a twelve-ounce bottle? "Okay, maybe I was a bit presumptuous. You looked uncomfortable. I rescued you."

I grind my stiletto heel into the floor. "You did no such thing, Ethan Barton. Don't you dare assume I needed your help."

He raises a hand defensively. "Alright, you were doing fine with the awkward scooting backward and avoiding eye contact. That was totally giving him the hint you weren't interested."

"Don't patronize me." I tug my arms close and turn away. "He's a family friend. I have to be nice to him."

Ethan audibly winces. "He's awfully handsy for a family friend."

My lips purse. "Is there something I can help you with? Or do you just like thinking you're a knight in shining armor?"

He shrugs. "If the shoe fits…"

"The shoe does not fit. You're hardly Cinderella in this scenario."

The corners of his eyes crease with unspoken laughter. "I can kill a man with my bare hands. I'm definitely more knight than Cinderella, princess."

"Is there something you want, Ethan Barton? Because at this point, you're wasting my time. If your only desire is to inconvenience me, I'm done."

A smirk tugs at his lips. "You'd rather go back to the guy with his hand on your leg?"

I roll my eyes. "If all you have to your credit is that you're slightly better than the person my mother wants me to date, I have zero interest in continuing this conversation." I stomp past him, thankful when he lets me leave.

"See you round, Eden," he calls as I march back into the other room—

Wham!

Strong arms grasp my shoulders, preventing me from falling. I stumble backward, eyes wide.

The person in front of me is an exact replica of the man I just left. Can I seriously not escape these Barton brothers?

"You okay?" His voice is thick with concern. "Eden Prince, right?"

I nod.

"Do you know who I am?"

I clear my throat. "Clifford Barton."

He chuckles. "Cliff, please. What're you running from? Something the matter?"

I swallow, still trying to settle my unease. Is there nowhere safe in this house? "It's nothing. I'm fine."

"You want a drink? Punch?"

"I'm not thirsty."

"Your dress is really pretty, Eden." He says it with simple kindness in his voice, but I feel sick. "I can't believe you're the same age as Noah. You're so grown-up. Where you heading so quickly?"

I step away. "That's none of your business."

"To see your date again?"

Was he watching too? Do they not have anything better to do than stalk me? Do they have any idea how weird and creepy that is?

"I have to go." I step around him and storm toward the buffet to grab a drink.

I don't know where Colton went, but thankfully, Noah freaking Barton isn't hovering by the food anymore. He's the last person I want to talk to.

My eyes flit around the area while I pour a cup of

punch.

The Bartons' New Year's Eve party is the highlight of Tourmaline society. Mr. Barton uses the profit from the basement blackjack tables to fund a local charity—this year, it's a small food bank downtown.

But tonight, the house is especially packed. Everyone wants to pay their respects after Dr. Barton's death.

In a far corner, Colton chats with my mother, and Mama smiles at him with an affection she rarely shows me.

God, my feet hurt.

I step away from the buffet to find somewhere to take off my heels. Mama insisted I look particularly nice tonight—I don't often wear dress clothes, and I wasn't nearly as tall the last time I wore this dress. If I remember correctly, there's a private seating area on the—

My glass slips from my hand at the abrupt stop, punch spraying everywhere.

This is the second time I've run into someone tonight.

My fingers grip the wall to keep from falling, and my eyes settle on the lump of a person—wet and pink from my punch—on the floor. I suppose it shouldn't surprise me anymore. The moment I aim to avoid the Barton brothers, I stumble on the last one.

Noah brushes the wavy blond hair from his eyes and slowly rises from the floor, patting himself off. He sighs at the punch all over his vest and shirt.

Finally, his cold-blue eyes turn to me. "Hi, Eden."

CHAPTER 7

NOAH

Eden raises her chin, pink lips scrunching into a pout. "Noah."

"You need to watch where you're going." I glance at the mess again. "How could you not see me?"

"I don't have the ability to see through walls, Barton." Irritation laces her voice. "Don't pretend this is my fault. You didn't see me either."

She cannot be serious.

"You literally walked into me."

Her lips twist into a sneer. "So did you." She taps her foot, one hand on her hip. "You're as much at fault as I am. If not more so. Don't walk into people carrying drinks."

I scoff but step closer, my irritation feeding off hers. "Right, because Eden Prince can't even share blame equally. You'll never admit when you're wrong."

"You can't admit something that isn't true."

She is the most ridiculous person I've ever met. It's been two months since I saw her, and the first thing she does is start an idiotic, sophomoric spat. What put her in such a foul mood?

I examine my shirt again and shoot her a glare. "God, what the hell is wrong with you, Prince? Accept the blame and apologize."

Her jaw clenches. "I have nothing to apologize for, Barton. Don't you dare try to convince me otherwise."

Obviously, this conversation is going well.

"Unbelievable." I turn away—the staircase is right behind me.

In the safety of my bedroom, I slowly undo the buttons of my vest and blue dress shirt, eyes clamped shut. The vest slides off first.

No matter how long it's been, Eden Prince gets under my skin in a way no one else can. She's insane. The most stubborn person I've ever met.

I drop the shirt on the floor. Breathe in, breathe out. Try to release the tension.

Why are Ethan and Cliff such an embarrassment? Were they harassing her? Really, what made Ethan think tonight would be a good night to hit on a seventeen-year-old? She's eight years younger than him.

I slump against the bed.

Tonight would be different if Mom were here. Not that she attended many of Dad's parties, but I could always sneak up to the roof and find the International

Space Station with her telescope. I kept careful track of it throughout the years.

Why did Dad insist the party go on?

The last two months have been horrible. Everything is tainted; New Year's Eve is no different.

Every visitor has made the time to tell me and my brothers how horrible and tragic the accident was, how sad they are for us, how they wish things could be different, how awful it must be to live without a mother. A conglomerate of passive-aggressive, "nice" people reminding me my mother is dead.

As if I could forget.

I run a hand through my loose waves.

Eden Prince is the only person who hasn't been uncharacteristically nice. I shouldn't be surprised, considering how antagonistic she typically is, but the interaction was oddly refreshing.

Her inability to understand social circumstances is strangely admirable.

Honestly, though, Eden has more admirable qualities than I'd ever admit aloud. She's easily the smartest person in our year, but she's never intimidated and she never holds back. She's intelligent, brave, honest. Her openness, while frustrating, is also compelling. She doesn't worry about being bossy or authoritarian. She takes action. She's sure of herself.

Meanwhile, I've never been sure of anything in my life.

Well, that's not entirely true.

I'm sure we would be better off if Mom were here.

Finally, I rise from the bed to locate another shirt. There's a lavender dress shirt near the front of my closet, and I tug it on. I don't want Ethan hammering on my door—or worse, Dad.

I go to the balcony instead of rejoining the party.

No one's outside in this weather. The temperature's supposed to hit negative five degrees tonight, but the cold is refreshing after the heated bodies inside. Dad wasn't prepared for this many guests; he didn't adjust the thermostat accordingly.

I lean against the railing, my fingers wrapping around the ice-covered bar.

The ground below is coated in a thick layer of snow. Icicles dangle from the ledges. All parking spots along the street are full, and our circle driveway is packed. Luckily, all our neighbors are here. Not sure there's room to drive on the street. Nearly everyone in Tourmaline is here. Everyone who's anyone.

My fingers tap the railing.

How long does my social appearance have to last? Why couldn't Dad and Ethan accept I have no interest in participating? As the host and event organizer, Dad's busy. He never would've known if I skipped.

Except, you know, if Ethan and Cliff told on me.

Behind me, the door jostles open. Maybe somebody needs a smoke.

"Ugh, it's you."

I turn at the voice.

Eden, her silky black hair released from the prim bun and swept over one shoulder, the sleek dress sparkling in the moonlight, her black stilettos linked in one hand, stumbles onto the balcony.

I return my attention to the view. "Go back inside. I don't want to see you either."

She huffs as the door slams shut, but she pads closer, wincing at the cold on her bare feet. "Your brothers are annoying." Her narrow toenails are painted a shiny black.

That's nothing new. They've annoyed me since the day I was born.

"Somehow, you're my best option tonight," she adds.

"Are we actually going to talk, Eden?"

For a moment, she doesn't speak—maybe weighing the options. "It wouldn't be the worst thing that's happened tonight."

I snort. "Same."

"You skipped the last month of school, Noah."

"I'm aware."

Does she always have to be so nosy? She knows exactly why I missed school, and I'm well aware of how behind I am. At least most of the teachers are understanding.

"You missed essays and lab reports. Poor Kevin didn't have a lab partner, so Mr. Libby paired him with me and Harmony." She says *poor* like it's an insult—not because his family has no money but because she didn't want to be stuck with an additional lab partner.

"How inconvenient for you."

"You will be back when school starts again, won't you?"

I shrug. I don't want to, but Dad already made up his mind. *You can't shirk your responsibilities forever,* he said.

"How can you shrug about that?" Eden's voice is sharp, aghast. "School is important. What about the STEM fair?

You're not backing out of that too, are you?"

I turn.

Her face is twisted with irritation. Or maybe confusion.

"Why, Eden," I say, my voice slow and pointed, "could you possibly miss me?"

She scoffs. "Don't be moronic. If there's anything I miss, it's the competition. It's no fun winning first place without having beaten you in the process."

I roll my eyes.

"Although"—she relaxes a bit—"I will add, you're slightly less irritating than your brothers."

Laughter bubbles in my throat. "Thanks, I think."

For a long minute, she doesn't speak. She drops the stilettos to the concrete and leans against the railing just out of reach. Her eyes study the view, and her boobs press together as she rests her elbows on the bar, creasing the dress. "Have you heard back from any colleges yet?"

I force myself to look away. "I got accepted to Archer Collins."

She bristles at the words. "Really." It's not a question.

"Yup."

"Shouldn't you be excited?"

I shrug. "I don't know if I'm going."

Eden turns on me, her grip on the railing tight. "How could you possibly not attend Archer Collins?" She scoffs. "It's the best science school on the East Coast. The fact that you were accepted speaks very highly of you. Besides, isn't it the same school your mother attended?"

My eyes flutter shut.

I don't want to talk about my mother. Not after every person tonight told me how sad they are for me and how they've kept our family in their prayers.

No, thanks.

"Do you have to be so nosy?" I snap, shooting her a glare. "Can't you mind your own business for once?"

Eden's determined brown eyes quiver as her face morphs into a sneer. "It was a simple question. You don't have to bite my head off."

Damn, she's an easy mark.

"I don't know why I bothered trying to be civil. You'd think—" She freezes, and her anger fades. "You want to distract me, don't you?"

I turn toward the dark vista before us.

Eden falls silent, but I can feel her eyes on me. When she does speak, her words are uncomfortably gentle: "Don't you have goals? Dreams? A desire to succeed? You can't give up every time something inconvenient happens."

My dreams and goals, my ambition, have all fallen to the wayside. Even my attempts to work on my STEM projects are halfhearted at best.

Wait, what?

It shouldn't be funny, but my laughter escapes without restraint. "You're the only person in the world who would say my mom dying is 'inconvenient.'"

Eden's face contorts into a frown. "Are you making fun of me?"

I settle my laughter, but my lips remain twisted into a smile. "It's actually…kind of nice."

Her frown deepens, and she looks away. "No one wants to force you to come back to school before you're ready, but it feels like you're giving up." For once, her voice lacks her normal authoritative tone.

I shake my head.

Because she's wrong.

Dad hates me staying home. He hates that I missed finals. He hates that I spent so long "moping" around the house instead of doing anything. He hates that I feel.

He was back at work three days after the accident. He had contracts and business associates waiting for his input. He had a million excuses. He moved on, acted like everything was normal.

And Ethan and Cliff? They didn't even make the memorial. Cliff had a football game to attend, and I don't have "clearance" to know what was involved in Ethan's Raider assessment.

No one else cared when Mom died. I was the only one who cried.

"Well," I say after a deep breath, "I'll be back when the new semester starts. You can have your competition back."

"I'll look forward to it." She pushes away from the railing with a deep sigh. "Time to make a social appearance. Mama's probably wondering where I ran off to." She dramatically tosses her stilettos over her shoulder and marches toward the door, her hips swaying with her determined walk.

When she's gone, I rest my chin on my knuckles and close my eyes. How much longer till I'm allowed to call it a night?

CHAPTER 8

EDEN

Mama's hatchback pulls up to the curb in front of Tourmaline High School, the first of a long line of cars dropping off students. She shifts into park and offers me a tight smile. "We will pick up your car after school."

I nod. I'll be glad for it—for what little semblance of independence I have—but I'm also glad for this moment. My hand rests on the door handle, but I hesitate.

"Thien?" Her voice twists with uncertainty more than concern.

With a determined breath, I turn my full attention to her, ignoring the line of cars behind us. "Mama, I've been meaning to talk to you about him…"

I struggle to say his name.

In my moment of hesitation, she presses further. "Papa?"

That forces my mouth to work. "No, Colton."

She nods in acknowledgment but doesn't say anything.

Perhaps because we haven't discussed Colton Danvers since we parted ways with him at the end of the Bartons' party.

My jaw clenches as I concentrate, but I don't know how to word what I want to say.

In any other position, with any other person, I know exactly how I feel and where I stand and what to say. That is a luxury I never had with Mama.

Instead, I diverge: "You know how I've been applying to colleges, right?"

She nods tightly, no emotion on her face.

"I've been, you know, keeping my options open so to speak."

Unfortunately, my attempts to keep it low-key don't concern her. Her face doesn't relax or intensify.

I clear my throat. "One of the places I applied to is Archer Collins—you know, where Colton goes? It's one of the best schools on the East Coast, and after New Year's Eve, I was thinking it could be cool to go to the same school." I swallow down my discomfort. "As Colton."

Mama's brown eyes widen slightly before returning to their natural narrow oval. "How would we pay for it? Your papa cannot—"

"I know, I know," I try to reassure her, but I doubt it does any good. "They're having this event next month. The second weekend in February. They invited qualifying prospective students to apply for their Trustee Scholarship. It could pay for up to thirty thousand dollars of my annual tuition." I bite my lip. "Then, I would be there at Archer Collins…where Colton is."

No point in bringing up the fact that he's graduating this year and might not live in Bethlehem anymore. I can't ruin this.

Mama blinks once, twice, then nods slowly. "How do you apply for the scholarship?"

"That's the thing, I have to go there. I know it's all the way in Pennsylvania, but everything is arranged by the school. I would stay in the dorms with another student, and they would provide meals for the weekend. All I have to do is get there."

"I have to work, Thien—"

"You wouldn't have to do anything, Mama. I can find money for a flight there and back. If you can drop me off and pick me up…" I shift uncomfortably, and my eyes drift toward the side-view mirror, taking in the waiting cars behind us.

Mama's voice is sharp and unconvinced when she speaks again. "I don't think flying by yourself—"

"Maybe," I interrupt, turning hopeful eyes on her, "Colton would want to get together while I'm there. I'd have a lot of free time outside my scholarship obligations. Do you think he'd want to have dinner or something?"

She lays her hands on the steering wheel, but her grip is relaxed. "You liked him, then?"

I try to stay nonchalant but optimistic. "We didn't get to spend a lot of time together. There were so many people at the party. Spending time alone would let us get to know each other better."

Mama nods. "True." After a moment of unbearable silence, she turns to me with a tight smile. "I promise you nothing, Thien, but I will consider it."

But that smile—even a tight one—is enough.

"Thank you, Mama." I grab my backpack and finally

push open my door. "See you at three?"

She gives a short nod, and I close the door and rush up the front steps of Tourmaline High School.

At the top, I glance back, but Mama's hatchback is gone.

My hope, however, is fully restored.

She may not have given explicit permission, but she was convinced. In February, I will be in Bethlehem, Pennsylvania, at Archer Collins, earning the goodwill of my future professors and administration, making my mark. I just wish I didn't have to lie to convince her.

Inside, I settle into my regular seat. I'm later than normal now, but I still beat Tinsley.

I pull out my French textbook, register the time via the analog clock on the far cafeteria wall, and begin to read the next chapter.

"Finally!" Tinsley collapses onto the bench beside me and lays her chin in her hand. "What's going on?"

I flip the page. "Nothing."

"Don't lie to me. You haven't texted me in two days."

My eyes flit to the clock again. The bell will ring in three minutes—and that's not soon enough. "I've spent the last two days breeding microorganisms at Kresge. Is that something you needed an update on?"

She groans. "You know exactly what I want to talk to you about, Edie. How was your date?"

I snap the book shut. "It was awkward, uncomfortable, and then, oddly okay."

All she does is cock an eyebrow.

"Something about him was off."

"What does he look like?"

I shrug. "Light-brown hair, hazel eyes. He was wearing a gray suit with a gold dress shirt."

Tinsley's laugh is loud despite the chatter of our fellow students. "You have no imagination, Edie. Did your skin tingle when he held your hand? Did he hold you in his strong arms while you danced? Did you get butterflies when he kissed you at midnight?" When I don't speak, she adds, "Was he at least cute?"

I tilt my head. "I hadn't considered it."

She nearly falls off the bench. "You didn't consider whether he's attractive?"

"Really, Tins, we talked about Archer Collins. That's the only reason I was interested in the conversation. But he didn't care for the subject matter." My lips twist into a frown, and my eyes drift across the expanse of the cafeteria. Noah said he would be back for the new semester, but I haven't seen him yet. "We didn't talk for long."

I hesitate to tell her everything, to explain the conversation with Mama, especially when Mama hasn't given me an explicit yes yet. But part of me desperately wants to discuss the prospect of seeing Colton again in February. I have no idea how I'm supposed to feel about it.

"Why's that?"

I turn back to Tinsley. "We were interrupted by Noah Barton's brothers."

"Speaking of Noah"—she scoots closer—"did you see him? Talk to him? How's he doing?"

I quirk my mouth to the side. "He was hiding most of the night."

Tinsley rolls her eyes. "Yeah, but was he sad or upset or

anything? I mean, how was he really?"

I open my mouth, but I'm not sure what sort of answer she's looking for. Yes, Noah Barton was sad and uninterested in the party, but I can't read his thoughts. He certainly didn't tell me any intimate details during our odd chat on the balcony.

Thankfully, I'm saved from answering by the bell ringing.

Finally.

I rise from the bench and slip the textbook inside my—

There he is.

Noah trudges down the side of the cafeteria, heading straight for the back hallway. His dirty-blond hair is tousled, his hands shoved deep in the front pocket of his gray hoody, his eyes glazed over like he can't see what's in front of him.

CHAPTER 9

NOAH

"How are you doing, Noah?"

I turn glossy eyes on Mrs. Tamson and force a smile. "I'm alright."

It's the same question everyone else has asked—other students, teachers, even the counselor has requested I stop by after school. I'm not looking forward to that conversation.

It's the same question and the same charade. I spout the same line, the same bullshit. Not because it's true but because it's what they want to hear. It's the line they need to feel better. They don't actually care, but they feel a certain obligation to ask. Just like I feel a certain obligation to placate them.

Mrs. Tamson smiles back, but it's a sad, pitying smile— one I've become increasingly familiar with. "That's good to hear. Let me know if there's anything I can do for you."

I nod. Because it's what I'm supposed to do. We both know I'll never request anything of her, though. Or any of them.

I send her one last smile before stepping out of the empty classroom. This is—no surprise—not the first time today a teacher has asked me to stay after class to check in, and I'm sure it won't be the last.

I'd give anything to still be at home. Dad, of course, wouldn't hear anything of it, and there's no point arguing with him. He's become even more stubborn and uncaring over the last couple months. I didn't realize that was possible.

The bell rings, but I don't head for Physics. The class is one of my favorites and Mr. Libby has been my guide and mentor, but this is too much social interaction for my first day.

Instead, I stop in the bathroom.

I drop my binder on the counter—there's a small dry space near the corner—and stare at the mirror. No one's in here. The next class has already started. And I relish that silence. The aloneness is welcome after the last few hours.

I run my hands under the faucet and rub cold water over my face, trying to push some semblance of life back into my veins.

The day has passed in a haze. I don't know what we've discussed or studied in class. All I remember are the awkward interactions like Mrs. Tamson and the note from the guidance counselor. I haven't been present all day.

I run a wet hand through my thick blond hair, mussing it to the side, and look at myself again.

Finally, there's a hint of pink to my cheeks.

Tourmaline is so small I could sneak out of the school without anyone noticing. It wouldn't be difficult. I mean, Mr. Libby would notice. And Mr. Grady, my history teacher in final block.

And Eden.

Eden Prince would notice if I missed Physics today.

She would know. She would remember.

And that would make me a liar.

I specifically told her I would be in class after the New Year. Skipping out on the second half of the day doesn't qualify, especially when that means skipping the only class we have together.

With a heavy sigh, I finally turn off the water and wipe my hands on my jeans before snatching up my binder and heading into the hallway.

I guess I'm going to class.

The classroom is empty when I arrive, the other students' books and bags resting on or against their desks, and the door to the lab is open.

With a heavy sigh, I drop off my things and peek my head inside.

Near the whiteboard, Mr. Libby preps his demo for our first experiment of the new semester. The other students gather around the first lab table, where a wide selection of supplies and accoutrements are spread out.

At the front of the group is Eden Prince, a pen clenched between her perfect teeth, her shiny black hair pulled up into a high ponytail. She drops the pen onto her notebook, resting on the countertop, and takes a deep breath. "Mr.

Libby, can we start?"

Mr. Libby pauses in the middle of jotting a line on the whiteboard, and irritation shoots up his neck. He recovers before facing the crowd, capping the dry erase marker as he turns. "Thank you for your enthusiasm, Eden. Unfortunately, you'll have to wait till after my demonstration to start the assignment."

Eden doesn't miss a beat. "How long until we start the demonstration?"

Mr. Libby's eyes darken, and I snicker in quiet amusement. At least I'm not the only one who finds her irritating.

Then, his gaze falls on me.

"Just a moment," he says to the class before crossing the lab to meet me by the door. "Noah." He keeps his voice quiet as we slip into the classroom, but a smile spreads across his thin lips. "We missed you."

I step farther from the lab. "I guess."

"I'm glad you're back." But concern tinges his hazel eyes. "Are you ready to be here?"

I shrug, trying to stay nonchalant, but Mr. Libby is the only teacher who sees right through me. "I couldn't stay home if I wanted to," I admit. "My dad didn't leave room for negotiation."

He squeezes my shoulder with a wan smile. "Let me know if you need anything, okay?"

I nod, but my gaze drifts toward the open door to the lab.

"You ready to do a thermodynamics lab?"

My eyes shift back to him, and I force a smile.

He doesn't buy it, but he doesn't say anything either. Instead, he nods me toward the lab, and I follow him inside.

Mr. Libby returns to the whiteboard and finishes writing *Thermodynamics* in big, bold letters, but I hang back.

Until Kevin Barnes spots me.

"Noah, man!" He raises his hand high above the crowd and motions me closer, even nudges a few people out of the way so I can join him at the front.

People part for me, and the chatter that was prominent when I first arrived fades away.

Kevin pulls me right up next to the counter, squeezing me between him and Eden—who doesn't look up from her notebook, where she's prepping the page for notes on Mr. Libby's demonstration. Her lab partner Harmony flashes me a smile over Eden's hunched form.

Mr. Libby begins: "Alright, folks, we're not going to waste any time just because it's the first day of a new semester. We're studying thermodynamics for the next couple weeks, but before we get into the 'boring details,' we'll start with an experiment." He swishes his arm through the air, indicating everything on the table.

Everyone scoots closer, but my focus is on Eden, her body and handwriting stiff at our close proximity.

"Between now and Wednesday, you need to read the chapter on the Laws of Thermodynamics to get a handle on the material. Have a firm understanding of Stoke's Law of Laminar Flow to calculate viscosity." He lifts one of the PVC pipes to show us. "The experiment is simple, but most of your work will be in the setup. Each group will have these materials…"

Eden shifts, her rich brown eyes darting in my direction before returning to her notebook, and the image of the high and mighty way she slung her stilettos over her shoulder and marched inside my house, determinedly leaving me alone on the balcony, her pert butt swaying with the movement, flashes through my head.

"Three one-meter lengths of clear PVC, caps for each side, primer, and pipe cement for the tubes." Mr. Libby indicates each material with the pipe. "Bottles of olive oil, corn syrup, and motor oil for our liquid. Ball bearings for each tube. A tall tub to fill with hot water"—he points to the large white tub inside the sink—"along with a thermometer and timer. Everyone following?"

Stiffly, Eden nudges her notebook farther onto the countertop, but there isn't much space.

To my left, Kevin grins at me, but rather than try to figure out why he's pretending to care, I lean onto the counter and jut out an elbow—right into the edge of her notebook. Her pen slips mid-word, drawing a long line across the page.

Eden turns to me with a glare.

I focus on Mr. Libby.

"As you can see," he says, leaning forward to grab the primer, "you will put together your own viscometers for the project. Make sure to apply enough primer and cement so the ends seal before your experiment." He wipes down the ends of the pipe and twists open the primer and cement. "If your viscometers aren't properly sealed, your data will be invalid."

I chance a glance at her.

It's a mistake.

Her hand is clenched into a fist atop her notebook, and her pretty oval eyes are narrowed into slits.

I raise an eyebrow.

Seething, she leans close, voice dangerously low, and whispers in my ear, "What the hell is your problem?"

"Eden…" Harmony's voice is barely a whisper, but she lays her hand on Eden's shoulder. "Leave him alone."

Eden shakes her off and turns on her. "I didn't ask you to butt in."

Her cheeks flush, and she looks down, falling silent.

"Eden…"

We turn toward the front of the room.

Mr. Libby's lips are pursed. "You're disrupting the class. Please be quiet during my demonstration."

Beside me, she nods once.

"After the cement dries, you can continue." He holds up the newly sealed pipe. "We have three liquids, one for each pipe, and then, you'll seal the other end. Feel free to leave your viscometers at your stations so they can dry between classes." His eyes dart from student to student before stopping at my left. "Kevin, can you help take off the lids for me and cap them again when I'm done?"

I rest on my elbows again, curiously eyeing Eden's hurried notes, decidedly messier after my interruption, and scoot nearer. "What put you in a foul mood today?" I murmur.

Her pink lips twist into a scowl, and when she looks up, her eyes widen at the closeness. "Someone"—she glares—"was rude and invasive."

Amusement tugs at my mouth. "You just told your lab partner to shut up. Sounds like you're the rude one."

She scoffs, then silences her irritation. "We're in class. Be quiet." She redirects her attention to her notes, struggling to catch up with Mr. Libby's presentation.

"Alright," Mr. Libby says, holding up the open bottle of motor oil that Kevin just handed him. "Next, you fill the tubes with the respective liquids..."

I spend a couple seconds trying to focus before my attention drifts.

The other students—Kevin, Harmony, Kelsey, among several others—look away if I catch their eyes. This is hardly the first time someone has stared today. Not the first time I've caught someone staring today either.

Slowly, I return to her.

Because Eden Prince doesn't acknowledge the elephant in the room. Not the same way as everyone else at least. She doesn't stare or give me that look. The one that says they pity me.

Eden is never anything but genuine, even if that means she genuinely dislikes me.

I press close to her ear to keep my voice low, and she freezes the moment I touch her shoulder. "You're going to rewrite that whole page just because of one accident, aren't you?"

I need that sort of genuineness now.

She doesn't turn or look this time. "I'm not convinced it was an accident."

I release a mocking gasp. "You think I marred your perfect paper on purpose?"

"I don't think. I know." She slaps her pen against the counter, giving up on the notes, and faces me. "I know you."

"You don't know me as well as you think you do, Prince."

She wets her lips, and they glisten under the fluorescent lights as she purses her mouth and clenches her jaw. "You're not that hard to figure out."

My hand clamps onto the edge of the countertop, and I straighten to my full height—nearly a whole foot above her. "You're not—"

"*Noah, Eden!*"

We don't listen.

I step closer, and any remaining separation disappears. "You—"

But Eden never backs down. "Get out of my space," she snaps, pushing me backward.

There's a murmur as I stumble.

I grab for the counter. No grip.

Her wrist. My fingers find purchase.

Trip over someone's foot.

Bump into something else I can't see.

Caught off guard, Eden loses her footing.

Something cold and wet rains down as I hit the floor, Eden between my legs, her face against my chest.

I cough.

Something stinks.

Dark droplets of liquid speckle my face and shirt. It's all over the floor too. Oil. Must be the motor oil. Kevin was putting the lid on.

But Eden, now struggling to sit up, took the brunt of the assault. The back of her low-cut striped shirt is soaked, beads form along her hairline, and the oil oozes down her neck and shoulder.

I watch, enthralled, as a viscous stream of golden oil trails down her exposed cleavage—

Her hand slips, and she falls, panting. My arm wraps around her waist reflexively, but it's an unnecessary attempt to catch her.

Across the expanse of my chest, wide brown eyes find mine, and my grip on her tightens, keeping her safe in my arms, not wanting to let go.

Someone clears their throat.

Because, you know, we're not alone.

Eden moves to sit up again, and this time, I help her.

When we rise from the floor, gripping the edge of the counter to keep from slipping, everyone is staring. And Mr. Libby looks unamused.

"Eden, Noah," he says, his voice eerily calm, "it's time to make a change."

CHAPTER 10

EDEN

I can't sit. The motor oil, slick and slimy, has coated my entire back, even down my jeans. So I stand while Mr. Libby settles into his desk chair and that asshole Noah freaking Barton drops onto a chair and massages his lower back.

Mr. Libby swivels his chair to face us properly, but his face is tight, grim. "How would you like to have new lab partners?"

Noah doesn't speak.

My eyes widen, and I step forward. "Really? Who? When? That would be amazing."

"Harmony and Kevin work well together," Mr. Libby says with a nod, his eyes drifting toward the door to the lab, where the rest of the class is putting together their viscometers. Harmony and Kevin are working together since Noah and I are stuck in here—getting behind on our work.

"They'll make a great team."

I frown. Why are we talking about Harmony and Kevin?

"So," Mr. Libby says, returning to us, "starting Wednesday, the two of you will be paired together."

"What?" The word is sharp and loud and echoes through the empty classroom.

Noah leans forward in the chair. "Is that a good idea?"

I shoot him a glare before turning to our teacher. "This will not work. It isn't even an option. You know this won't work. This is completely unacceptable."

He sighs and taps his index finger on his knee. "Eden, we've had this discussion before…"

"No." I stamp my foot to make a point, but I can feel globules of oil slide down at the sharp movement. "We have not discussed your switching our partners in the middle of the school year. Why should we work together? That makes no sense whatsoever. Did you miss the mess we just made?" I throw my arm in the direction of the lab before gesturing to my own state. "Can you not see the mess we're in right now?"

Mr. Libby purses his lips. "No, Eden, I noticed your mess—a mess you'll be cleaning up while everyone else preps for Wednesday's lab. But we have had a serious conversation about respect, haven't we?"

Heat rises to my cheeks, but my hesitation is short-lived. "That's not an explanation. I was unaware of any need for a new system. As the Senior Class President, I demand an explanation."

He scowls. "I'm happy to give one, Eden, but asking would've been a better approach, don't you think?"

I return his scowl with a fierce glare and cross my arms. "What is it then?"

He hesitates, glancing between us. "You two have been disrupting class since the moment I met you. This unacceptable behavior is a serious impediment to teaching, and I will tolerate it no longer. You're both highly intelligent individuals, and I love that the competition encourages you to excel, but no one else can excel with your constant interruptions and distractions."

Noah frowns. "How is pairing us together supposed to make that better?"

"This isn't right!" My eyes narrow into slits, and my nose and mouth twist with anger. "You cannot partner us together. This is ridiculous."

Mr. Libby leans back with a sigh. "I'm surprised at you, Eden." His tone specifically indicates he isn't. "Don't you want the most appropriate and skilled partner? You two are my best students. If you could ever manage to get along, you would make excellent partners." He quirks an irritating little smile. "So we're going to spend the rest of the school year finding out."

I scoff. "Harmony has been a perfectly fine partner. She's always cooperative."

He levels me with an unimpressed glower. "You forgot to include Harmony's name on your last lab report. You never allow her to participate in the experiments or write any of the reports. That behavior stops now."

"But Mr. Libby—"

"No, Eden. Class President or not, I am your teacher. I make the decisions." He pushes up from the chair, moving on. "Now, let's get back in there, and I'll grab you two some cleaning supplies…"

Noah rises too, a hand in his pocket, no real reaction to the situation. How can he not care?

"Do the two of you need to make a phone call for some extra clothes?"

Noah glances at himself—he's practically clean compared to the mess covering me—and shrugs. "I might have another shirt in my locker."

Instead of answering, I march toward my desk and gather up my things. I'm not going to stay here to clean up a mess that was barely my fault. There's motor oil covering half my body, and it's Noah fucking Barton's fault. Not mine.

"Eden…"

I ignore Mr. Libby's calls as I storm out of the classroom, heading for the front of the school.

I'm not staying here.

I'm going home, taking a shower, and putting on fresh clothes. These are ruined.

I stop at my locker and tear open my purse, but the keys are missing.

Dammit.

My car's at the shop to replace the exhaust manifold. Mama dropped me off this morning.

Leaving me no means of escape.

Dammit.

I slam my locker shut and click the lock into place.

Inside the classroom, Mr. Libby waits for me by the door, alone. Like he knew I'd be back. I stop in front of him.

"You dropped your phone, Eden." He offers it to me.

I snatch it from his hands, irritation rearing its head again, but I swallow it down. "Can I call my mom?"

A small, reassuring smile graces his face. "Of course." He steps away, heading toward the lab again. "You'll help clean while you wait for her to get here."

Mama's russet-brown eyes assess me, but I have nothing to say. I grab the bag of clothing from her hands and leave the front office. The bathroom is only twenty feet down. I can change and clean myself as best I can there.

Mama follows.

She hovers by the sinks while I shut myself in a stall and tear off my shirt. She clears her throat. "Thien, explain this to me."

I run the shirt over my hair, but the motor oil—the feel of it and the smell—has permeated everything. "I explained over the phone, Mama. We were working on an experiment, and one of the liquids spilled."

The shirt she brought me is a simple green tee with an image of the Earth and the words *Make Earth Day Every Day*. She probably grabbed the first thing she saw.

"How?"

I pause with the new shirt halfway on, then finish tugging it down and flatten it against my sides. "Noah knocked it over."

No sense in lying to her more than necessary.

She clucks her tongue. "On purpose?"

"Not exactly."

The jeans are next, and I switch them for the black

skinny jeans she brought, slipping my feet out of my sneakers to do so.

"What does that mean?" Mama asks.

I bite my lip, then busy myself with stuffing the dirty clothes inside the now empty bag, covering up any opportunity to respond. I hang the bag onto the door hook and pull my sneakers back on, taking a moment to tighten and retie the laces.

Only when I unlock the door and exit the stall, bag in hand, do I answer: "He didn't mean to spill the oil. He was trying to annoy me."

Mama raises an eyebrow.

And you know, I may have pushed him a little bit.

I set the bag on the counter, then grab a paper towel, run it under hot water, and add a little soap. I shoot a sideways glance in her direction, but she isn't focusing on me, and I turn back to the mirrors and begin to scrub at my face.

Mama crosses and uncrosses her arms with a heavy sigh. "Do you want to visit your papa after we pick up your car? You haven't—"

"I've been busy, Mama." I drop the towel in the trash and lean over the sink to splash cold water on myself. "I'll visit later." I don't bother looking at her as I pat my face dry. Instead, I examine my flushed cheeks in the mirror. No more makeup today apparently. I'll survive.

"There are more important things than your experiments, Thien."

I shoot a glance in her direction before turning back to my face in the mirror, slowly fading back to its natural warm fawn tone. "I'll visit him when I can. I…I have to get back to class."

She doesn't say anything else.

Not even goodbye when we part ways at the bathroom entrance, she for the school entrance and myself for the hallway leading back to the classrooms.

CHAPTER 11

NOAH

Dad isn't usually home this early, but his car's in the garage when I park my bike and he's sifting through the freezer when I enter the kitchen. He glances over as I lay my backpack on the counter. "How was school?"

I push past him to grab a soda from the fridge door. "Fine."

It's not like he wants to know. He wouldn't listen when I asked to stay home this morning. I don't want to deal with everything—the watching, the whispers, the overly nice attitudes.

But that's not the reason my stomach is a swirl of energy and confusion. What stands out the most from today isn't the awkwardness or the stares. It's not even the mess we made, the bruise forming on my lower back from hitting the hard concrete floor, or the fact that I have a new lab partner I'm not looking forward to working with.

No, what stands out is lying there with Eden on top of me. Covered in motor oil, surprised, and breathless, she finally had nothing snobby or authoritarian to say.

There was something in the way she looked at me, something about how she fit in my arms. I can't put my finger on it.

I don't think I want to.

Dad pulls a couple frozen pizzas out and glances between them. "Which do you want for dinner?"

"Why not both?"

"Your brothers are heading out soon." He purses his lips, not meeting my eyes. "Cliff needs to get back early for practice, so Ethan's dropping him off on his way to the base. They're packing."

Ah, that's why he's home early.

"Can we talk about February again?"

Dad's back stiffens. "What about it?"

"Have you thought more about the scholarship weekend? It doesn't cost anything to attend. I'd stay in the dorms with a student sponsor. It wouldn't be inconvenient."

He sighs. "That's not true, and you know it. I'm traveling that weekend. How would you get there?"

I bite my lip. "I could take a plane down by myself. I'm seventeen. I'm practically an adult."

Dad shoves one of the pizza boxes back in the freezer. "You're not an adult yet."

I run a hand through my loose blond bangs. "Dad, this is my future. Archer Collins means a lot to me. This weekend could get me an amazing scholarship. Why don't you understand that?"

"Noah, you're being melodramatic." Finally, he turns.

"Missing out on this weekend is not the end of the world. You future doesn't hinge on one event."

"Could you at least consider it for more than a split second?"

"You think I haven't considered it in the two weeks since you first brought it up?" Dad's veins pulse when he clenches his jaw. "Of course I've considered it, but that doesn't change my answer."

There's no reasoning with him.

I grab my backpack off the counter and head upstairs. The solitude will be a relief after the day I've had.

Unfortunately, there's no relief when I reach the second floor.

Both Cliff and Ethan's doors are open, and the heavy thump of Metallica's "Whiskey in the Jar" blares throughout the upstairs. Great. Hopefully, the music is loud enough they don't register my arrival.

I hide in my room and lay my things on the bed.

After an arduous discussion with the school counselor this afternoon, I have a proper understanding of how to proceed with my incompletes last semester. My teachers have been generous under the circumstances—I need to write a couple essays. Tedious but very doable. Better to get it out of the way.

I sit at my desktop with the notes from my meeting, but even with the door shut, the music is too loud to focus.

Finally, Metallica fades...

Only to be replaced by Breaking Benjamin.

When did Dad say they're leaving? At least when

they're not home, things are quiet and Dad's never here. The silence is welcome compared to this madness...though I'm not sure I want the moments of reflection that come with that silence.

I don't want to reflect on my day.

To reflect on Eden.

A frown tugs at my lips, and I rub my face in an attempt to push away the exhaustion.

Unsuccessful.

I can't close my eyes. Even with the music going, all I see is Eden Prince on top of me, dripping, panting, pretty brown eyes staring.

Plus, that view down her shirt.

I shouldn't have looked. That was inappropriate. Weird.

But now, I can't stop picturing it.

Hormones. It has to be hormones.

I'm seventeen. It was bound to happen sometime. Just, you know, not with Eden Prince.

Arguing with her is a convenient distraction, but things were never supposed to get out of hand.

Knock, knock.

I twist toward the door as it creaks open, almost eager for the interruption.

Ethan pokes his head in. "Oh, good, you're here." He steps inside, and he practically has to yell over Cliff's music. "Didn't know when you'd be back from school. Dad says you've been going by the park a lot."

"I had a couple meetings today." I turn back to the desktop and open a new Word document. "Stuff I had to take care of."

"Right."

"Something I can help you with?"

Ethan closes the door, shutting out the music again, and collapses on my bed. "We're gonna head out here in about fifteen. I just put my bag in the rental."

"Yeah, Dad mentioned you were leaving soon. Gotta be at the base by midnight?"

"You can call me to talk if you ever need to, you know." His voice is softer now, harder to hear over the pounding bass.

I focus on the bright screen. "Yeah, sure."

He says that like we're close, like he has even a minute understanding of me.

The silence between us is heavy, and after a minute, he slaps his knee and pushes off. "So I guess we're gonna head out. Not sure when I'll have more leave—not till after phase two of my assessment—but I'll see you."

"Right. See you," I call after him as he slips from my room.

A moment later, the music shuts off, and their footfalls pass my door, then continue downstairs.

Alone at last.

Alone with my traitorous thoughts.

CHAPTER 12

EDEN

MY FINGERS THRUM AGAINST THE COUNTERTOP, STRIKING a heavy beat on the metal surface.

Kresge Laboratories, owned and operated by Dr. Edith Langston and Dr. Emily Hook, is the only real lab in tiny Tourmaline, Maine. The doctors primarily perform medical research, and because of their work in the community, they became good friends with Papa.

He was, after all, mayor of Tourmaline for nine years. He would have kept the position if his health hadn't begun to deteriorate.

I replace the slide on the microscope stage and flip on the illuminator. The microorganisms have grown tremendously in only the last couple days.

But my fingers still drum, drum, drum on the counter. "You look agitated."

As Dr. Emily Hook pauses by my lab station, I look up,

offering her little more than a shrug.

When I first planned this experiment, I had no idea how to proceed. STEM fair regulations require all experiments of this nature to be performed in a laboratory. They can't be done at home—and Mama wouldn't have allowed that.

Visiting Papa reminded me we still have his connections, even if he hasn't been the Mayor of Tourmaline in five years. I contacted Dr. Hook immediately, and when I presented my case, she okayed the experiment. I started setting up the following Monday.

"Is your experiment not going well?" She pulls out the stool beside me.

I look back through the microscope. "Their growth is on target—better than target, really."

Dr. Hook flashes me her teeth in a wide smile. "That's wonderful, Eden."

I nod.

"So what's the matter?"

My fingers finish a final beat on the metal countertop, and I flip off the microscope's light. "School things." When she raises an eyebrow, I continue. "I got in an argument yesterday, and my Physics lab partner was reassigned to someone else."

"Oh? Are you working alone then?"

I wish.

A scoff escapes my lips. "Of course not. Mr. Libby assigned me to work with him." I cannot hide the vehemence.

Dr. Hook shoots me a little bemused smile. "Who?"

Here, though, I hesitate. Not because I have any guilt

or remorse when it comes to my antagonistic relationship with Noah Barton, but because of the multiple times I've been reminded it's rude to speak ill of someone after their mother just died. I don't see how one has to do with the other, but that doesn't stop people—mostly Tinsley—from telling me to "be nice."

"Noah Barton," I say in a hushed voice. "He threw motor oil on me."

Her eyes light up with recognition. "Ginny's youngest?" A small smile flashes across her lips, then disappears. "I haven't seen him since he was five or six. Dr. Barton did a little work here at the time, you know."

I didn't know. I was in kindergarten.

"Why did he throw motor oil on you?"

I scowl.

Perhaps he was enjoying irritating me. Or he was bored listening to the instructions. Or he wanted the perfect view down my shirt.

Or you know, maybe it was somewhat of an accident.

I guess.

"Well," I say with a sigh, "it may have been an accident."

"Then why are you so upset about it?"

"We have our first lab experiment tomorrow morning. He's the reason I got in trouble, and then we have to work together? It's ridiculous." I huff, then turn back to the microscope, even if I don't feel like working. "I don't understand why Mr. Libby thinks working together will make us get along. It'll only make things worse."

"Or you could give him a break, Eden." Her voice is soft, gentle, but it sends a shiver down my spine. "His mother just died. Don't you think he could use a friend now more than ever?"

I frown.

I'm not sure Noah Barton wants a friend. He seems to enjoy arguing with me more than all the nice things people have said or done after Dr. Barton died.

In the morning, the cafeteria is loud, overwhelming, and I'd prefer not to be here today. I already had an intense early Student Council meeting, during which we achieved absolutely nothing.

Now, the bell is about to ring, and Tinsley still isn't here.

And worst of all?

Today, Noah and I must complete an experiment without breaking anything.

"Sorry, sorry." Tinsley drops onto the bench beside me and leans her head on my shoulder. "It's been a long morning."

The bell rings.

I nudge her off my shoulder. "It's not even eight in the morning, Tins. What could've possibly happened already?" I rise from the bench and grab my backpack. "Did you forget I have an experiment with Noah freaking Barton today? Can you believe it?"

She sighs. "It's not a big deal, Edie."

My jaw tightens. "You relish my pain."

Subdued laughter bubbles from her lips, and she stands too, holding her bag over one shoulder. "No, you're melodramatic."

I narrow my eyes, then turn on my heel and head

toward the classrooms. We move with the crowd, Tinsley on my heels.

Our first classes are next to each other, but our lockers are half a hallway apart—they're arranged alphabetically, and *Edwards* is decidedly earlier in the alphabet than *Prince*.

"I am not melodramatic, Tins." I stop next to her locker as she fiddles with the lock. "Why can't you see this is huge?"

She rolls her eyes, and the lock comes loose. "You and Noah could work well together if you sucked it up and stopped being idiots." She hangs her bag inside and pulls out the books and binder for her first two classes.

I huff. "We're not idiots, thank you. We're the top two students in our year with above average IQs."

The locker slams shut, and she shoots me a glare as she reattaches the lock. "Right, so you're both giant nerds."

"Did I mention we've both been accepted to Archer Collins?"

Tinsley starts down the hallway again. "You've only mentioned it a million times. Do we really need is to extend this rivalry for another four years? One of you could go to a different school. Seriously, give the rest of the world a break."

We stop again, but Elise Porter is making out with her boyfriend against my locker.

"I'm not going anywhere but Archer Collins," I say loudly. "He can go somewhere else."

Elise and Ramon don't get the hint.

"Excuse you!" I snap my fingers near their faces. "Stop exchanging fluids, and get out of the way."

Behind me, Tinsley snickers as they finally separate and, irritated, scoot out of my path.

I put in the combination and tear open my locker. The contents are perfectly organized: textbooks on the top shelf, my jacket and backpack hanging from the hooks, my lunch box on the bottom, and an eight-by-eleven-inch calendar attached to the inside of my door.

Now that we're alone—relatively—it's Tinsley's turn to lean against the lockers while I grab my statistics and physics books. "Edie, I'm pretty sure Noah's school choice was because his mom went there. I don't think he'll change his mind."

I scoff. "Well, I'm not changing mine."

"You can be really rude, you know?"

I pause.

Her words are harsher than normal. She's rarely angry with me for fighting with Noah—she typically finds it entertaining. How is this different?

I purse my lips and slam my locker. "So can you, Tins."

Time for class.

I sit at station number six per usual.

Unfortunately, that's the only usual thing about Physics today.

Instead of sitting with me, Harmony joins Kevin at station four, and a good minute after the tardy bell rings, Noah Barton collapses onto the stool beside me.

"What took you so long?"

He rolls his eyes. "What do you care?"

I scoff. "When you're late, you make the entire class take longer, and as my partner, you're an impediment to our project."

For a minute, he simply stares—while Mr. Libby stands at the head of the lab, talking about the project—and then, he laughs.

"What?" I hiss.

Noah's lips curl into a smile. "I'm so sorry to inconvenience you, Eden. Those thirty seconds before Mr. Libby started class definitely impeded the project."

I grit my teeth. Great. What I really need is another person treating me like I'm melodramatic and insane.

Before I say anything, he directs his attention to Mr. Libby, and I force myself to focus as well.

"As you know," Mr. Libby says, "the purpose of this project is to study the effect of temperature on a liquid's viscosity and determine whether there is a universal relationship between viscosity and temperature. We'll work on this experiment today, and your lab reports will be due next Wednesday. Any questions?"

Two people raise their hands.

I turn back to our station. I have no patience for idiotic questions.

Our tub is in the sink already, but the viscometers we made last time are sitting upright to finish drying—we barely managed to finish them before the bell rang. The liquids inside are at room temperature. We should time their viscosity now for a control group.

I pull out my notes from last class—rewritten and reorganized on a fresh page.

At the front of the lab, Mr. Libby's done with questions.

"Get to work. I'll be checking on you throughout class."

I'm ready.

"You can flip the viscometers." I grab the timer from the countertop, ready to press the button as soon as he proceeds. "I'll keep track of the times in my notes."

Across from me, Noah purses his lips. "What, do you not trust me to operate the timer correctly?"

I frown.

Honestly, I don't trust anyone to operate the timer correctly. Tinsley rolls her eyes at my perfectionism, but I'm being realistic. Other people rarely live up to my expectations.

"Yeah, that's what I thought." Instead of flipping over the first viscometer, he twists on the hot water.

True, we need to fill the tub, but shouldn't we measure the control group first? Is he doing this out of order to annoy me?

I wouldn't put it past him.

Noah pokes a finger in the water, but it's not hot enough because he turns his attention to the viscometers. "Which order?"

"What?"

He shoots me an irritated glance. "Olive oil, corn syrup, and motor oil. Which order do you want to go in? I imagine you'll be particular about these experiments."

I roll my eyes. "Olive oil, motor oil, then corn syrup. We should go in the order of highest viscosity to lowest, obviously."

He checks the temperature again—it's steaming now—and spins the faucet to fill the tub.

"Do you have a hypothesis about the results?"

Noah chuckles as he wipes his hands on a paper towel. "Liquid viscosity is inversely proportional to its temperature, and you know that, Eden."

Of course I do.

He grabs the viscometer of olive oil and meets my eyes. "You ready?"

With the timer in my left hand and a pen in my right, I nod.

"Let's get to work."

Despite our disagreements, we're still the first to finish. The other groups took too long to start the experiment.

As expected, the liquids were least viscous when we first put them in the hot water, and as the water cooled, they thickened up. Now, we use Stoke's Law of Laminar Flow to calculate the viscosity based on the time it took the ball bearing to fall through the tube.

After that, we only have the actual report. I can get that done over the weekend. We'll get extra credit for turning it in early.

I close my notes while Noah organizes his things on the other side of the classroom—everyone else is still in the lab next door. "You took notes too, right?"

He glances over. "Of course. You saw me."

"Give them to me. I'll do the lab report over the weekend. You can look over it on Monday before we turn it in."

Noah gapes. "That's ridiculous."

"It's efficient."

He stops packing up, and his eyes narrow. "You're not

writing the report without me, Eden. This is a partner project, and I won't allow you to take control of our assignments. We do this together or not at all."

"Why do you want to play by Mr. Libby's rules?" I cross one leg over the other. "We're faster if we work separately. You know that. You can write our next report."

He raises an eyebrow, amusement etched on his features. "You would never let me be in charge of an entire report. Eden Prince doesn't relinquish control if her life depends on it."

I purse my lips. "As irritating as you may be, I've seen your reports. They're almost as good as mine."

He laughs—a full hearty laugh that lights up his eyes, a laugh I doubt anyone has heard in a few months. "Gee, thanks. I feel so reassured." He shakes his head. "I'm still not letting you write the report alone. I will complain to Mr. Libby that you're ignoring the parameters of the assignment. I'm sure he'd be willing to take action." He shrugs, nonchalant, and continues packing. "Who knows, he may even fail you."

My eyes widen, and I clutch my notebook to my chest. I cannot afford to fail the assignment, even if Mr. Libby's requirements are insulting and ridiculous.

"Let's get together this weekend."

I shake my head. "You can't come over."

My mom would flip if she found out I had a boy over, even for a class project.

"Fine." He zips his bag closed. "You can come to mine. You have a car, right?"

I nod. "I'm busy Saturday morning and all of Sunday. When are you available?"

"Whenever. Saturday afternoon." Noah shoulders his bag, even though the bell hasn't rung. "Or Friday night if that doesn't work."

I scowl. "Saturday afternoon should be fine. Two o'clock?"

"Great."

I heave a sigh. "Glad we agree."

He snorts. "Sure you are."

CHAPTER 13

NOAH

DAD NORMALLY WORKS ON THE WEEKENDS, BUT WHEN Eden's white Prius parks in our driveway, he's still here. God, the last thing I need is for him to make this more unbearable. Why isn't he working?

She climbs out of her car and pulls her backpack from the passenger seat.

I meet her at the door before she can ring the bell.

Eden's brown eyes widen when I tear open the door, her hand poised to press the button. Her lips, painted with a thick pink gloss, twist into a frown. "That was cree—"

I snatch her upheld hand, thread our fingers together, and drag her inside the house. "Hush."

The door closes behind her, and I tug her across the entryway toward the nearby stairs. She follows, her sneaker-covered feet stumbling over the maroon rug, but she doesn't fall.

Dad is in the kitchen. If we hurry, we can sneak upstairs without him noticing.

"Where are we going?"

God, doesn't she know when to be quiet?

I shush her again; this time, she listens.

Once we reach my bedroom, I lock the door behind us.

She tears away from me. "What the hell?"

I flip on the light and turn to her, hesitant. "My stuff's all up here."

Eden crosses her arms, and finally, her eyes flit around the room, examining her surroundings. "This is your bedroom." The words are contemplative—and they quiver with concern.

I did just lock her in my bedroom.

"Uh, yeah." I take a seat at my desk to give her space. The computer's already on, and my notes sit on the desk by the keyboard. "Where do you want to begin?"

Finally, she settles on my bed, her mouth taut, her eyes continually scanning the room.

The contents are minimal: a queen bed with blue and gray bedding, a desk with my computer, a nightstand, and a closet. My decorations are minimal—glow-in-the-dark stars on the ceiling, an Archer Collins pennant pinned to a corkboard, a couple picture frames. I don't keep much, and I don't need much. This has always been my haven from Dad's judgmental looks, from Ethan's commentary, from the world wondering what I'll do now.

Not many people have seen my bedroom.

Eden slips off her backpack and unzips the bag. "I already started the report, so maybe you should read over what I've written."

"Are you serious?" A scowl contorts my mouth. "We need to do this together. That's what partnership means."

She doesn't look up. "I don't want to be your partner. Why would you prolong this process by making us rewrite the work I've already done?"

"You don't get to be right all the time. You may not like it, but that doesn't change that we're partners." I heave a sigh. "Give it here, then."

She wakes her laptop from hibernation, and the document is open when she logs in. "Come and read it."

I join her on the bed with an irritated huff, scooting close enough to see the screen. She still holds onto the computer, her body stiffening—but if she won't let me hold it, being close is the only way I can read what she's written. Maybe she's hoping I'll give up. Not a chance.

Her eyes flit in my direction, but she doesn't look at me. "What do you think?"

I blink. I've barely looked at her words—and she's well aware. I clear my throat and lean closer, skimming over the partially written report.

She skipped the introduction and went right into the procedure, a compilation of our worksheet and her notes. Below that, she has a chart listing our data. She could use adding in more details, but the work itself is sound. You know, because the procedure is the easiest part to write.

I lean back, putting more space between us. "Looks good."

"Did I miss anything?"

The words are a challenge. She wants me to admit she was right and should finish it on her own.

I won't let her have the satisfaction.

"The title would be a good thing to have, right?" I shrug, trying to be blasé.

Eden flushes—more from frustration than embarrassment—and types out a quick title below our names and the date. What's more impressive is that she included my name at all.

I grab my notes from the desk and sit on the bed, giving her most of the queen-sized mattress. "We still have the introduction, results, and conclusion. We need to discuss any factors that influenced the experiment."

"I wrote down a few." She pulls out her notebook and reads off a couple options: "What would happen if we mismeasured the diameter of the ball bearings. What would happen if the water started at a lower temperature. What would happen if we incorrectly computed the viscosity. What would—"

"If we used the timer incorrectly." I shoot her a challenging look—I can list off a bunch of human errors too. "If we used liquids with closer viscosity. If the tubes weren't properly sealed. There are a lot of options."

She nods, lips pursed. "I'm sure there are many potential errors we can include."

"Especially for the person keeping track of the data."

Eden narrows her eyes—that was her job, after all. "We have a lot of work to do."

I lie back, holding my notebook above my head. "Obviously, the olive oil was most viscous, corn syrup the least, and motor oil was in between. As predicted, the viscosity decreased as the temperature increased..."

"But," Eden says, taking control yet again, "the data doesn't support the secondary hypothesis: There's no universal viscosity-versus-temperature curve, and the magnitude of the effect that temperature has on liquid viscosity is not directly proportional to the average viscosity."

"Right."

A knock sounds on the door.

I look up, eyes wide. What does Dad want?

"Noah, you in there? There's a weird car—"

I jump up, unlock the door, and stumble out into the hallway, slamming the door behind me. "What, Dad?"

Eyes dilated in the darkness of the hallway, Dad frowns. "Everything okay, Noah?"

"Uh, yeah. How can I help you?"

He takes a moment to decide whether or not to believe me. "There's a car I don't recognize in the driveway. Any idea who it belongs to? Do you have someone over?"

I open my mouth but hesitate. "Um, we're working on a Physics report. It's no big deal."

Dad raises an eyebrow. "Does your friend want to stay for dinner? I've got some frozen lasagna to shove in the oven."

"No, no, Dad, she can't stay that long."

The other thick eyebrow darts up. "'She'? Do you have a girl in your room?"

Heat rises to my cheeks. "We're working on a project."

"Right, 'working on a project.'" His lips purse in amusement. "Do you need condoms?"

My jaw drops. "You can't be serious. We're not even friends, Dad. We're not going to…you know."

Dad shakes his head. "There's no harm in talking about

sex, Noah."

I pinch the bridge of my nose and close my eyes, my back against the door. "No offense, Dad, but if sex were on my radar, you're the last person I'd want to discuss it with."

He chuckles. "So you do like her."

"What? I didn't say that." I don't imagine my hot cheeks give him the right impression, though.

"You don't have to." Dad lays a hand on my shoulder in a way I imagine is meant to be encouraging. "Attraction—sex—is completely natural. You should never be ashamed of these feelings."

"We're working on a lab report." I take a calming breath and meet his eyes. "We'll be done before dinner, so Eden won't be able to stay." I force my irritation into the words. Maybe he'll realize I want him to go away.

He pulls back, eyebrows raised. "Eden Prince? The Vietnamese girl?"

Shit.

"Yes, Eden Prince."

"She's pretty," he says, nodding.

"I hadn't noticed." But my cheeks are still flushed—especially at the vivid memory of slick oil dripping down her exposed cleavage, her shallow hot breath grazing my face. "We don't get along, you know. We argue all the time."

"Most people call that foreplay." Dad winks, a grin on his tawny face. "I'll let you get back to it then, and I'll buy you a pack of condoms…just in case."

When he's gone, I press my forehead to my bedroom door and shut my eyes.

What the ever-loving hell was that? Why would he assume I'm interested in her just because she's in my room?

I brought her up here to avoid awkwardness, but of course, my luck is nonexistent.

Although, I suppose, when have I had a girl in my bedroom before?

The worst part is, there's no way she missed that conversation. We were talking right in front of the door, and Dad's voice is loud when he whispers. He wasn't whispering.

After a few calming breaths, I push inside my room. "Uh, sorry about that." I hesitate, then slowly close the door.

Eden can't look at me. Or speak apparently. And her cheeks are tinged pink.

Huh.

After knowing each other for over ten years, I finally found a way to render Eden Prince speechless.

I clear my throat as I sit on the bed beside her, grabbing my notebook from where I abandoned it. "Right, where were we?"

Eden sits up and shifts to put some distance between us. She pulls her laptop closer. "I'm not having sex with you."

I frown. "I didn't ask you to."

"You brought me to your bedroom and locked the door." She sighs. "I'm flattered or whatever, but it's not happening."

I heave a sigh. "Look, I'm sorry about that. I hadn't expected my dad to be home when we discussed meeting, and I didn't want him to bother us."

She shoots me a skeptical glance. "While you were seducing me?"

I scowl. "I don't know, Eden. Have I tried seducing

you?"

"I wouldn't expect you to be good at it. Do you know how?"

"Would you recognize someone trying to seduce you?"

"What the hell is that supposed to mean?"

"No one's ever tried, so why would you know what flirting looks like?" I shrug, trying to seem nonchalant. "Let alone someone wanting to sleep with you. Most people find you annoying."

Her jaw clenches, but she closes her laptop with absolute precision. "Plenty of people want to sleep with me, thanks."

I blink away the thought of her petite body in my arms, the golden oil dripping into regions unexplored.

I'm not supposed to think about that. To think about her like that.

When I look at her again, unable to argue, her pale face has turned a deep pink. Refusing to look at me, she slips off the bed and slides her laptop and notebook inside her backpack. "I'll finish the report over the weekend."

I scoff. "This is a partner assignment."

"Next time, don't lock me in your bedroom," she snaps. "Maybe don't stare at my boobs after dumping a quart of motor oil all over me."

I flush. I didn't realize she noticed me checking her out.

No, not checking her out.

Looking.

Just looking.

She meets my eyes as she pulls her backpack over her shoulder. "I'll see you Monday in class. You can look over the report then."

My eyes narrow into a glare. "If you finish the report by yourself, I'm turning in my own. You barely let me look at it."

Eden laughs as she marches to the door. "You won't. That wouldn't be in your own self-interest, and you're no fool." She slips out with a confidence in her step I don't possess.

I sigh.

She may think I'm a fool—and hell, I might be one—but I'm writing my own damn report.

CHAPTER 14

EDEN

I'M THE FIRST PERSON IN THE PHYSICS CLASSROOM THE following Wednesday, and I organize my desk and pull out the seventeen-page lab report.

At the back of the room, Mr. Libby types away on his desktop, not even looking as the rest of the class slowly files into the room.

I flip through my report—our report—to make sure I didn't miss anything. Not that I could change anything if I had. They're due today, and I've double-checked it at least five times since I finished it over the weekend.

I asked Noah to check it Monday like I said I would, but he had zero input. He thumbed through the pages, his mouth set in a firm line, and handed it back. He didn't say a thing.

To be fair, Noah hasn't been particularly pleasant during the short moments we've been forced to interact.

Which means today is going to be fun.

The tardy bell rings, and I glance around and release a sigh as Noah slides into the classroom seconds after the bell. We're supposed to spend this period studying with our lab partners for the thermodynamics test on Monday.

I would've preferred to study by myself.

And I would've preferred if he weren't here when I turn in our report.

Mr. Libby meanders up to the whiteboard and jots down a few phrases. "This is our last class before the section test," he says, capping the dry-erase marker and twirling it between his fingers. "Can everyone pass your lab reports to the front of the class?"

Hesitant, I hand Anna my—our—report and watch as the papers move toward the front of the room.

Mr. Libby collects the reports from the first person in each row, straightening them in his hands, before returning to the whiteboard. "Alright, you all have your guides. Any questions before you divide into study groups?"

Kelsey, who sits in the first row, raises her manicured hand. "Mr. Libby, can you go over the different types of heat transfer again?"

I roll my eyes.

Kelsey is the only sophomore in the class, and I don't know how she managed to get into such an advanced class. That queen bee type barely has any brains between her ears.

As he launches into a short explanation, I tune him out and flip through my careful notes. All the answers I could need for Monday's test are here.

I shoot a quick glance toward Noah, who's reading his textbook. He hasn't looked in my direction.

Not that I've been paying attention.

Why would I?

At last, Mr. Libby finishes and heads to his corner desk at the back of the room. "Find your partner," he adds as he lays down the stack of lab reports. "Call on me if you have any questions."

Everyone moves their chairs to pair up with their respective lab partners.

I don't move. Noah's seat is on the opposite side of the classroom near the hallway—seats are assigned by the alphabetical order of our last names—but there's far more room near my seat. He can join me.

After an aggravating moment, he scoots a nearby desk closer and sits. But he doesn't look at me. He doesn't speak. He's still mad about something that happened five days ago.

I focus on our textbook's table of contents. "Should we start with the Laws of Thermodynamics?" I pause, but he doesn't answer. "Do you want to read over them individually? Or ask each other questions?"

Noah shrugs, lips pursed. Instead of answering, he tugs his textbook closer and starts to read the first section chapter.

"Right," I murmur.

There's no reason we need to study together anyway. We're both capable of passing the test on Monday.

I don't know how to study with a partner anyway.

And if I did, why would I want to study with Noah Barton? I don't want to talk to him. I don't want to do anything with him.

I flip open my notebook and find my thermodynamics

notes.

He's not supposed to ignore me. Why isn't he nee-
dling me, irritating me, trying to distract me? Why isn't
he arguing with me?

Oddly, the arguing, the disagreements, the spats, are
strangely comforting. No matter how ridiculous our fights
are, the fact that we fight tells me he cares. Not about me,
but he cares about the science. It's nice to have someone
who cares about the science as much as I do, even if he
prefers astrophysics to biology or ecology.

Noah flips the page in his textbook. The sound of the
flimsy paper grates on my nerves.

But this behavior is something else entirely.

He doesn't want to argue. He doesn't want to talk. He's
not interested. He doesn't care about the science. How can
he be enthusiastic one day and uninterested the next?

He nips his chapped lip.

How can he not care?

His fingers, nails torn short, tap gently on the desk.

My eyes narrow. "What is your problem?"

Noah's head jolts up. "What?"

"What is your problem with me?"

He quirks his head. "I don't understand, Eden. I don't
have a problem with you."

I scoff.

"We've never gotten along, but I don't have a particular
problem with you."

"Why are you acting so weird? This"—I gesture up and
down his form—"is weird."

His Adam's apple bobs when he swallows. "I'm not
acting weird."

I chew the inside of my cheek before venturing to say the next thing that comes to mind: "Then why aren't you arguing with me? Are you still mad about last weekend?"

His brow furrows. "You want to argue?"

"Of course not." I clear my throat. Need to regroup. "We normally argue, so the fact that you're refusing to is unsettling. It's not like I enjoy arguing with you. Don't get the wrong idea."

One eyebrow shoots up, curious.

But I can't clarify. I don't know what "wrong idea" he might get from the fact that I enjoy arguing with him. Because frankly, I do. It's a convenient emotional release.

"I'm sorry…?" His words come out quiet, unsure—like a question.

To be fair, I don't know why he's apologizing either. Our disagreement over the weekend wasn't any more his fault than mine.

I shift my attention back to my notes. This is suddenly awkward, and I'm not sure why. I clear my throat. "The Trustee Banquet at Archer Collins is this weekend. You're going, right? You got invited?"

For a long moment, Noah doesn't speak.

I'm too nervous to look up.

Then: "Nah, I'm staying home. Figured it was more important to get ahead on my STEM project, you know?"

I frown.

How is the New England STEM Fair more important than a college scholarship? The Trustee Scholarship is awarded to several students in varying amounts—he has a realistic shot at receiving the financial assistance. How can he pass on this?

"Oh" is all I can say.

He returns to his textbook, and I—

"Eden, Noah…" Mr. Libby approaches quietly. "Could the two of you stay after class for a few minutes?"

CHAPTER 15

NOAH

When the bell rings, everyone heads for their next class.

Everyone except me and Eden.

And she looks concerned.

Slowly, I stack my binder and textbook, waiting out the seconds until Mr. Libby sits with us to explain.

To be fair, I already know why we're staying after, and Eden would too if she believed me. But apparently, she thought I was being dramatic when I said I'd write my own lab report.

Once all the other students have gone, Mr. Libby rolls his chair toward us—I'm still sitting by Eden's desk—and clasps his hands over his lap. "Well, you've completed one assignment," he says, relaxed, amiable. "What do you think of the arrangement? How do you think the partnership is going?"

Eden sits up straight. "It's perfectly fine. We're working things out, and as you can see from our report, we completed everything without an issue."

Mr. Libby turns to me. "And Noah? How do you think the partnership is progressing?"

I hesitate—the question is a trap. We all know the supposed partnership is in shambles. Eden is the only person who thinks she can fool the world by pretending everything is okay.

"I'm not sure I need to say anything," I finally settle on. "All you need to do is look at our lab reports to see how well we work together." I glance at Eden, but she doesn't seem to catch the plural.

Mr. Libby, however, has. He rolls back to the desk, then returns, carrying the two reports. "Thank you both for bringing them up." He glances between the two stapled documents with a tight frown. "Obviously, this is what I want to discuss."

Eden can't stop staring, her mouth agape.

She genuinely didn't believe my threat.

"Can you explain why I was given two different reports for your team?" He scrutinizes the top of the page. "Noah, your name is on both of these."

I offer him a rueful smile. "Yeah, I don't think we've worked out all the kinks yet."

"Why did you write a second report?"

"I had to. On principle. The first report doesn't reflect our full capabilities as a team—that would require me to have participated in writing it," I say with a shrug. "Eden wasn't splitting things appropriately, and I felt obligated to do my part."

Mr. Libby nods before turning to her. "Eden, do you have anything to say? Did you know Noah was writing his own report?"

All she can do is shake her head.

He gives her another moment, but her speechlessness doesn't wane. He continues:

"Alright, here's the problem. When you have a lab partner, you are supposed to be a team. You must work together and rely on each other. This sort of behavior"—he raises the two reports—"is unacceptable. This is not teamwork." He drops the papers on his lap again and heaves a sigh. "So here's what we'll do: You didn't meet the parameters of the assignment. I'm docking both of you two grades on this report, making your highest possible score eighty percent."

"What?"

Apparently, that's enough to pull Eden out of shock.

Mr. Libby ignores her. "I'm sure you both put together excellent lab reports, but next time, there will be only one—and it will be written by both of you. If this happens again, I won't hesitate to fail both of you."

I nod, solemn.

Not my preferred result, but I knew the risk when I made the decision. And I'd rather have this outcome than Eden writing every report—and we usually have one or two experiments a month.

"Do I make myself clear?"

"Yes," Eden slowly says.

"Crystal."

A smile spreads across Mr. Libby's face. "Good. Then, I'll see you in class Friday." He rolls his chair back to his desk, a dismissal.

I grab my things and rise from the desk, and Eden rushes to follow.

Only ten feet down the hallway, Eden catches up, clasping her hand on my arm and spinning me around. "What the hell was that? I can't believe you lost us twenty percent. How can you—?"

I tug away, silencing her with a glare. "Eden, I told you exactly what I would do. You chose to write the report without me. That's on you."

"You didn't have to say anything. You didn't have to turn in that extra lab report. You didn't have to screw me over like this."

"You have the best grade in our class. I'm sure one B- on one assignment won't ruin your GPA."

"The only reason I have the highest GPA right now is because you missed over a month of classes last semester, and you know that." Her eyes dart around the empty hallway—everyone else is in their respective classrooms or at lunch, which is where I should be now. "You should have warned me."

I scowl. "I did. You chose not to believe me."

"That wasn't—"

"Cut the crap, Eden."

She falls silent, and her eyes drift to the floor, a strand of glossy black hair falling in her eyes.

I close the distance until there's nothing separating us. "I'd rather fail than let you get your way on the next report."

Her eyes lift to mine. "It's that important to you?"

"We work together on the next report, or we both fail."

She heaves a sigh. "I don't understand why we have to play by Mr. Libby's rules. We could take turns. We could write the individual sections without getting together outside of school."

"Because I don't like people who think they're exempt from the rules. So yes, this is important to me." I study her for a moment, but she doesn't speak. Against my better judgment, I tuck the loose strand behind her ear, and her eyes flit to my face at the contact, a frown on her soft features. "Good luck at Archer Collins this weekend," I murmur, then walk away, heading for the cafeteria.

CHAPTER 16

EDEN

I FLIP OFF THE ILLUMINATOR AND HEAVE A SIGH. I HATE having to leave the project for the weekend, but even the STEM fair isn't important enough to miss this scholarship opportunity. Even if it means spending an evening with Colton.

Sacrifices must be made.

I can only hope the microorganisms' growth will progress while I'm away. For now, they're on target. Let's hope they stay that way.

I return the slides to their case and begin to clear the area. I didn't make much of a mess, but I still pulled out supplies and disorganized things.

"Leaving so soon?"

I glance up. "Yeah."

Dr. Emily Hook smiles. "You're usually here for several hours each night you come in."

I flash her a small smile. "I wanted to do a final check before I'm gone for the weekend."

She raises an eyebrow.

"I'm flying down to Archer Collins tomorrow right after school. They invited a bunch of prospective students to apply for their Trustee Scholarship, which could help pay for my tuition." I send her a hesitant smile. My nerves aren't exactly under control right now.

"Congratulations." She leans against the counter beside me. "That's phenomenal, Eden."

I nod, trying to keep my words to myself. It's not often I'm able to keep my excitement at bay—not when it comes to Archer Collins.

"So what's the verdict?" Her mouth twists into a teasing smile. "How was partnering with Noah for the lab experiment?"

I scoot the microscope away from the counter's edge with a deep sigh. "Worse than I hoped, but better than I expected."

Dr. Hook chuckles.

"We got in trouble for not working together as a team. Mr. Libby docked our grades because we each turned in a lab report instead of writing one together." I pause beside her. I'm already done, since this was a simple checkup. "Noah wouldn't listen. He wouldn't let me do anything. He…"

He wouldn't even make a move. He held my hand and escorted me to his bedroom—and then, he did nothing.

Not that I wanted him to make a move. Why would I?

But he didn't have to say those hurtful things either. He didn't have to remind me the only guy attracted to me is four and a half years older and not even remotely interesting enough to warrant my attention. A guy I have to see when he picks me up at the airport and drives me to Archer Collins tomorrow.

As frustrating and aggravating as Noah Barton is, I couldn't possibly call him boring.

Beside me, Dr. Hook squeezes my shoulder. "Sounds like the two of you have your work cut out for you."

I release a breathy chuckle. "Something like that."

Mama tears open the front door the moment she hears my car door close. "Thien, where have you been?"

I pause in the middle of pulling my backpack from the passenger seat. "I stopped by the lab to check on my experiment. Is something wrong?"

Was she worried?

She releases an irritated huff and says, "You haven't started packing," before returning to the house, leaving the door open.

I frown. Did she go through my room?

When I get inside and head upstairs, she's on the top landing, arms crossed. "I'm taking you to school in the morning. We need to drive to Portland the moment class releases."

I nod. I figured that would be the easiest option with my flight scheduled for 6:35, but that doesn't have anything to do with her going through my bedroom.

I pass her on the way to my door, cracked open—definitely not how I left it.

Inside, she has my suitcase open on the bed, next to a pile of laundry I didn't wash myself. She follows me to the doorway and hovers while I put away my textbooks and pull out the homework I need to complete before Monday. I don't know whether I'll have time over the weekend, so I need to finish it tonight while I can.

She tsk tsks from the doorway. "Why is your room a mess, Thien? You should at least keep it tidy." Her severe gaze scrutinizes my desk and shelves, covered in haphazard papers and disorganized books. "Packing would be faster if you were organized."

I stifle an irritated sigh and turn my attention to the suitcase. "Don't worry, Mama. I have the whole night to pack for two days. It'll take twenty minutes."

Surprisingly, Mama is more excited about my trip to Archer Collins than I am.

But it's no surprise why.

"It's almost as if you don't want to see Colton again." She purses her lips. "He's going out of his way to pick you up tomorrow night. That was your idea."

Kind of.

The white lie was completely necessary. Why else would she let me go to the Trustee Weekend? She adores Colton—she's already planning our wedding in her head, no matter how boring or unpleasant he is.

"I just want to make sure I'm fully caught up before the weekend," I say. "That way I can enjoy my time there."

Mama's glare is harsh, despite my attempt to placate her. "Pack. You will not waste this opportunity to get to know Colton."

"Of course, Mama."

"And put away your laundry," she says as a goodbye as she slips from my bedroom.

She's right, of course.

Packing is important. I won't have time tomorrow, and there is so much I need to prepare for. I need to dress professionally and be witty and intelligent and convince them to give me a butt-ton of money so I can convince Mama to let me attend Archer Collins.

Literally none of my reasons are to make a good impression on Colton Danvers.

I almost laugh.

I certainly can't tell her that.

To Mama, Colton Danvers is everything a man of his age ought to be: He's attractive. He's intelligent. He's healthy. He's financially stable. He doesn't dillydally with unimportant side projects. He doesn't take unnecessary risks. He can afford to take care of a family. He can afford to take care of me.

After what happened to Papa, she would do anything to guarantee my security, even if that means sacrificing my overall happiness. Financial and physical security are more important.

And I suppose she would know. She grew up in poverty, watching her family fall to pieces in a country still recovering from civil war. It was a little bit luck but mostly Mama's own tenacity that introduced her to Papa—and an opportunity for a better future.

Now, I have opportunities she never had, simply by living here.

With a sigh, I lean over the pile of laundry, still warm from the dryer, and pull out a few pieces to fold.

That means nothing to her.

Maybe if I play up interest in Colton, she might be enthusiastic about college. Maybe she'll jump at the chance for me to attend a school near where he lives.

CHAPTER 17

NOAH

I wet my lips and squint at the screen. I may be stuck at home for the weekend—alone since Dad is on a business trip—but I can at least spend the time tweaking my project instead of wallowing in self-pity.

Eden was right.

It's been too long since I allowed myself to dream, to have goals, to make plans for my future. This project is all I have.

If I can perfect this program, spacecrafts can plot a more efficient course for interplanetary missions. Hell, manned interplanetary missions would be a lot more feasible, and boy would I love to be on one of those.

This is the first step in a long process.

I glance at the clock at the bottom of the screen. It's nearly seven on a Friday night. This is the start of a long weekend.

A weekend I'll have to spend trying not to think about everyone at the Trustee Banquet. About Eden Prince winning over the Archer Collins faculty before I have the chance. About the opportunities I'm missing.

"Why's it so dark in here?"

I spin toward the open door, slipping off the swivel chair.

Landing flat on my ass.

In the darkened doorway, Ethan grips the door jamb. "Damn, String Bean. You alright?"

"Jesus, Ethan, what are you doing here?" It takes a moment to catch my breath.

He snickers. "Scaring you, apparently."

"You'd be scared too. I was supposed to be alone. Shouldn't you be on base?"

"I got leave for the weekend and decided…why not visit my scrawny little bro?" He flips on the light. "Dad's away for the weekend. Someone might as well keep you company."

I squint, suddenly blind. "You could've let me know. I'm working on my STEM project the whole weekend. You'll be bored."

Ethan laughs. "Or you could entertain me. I came all the way here instead of—"

"What?" I raise an eyebrow.

Now that he and Meredith are broken up, what would he do on leave? He doesn't have many friends outside the military, and we don't have much of an extended family.

He could've saved up his leave for something more important than a random weekend without Dad. Why would he waste leave time on his "scrawny little bro"? I've always been an inconvenience anyway.

"Instead of getting laid," he adds with a laugh.

I roll my eyes. "You and Meredith back together?"

"Nah."

Okay, then.

I'm not going to ask.

Ethan plops onto my bed and hums the beginning notes of a familiar tune while I return to the computer. Is he trying to break my concentration?

I groan.

Of course he is. This is Ethan. God forbid he learn how to entertain himself. Don't most children know how to do that? How is he more of a child than I am?

"Will you be quiet?"

His humming grows louder.

Then, I recognize it.

Is he seriously humming the *Pokémon* theme song?

"You could put on a movie or something. Football?" I glance over, but he doesn't react. "Or you could visit Cliff. He'd be happy to see you."

Finally, Ethan's rough melody comes to a close. "Cliff's got a game, kiddo. And I'm not hanging round his dingy apartment while he practices or does homework. Boring."

I roll my eyes. "You know I'm doing homework too, right?"

"Nah, you're working on your little project. The science fair isn't till April, right? You've got time to take a break."

"So I can entertain you?"

He smirks.

How entitled can you get?

"You eaten dinner yet?"

I glance at the clock again. It's 7:13 now. I hadn't considered dinner. "No."

"You wanna grab a couple pizzas and play *Call of Duty?*"

I shoot a skeptical look in his direction. "*Call of Duty?* Really?"

He shrugs. "So?"

"Cliff took that with him to college. Besides, first-person shooter games are overrated."

Ethan snickers. "What would you rather play, String Bean?"

I don't play video games often, but there are a few games I enjoy. "*Diablo?*"

He raises an eyebrow, forehead creased, but tugs his keys from his pocket. "Get your coat. Let's grab some pizza."

"What do you want, String Bean?" Ethan examines the menu under the harsh fluorescent lights and hums in consideration. "Pepperoni? Cheeseburger? Supreme? Meat lovers?"

I glance at the menu before scanning the concrete building with disinterest. "I don't care. Whatever you want."

He shoots me a glare. "You have to eat something. You can't starve because you're moping about your fancy college weekend."

Irritation tugs at my stomach. "It was hardly a 'fancy college weekend,' Ethan." I shake my head, but the irritation doesn't wane. "This was a serious opportunity."

But like normal, none of them care.

Mom was the only one who cared.

Now, she's gone.

Beside me, Ethan glowers. "Come on, Noah, let's order the pizza."

Grudgingly, I peruse the menu again and finally say, "Supreme's fine. Just hurry up." Without another word, I take a seat near the exit while he waits in line.

Ethan puts in our order after a woman in the floral dress and sits beside me, but he knows better than to strike up a conversation. He flips through the contents of his phone, lips pursed.

The nearby bell chimes as the door pulls open.

I lean forward to look at the receipt on Ethan's lap. He got a large supreme, a large pepperoni, and some breadsticks. Apparently, we're going to have leftovers.

"Noah?"

My gaze shifts up at my name. "Mr. Libby…hey."

He offers me a soft smile. "You must be heading to the Trustee Weekend in the morning. Getting pizza with your…friend?"

I clear my throat. "My brother Ethan. The one in the Marines, you know?" I don't have the heart to correct him about the Trustee Weekend.

Mr. Libby nods, his dark-brown hair flopping lazily. "Of course."

Ethan sits up and offers his hand. "Ethan Barton. You are?"

"Michael Libby." Hesitantly, he takes Ethan's hand, and they shake to an uncomfortably slow rhythm before finally separating. "I teach Noah's physics class."

Ethan assesses him for a long minute, and Mr. Libby shifts uneasily under his gaze. "Aren't you a little young to be a teacher?"

Mr. Libby releases a strangled laugh. "That's what most of the parents say."

"I'm not a parent." Ethan cocks his head, his lips flattening into a thin line. "Actually, you look my age."

Instead of answering, Mr. Libby turns to me, a pink flush lighting up his cheeks. "Anyway, I need to grab dinner and get back to grading papers." He shuffles toward the line, then pauses to look over his shoulder. "Remember, we're studying reflection and refraction on Monday. Have a good weekend at Archer Collins."

When he reaches the register, pulling out his wallet, I turn my attention to Ethan again.

He still watches Mr. Libby with a curious eye. "He's seriously young to be a teacher. What is he—twenty-five or something?"

I raise an eyebrow. "I don't know."

It never mattered before, and I'm not sure why it matters now.

Finally, Ethan clears his throat and shifts toward me. "Why'd you lie to him? You're not going to Archer Collins this weekend."

I frown. I was hoping he wouldn't ask that. "I dunno. He always looks out for me, roots for me. I don't want to disappoint him."

A little smile plays on Ethan's lips, and his eyes drift back toward Mr. Libby. "Sounds like a good teacher."

I clear my throat.

Ethan looks back and laughs. "So your science project, huh?"

"What about it?"

"What are you doing it on?"

I frown—why the sudden interest? "You wouldn't understand."

"I'm not an idiot, String Bean," he says with a glare, "and you better remember that."

My jaw clenches. "It's a computer program to calculate interplanetary superhighways—ways to make travel faster and safer for spacecrafts, manned or unmanned."

Ethan's body relaxes slowly. "Safer, huh?"

"Yeah."

"Do you—?"

"*Barton!* Order up."

Ethan's head shoots up, and he practically jumps from the chair to grab the three boxes, pausing to give Mr. Libby a once-over as he returns to me.

Relief floods my body.

The last thing I want to talk to Ethan about is my project—and how much of my inspiration is Mom. He wouldn't understand. No one understands. Not Ethan or Cliff. Certainly not Dad.

The hot cheese stretches as I shove the slice in my mouth. The sauce burns the roof of my mouth, but I don't care. Too hungry.

"What was the game?" Ethan drops to his knees by the console and runs his finger along the cases. "Diaboromon?"

I swallow. "*Diablo III*, moron. It's multiplayer, don't worry."

"Remember, don't insult the big brother who feeds you."

He tugs the case out—and grimaces at the cover. "What the hell is this?"

I stifle a laugh. "Dungeon crawler. We have to defeat the Lord of Terror."

He turns the front to face me. "That's this asshole, right?"

"Oh yeah." I return to my pizza as he inserts the disk.

I'm not sure what to expect from tonight. The pizza's delicious, and it's a decent game, but spending the weekend with only Ethan for company? Why is he here?

Besides, I have so much work to do.

"So," Ethan says as he drops onto the couch, "your physics teacher—does he know about your science project?"

I shoot him a frown. "I've mentioned it once or twice, but that was before…" The words fail me, and Ethan doesn't press. He knows what I mean.

"Kinda surprised you're still working on it. You missed a whole month of school. A lot to make up." He offers me one of the controllers. "Do you have time for this project too?"

Irritation wells in my chest. "What do you care?"

Ethan doesn't look at me. Or speak.

No surprise there.

I grab the controller from his hand. "Come on. Let's play."

CHAPTER 18

EDEN

I SHIFT UNCOMFORTABLY IN THE PASSENGER SEAT OF Colton's Jeep Wrangler. He has the windows and top down, and the wind whips my hair across my face, in my eyes. Completely ruining the delicate waves Mama put in before school.

Colton flashes me a grin—one I can barely see through the strands of hair stuck to my lipgloss—and shifts gears as we barrel through an intersection.

"Thanks for picking me up," I say over the sound of the road.

It's not the first time I've thanked him, but honestly, I don't know what else to say.

"Of course, of course." He releases the stick to squeeze my thigh, thankfully covered by a pair of thick skinny jeans. "I was glad you called me. I don't know...I wasn't really expecting to hear from you."

I give a short nod, keeping my smile small, and push thick sections of hair behind my ear again. "Well, I'm glad you said yes. I've been looking forward to this weekend for months now."

Technically true, though it has nothing to do with him.

His hand squeezes and massages my thigh for a moment, then he pulls back to shift gears again.

I cross my legs and look out the window. "How far to Archer Collins?"

"Maybe ten minutes now."

Thank god.

I've been looking forward to this moment for a hell of a lot longer than "months"—the moment I can finally see Archer Collins in person. That will make this whole ordeal worth it.

"What all do you have to do tonight?" He flashes me a grin.

I look back out the window, waiting for the university to come into view, even if we're still ten minutes away. "My student sponsor is supposed to meet me outside Gadsden Hall so I can get settled into the dorm room. After that, I don't know. There aren't any official plans."

"You ever been here before?"

I shake my head.

"I could give you a sort of…personal tour." He chuckles. "I know the place pretty well by now."

The wind whips my hair away from my ear again, and I tug it back. "I don't know. After the flight, I'm kind of tired, but if I'm feeling up to it, sure."

Colton points out my window. "Take a look. This is the edge of campus. It doesn't look like much, but these are the upperclassmen houses."

My lips form an *O* as the pretty cottages fly past. "Which one's yours?"

He laughs, and his hand finds my leg again. "Mine's on the other side of campus. I can show you while you're here if you like."

Outside, the campus cottages transition into larger, modern houses with multiple stories and pristine paint. It's cold here too, but the landscaping is beautiful and perfect.

Then, there it is.

I tear off my seat belt and rise to look out the top of the Jeep.

"Whoa, what are you doing, Eden? Sit back down!"

The car slows but doesn't stop.

Ahead of us, enormous iron gates rise against the nighttime city lights, and spotlights brighten the words *Archer Collins* at the top of the arch, split in the middle by the iconic archer.

Colton flicks on his blinker and turns down the driveway, slowing to a stop just inside the open gate. "Hey, get back in the car."

I take a long deep breath, and laughter bubbles in my throat.

This is the moment I've been waiting for my entire life.

Archer Collins is beautiful, even in this dark lighting, and I cannot imagine attending anywhere but here. The campus is stunning, the location historical, the feel of the place lonely and nostalgic.

Emotions overwhelm me, and I collapse onto the seat with a weight on my chest.

"You alright?"

A sigh escapes my lips. "Yeah. Let's go."

I only wish I had better company for the momentous occasion.

"Right over here." Kayla, my student sponsor, who like she agreed, met me outside Gadsden Hall, leads me down the second floor hallway. "We're right by the fire exit, so make sure to only use the main entrance. These doors"—she gestures toward the doors at the end of the hall—"will set off alarms if you open them."

She turns to the right and enters an open doorway, and I follow her inside a small alcove.

There are four doors, three of them shut, one open, and she flips on the light and nods me inside the room.

"This is yours for the weekend," she says, motioning around the small room.

A bed is pressed against one wall with a desk and small shelf opposite, and there's a dresser and a closet in one corner. A set of sheets and a pillow sit atop the bed, ready to be stretched across the mattress, but there's nothing else in the room.

"It's not much," Kayla adds, hovering by the doorway as I drop my bag on the bare mattress, "but it's a decent room. Mine is right next door, so holler if you need anything."

I pull my suitcase close and open the latch, ready to pull out everything I need for the rest of the evening.

"How do you know Colton?"

I pause.

She's still in the doorway.

"Colton Danvers?" I clarify, glancing at her.

Kayla nods. "I never would have expected him to pick up a high schooler."

I frown. "He's a family friend. My mom wanted someone she trusted to make sure I got here and back, so he picked me up at the airport." I withdraw my pajamas from the suitcase and lay them atop the dresser.

She hums skeptically. "So you're not dating him?"

I freeze. "What?"

To be fair, when he said goodbye outside the dormitory, he got out of the Jeep to help me unload and give me a tight hug. His hand hovered at the small of my back as Kayla introduced herself, and he gave me a kiss on the cheek before diving back into his car.

I clear my throat. "No, definitely not dating."

No matter how much Mama wants us to.

"What do you usually do on a Friday night?" I ask, desperate to redirect the conversation. "What's the social scene like?"

Kayla raises an eyebrow. "You really social? Have a lot of friends?"

I shrug. Not even remotely. I care more about how distracting everyone will be. I have no intention to leave my dorm room on the weekends, except to replenish my food stash and pee.

"There are a few people—I mean, we have frats—who party on the weekends," she says slowly, but there's something about her tone that makes me doubt the validity of her words. How honest is she being?

"Right."

"What's your first event in the morning?"

I pull out my phone and open the calendar. "There's a special breakfast for everyone staying on campus. The interviews start immediately afterward. Mine's at 3:45 p.m." I drop my phone on the desk and return to unpacking. "Then, there's the dinner tomorrow night and a goodbye brunch Sunday." That gives them time to fit in some interviews in the morning too.

"You nervous?"

I scoff. I don't get nervous.

My phone buzzes.

I pause to grab it. A text from Colton.

Hey, what time's your dinner over tomorrow? it says. *I wanna show you around campus.*

I frown. How much could he show me at eight o'clock at night? How much can I see? I doubt we could go into any of the administrative or education buildings, and I don't care much about housing aside from the freshman dorms.

Another text: *We could chill with a few friends at my house afterward if you like.*

Unease settles in my stomach.

No, I was wrong.

A few select things can make me nervous.

Colton offers me a small smile and his hand, and he leads the way along one of Archer Collins' many sidewalks. "How was your dinner?"

I try to stay nonchalant, but that's hard to do in a black dress and stiletto heels. "It was nice to talk to some alumni about their experience with the Trustee Scholarship. We talked about our interviews."

"Speaking of..." He releases my hand—I stretch my fingers to rid myself of the feel of his grasp—and throws his arm around my bare shoulders.

"The interview?"

"Yeah. How do you think you did?"

Pride swells my chest, and a grin spreads across my face. "It was perfect. I know I got it." But it's also a question of how much they'll award me since it varies. "I'm not worried about a thing."

Colton chuckles. "So confident."

"Of course." But my eyes dart around the barely lit campus. "What are these buildings?"

He nods to each as he names them: "Baker Hall, Macy Hall, and Kinsey Hall. They're education buildings. Where most of the legal and business classes are. I spend a lot of time in Kinsey."

I move on.

They're not something I'm interested in.

But Colton tugs me to a stop. "This way." He nods me toward a small green space with a white gazebo. "This is one of my favorite places," he says as he leads me through the narrow doorway and under the roof. "Beautiful, isn't it?"

My eyes dart around the dark secluded area, tucked between Macy and Kinsey Hall. "It's nice."

His arm, which loosened so we could fit through the opening, tightens around my shoulders and tugs me to him. "You know, I'm really glad you came down here, Eden. It's good to see you."

I smile, but he's uncomfortably close. "I'm glad I'm here

too."

Not that that has anything to do with him.

He raises his other hand to my cheek, his eyes meet mine, and he leans his forehead close to mine. "You look beautiful in this dress." The hand at my shoulders runs down my back, then up again, wrinkling the sheer material and unintentionally raising the back of the skirt. "You're beautiful."

"Thanks," I murmur, swallowing down the distress.

This is what I'm supposed to do. I'm supposed to be here with him. I'm supposed to enjoy talking to him. I'm supposed to feel like these ridiculous compliments are genuine. And I'm supposed to kiss him when he presses his lips to mine.

Instead, I slip away.

A kiss is something I refuse to be disingenuous about. Wanting to kiss him isn't something I can fake. Happiness, joy, pleasure—these aren't things I can lie about. They aren't things I want to lie about.

Even if it breaks Mama's heart.

I wet my lips as I slip from the gazebo. "Where are the science buildings? I'm majoring in Bio and Ecology. I'd love to see where I'm going to study."

CHAPTER 19

NOAH

It's not the first time Ethan's eyes dart toward the door behind me and his lips twist in irritation. And it's certainly not the first time this behavior has become annoying.

But it is the first time he blatantly heaves a sigh as he returns to his plate of lobster rolls—yes, he needed two.

I spin the straw in my cup, knocking the ice repeatedly against the hard plastic. "Are you expecting someone?"

"Course not." He takes a large bite of his sandwich, and the creamy lobster pieces inside squish and drip.

"Right." I slurp at my straw and nudge away the rest of my fish and chips. "But you were hoping to see someone. Who?"

He shrugs, still chewing.

"Who do you even know here? Not many people stay after they graduate high school."

He shoots me a glare but takes another bite. Stuffing his face to avoid the questions.

"I can't believe it," I say, shaking my head.

"What?" The word is barely intelligible through a mouthful of lobster.

"You and Meredith only just broke up, and you already have your sights on somebody else."

Ethan scowls and wipes his mouth. "First of all, Meredith and I broke up seven weeks ago, and it'd been going south for a good six months before that."

"And second of all?"

His eyes narrow. "I don't have my 'sights' on anyone."

A little smile tugs at my lips. "Only because they're not here. And you're disappointed about that." I pause, considering. "Who would you expect to find at Pearl's on a Sunday night?"

Irritation lights up Ethan's eyes, and he clasps his hands atop the table, leaning close. "What about you, String Bean?"

I cock my head. "What about me?"

He dons a devious grin. "You know, Dad mentioned something pretty interesting last week. He said you had a girl in your bedroom—with the door locked."

Heat rises to my cheeks, and I lean back. "I wanted to save her the awkwardness of running into Dad. Nothing happened."

"Hmm, but you wanted it to, didn't you?"

I will not justify that with a response.

"And it got even more interesting when he mentioned who the girl was." With a smirk, he snatches up his sandwich again and brandishes it toward me. "I thought Eden

Prince was eternally annoying? That she's 'conceited' and 'completely insane'?"

"She is," I murmur.

"Then why are you hiding her in your bedroom for two hours at a time?" He waggles his eyebrows and chomps down on the remnants of his first sandwich.

I heave a sigh. "We're lab partners. We were writing up a report on how temperature affects liquid viscosity."

But that doesn't stop his stupid smirk. "Oh, really? Does how hot she is affect your...ahem, liquid viscosity?"

I roll my eyes. "Stop trying to make physics sound dirty. Do you even know what *viscosity* is?"

"I don't have to." He finishes off the final bite of his first sandwich, then plucks up the second. "You have condoms, right? Do you need somebody to buy them for you?"

"Dad already offered, thanks," I say, trying not to cringe. "I don't plan to take him up on it either. Like I said, there's nothing going on between us. We're lab partners, and we're not even good lab partners."

Ethan raises an eyebrow. "How can you be a bad lab partner?"

"By not working together." I release a strangled sigh and slump against the tabletop. "She's so stubborn she'd rather we both fail than learn to work together."

He shrugs. "She'd be a lot more reasonable after a good orgasm."

My mouth drops open, and I stare, eyes wide, as he scarfs down the ends of his food.

"What?" He swallows the final bite. "Don't tell me you've never thought about it."

Any heat that faded from my cheeks comes back

tenfold. "N-no, of course not. There's nothing—"

"Your red face tells a different story, String Bean." Ethan smirks, then rises slightly to pull his wallet from his back pocket. "When are you going to suck it up and ask her out?"

I purse my lips. "I'm not. Like I said, there's nothing between us."

"Right," he says with a snort, rising from his seat. "Not yet."

Irritation rises in my stomach, and I follow him to the register to pay.

An hour later, I climb the stairs alone and slide open the window at the top of the stairwell. It's the easiest way to get to the roof.

From the roof, I watch Ethan's rental car zoom out of the driveway and head toward town. He's a couple hours out, and he has to get back to the base by midnight, so I can't blame him for the speed.

I might almost miss him this time.

I drop down on the roof beside the Schmidt-Cassegrain telescope, draped with a plastic tarp to keep the rain and snow off the beautiful machine. The bulky thing has a 250-millimeter scope and a maximum magnification of 500x—assuming it's a nice clear night, which it usually isn't.

Mom's telescope.

I used to look through it every night. Watch the stars. Find her current location. It's not hard with this thing.

But there isn't much point in doing that anymore, is there?

I push up onto my knees and slowly peel the plastic off the machine, revealing the sleek tripod legs, the long black tube, and the scope and eyepiece near the closest end. The glass lens at the opposite end is covered by a dust cap, which I gingerly release and set on the roof beside me.

Instead of pointing it toward the stars, I tilt the telescope toward the roads of Tourmaline below. Maybe I can catch a final glimpse of Ethan's rental car before he's out of sight.

I press against the eyepiece and swallow slowly as I adjust the magnification and focus.

Ethan, though, is gone from view. The car is nowhere on any visible roads. I'm sure he was in a hurry since he left so late.

With a sigh, I tilt the telescope back up toward the sky and close my eyes.

It'll be blurry and unfocused—I did just adjust for looking at the ground—but I'm still not prepared to examine the sparkling balls of gas and fire dotting the sky.

I'm not prepared to look at that sky knowing Mom isn't up there anymore.

CHAPTER 20

EDEN

Across from me, Noah narrows his eyes at the list of supplies. "We have a pencil and the three sheets of paper...we need the glass, the plexiglass, protractor, laser pointer, and one of the clear tubs for water."

I roll my eyes. We went over the supplies and procedure during Mr. Libby's demonstration last class. Why does he need to go over it again? Nothing's new.

He glances toward the front lab station, where Mr. Libby has a collection of all our specialty materials. "Which one of us is going to get them?"

"You can't be serious." I cross my arms and scowl. "Obviously you, since you just listed them off—as if we didn't already know. Is your memory that bad you forgot what we needed between Friday and today? Why are you wasting my time?"

Noah purses his lips. "What's put you in such a foul

mood?"

I scoff. "Nothing." He's more perceptive than I'd like.

The Trustee Weekend ended perfectly fine. Colton didn't try to kiss me again—well, aside from the short peck on the cheek when he dropped me off at the airport—but that wasn't the difficult part.

No, that was the way Mama's face lit up the moment she saw me.

For a moment, I thought maybe she was excited to see me. Maybe she missed me. But after a short hug, instigated by me, all her questions were about Colton. About how much time we were able to spend together instead of my being wrapped up in silly scholarship-required activities. About whether things between the two of us were starting to develop into something serious.

And what could I say to her?

All I could do, all I could say, was lie.

I lied to her about how much fun we had. I lied to her about how much I enjoyed his company. I lied to her about how comfortable I was around him. I lied to her about how much I want to see him again.

I felt sick, but I didn't know what else to do.

"How are you doing, Eden? Noah?"

I blink and turn my attention to Mr. Libby. When did he come to our station?

Noah shoots me a skeptical glance. "We haven't decided which of us should grab the supplies."

The edge of Mr. Libby's mouth pinches with amusement, but he restrains himself. "Surely, you two are capable of deciding who will get the necessary materials for the experiment. Need I remind you the consequences of another slipup?"

I look away, discomfort teasing at my stomach.

"How was the Trustee Weekend?" Mr. Libby glances between us, excitement in his eyes.

Doesn't he know Noah didn't go?

Across from me, Noah's stool squeaks as he moves, anxiety etched on his face. "Uh, well…"

I push away from the counter. "Fine, I'll get the materials." I hop down and march around them to reach the front lab station.

What all did we need again?

On the counter, there remains one of each material—everyone else has already grabbed their supplies. One protractor. One laser pointer. One inch-thick rectangle of glass. One inch-thick rectangle of plexiglass. One clear rectangular tub to fill with one inch of water.

I gather the supplies in my arms and return to the table, but with their backs to me, Noah and Mr. Libby don't register my approach.

"…he wouldn't let me go since no one could go with me." Noah's eyes study the countertop. His voice cracks.

Mr. Libby presses a hand on his shoulder and squeezes gently. "Couldn't your brother have taken you? He was here for the weekend."

I pause.

Noah shakes his head. "Ethan came here to keep me out of trouble. If my dad can't trust me to travel by myself, he can't trust me to stay home by myself either. They think I'm a child."

"It's because he cares, Noah."

He scoffs. "No, he doesn't."

The blocks of glass and plexiglass dig into my palm, and I can't stand here awkwardly anymore. I push past them and deposit everything on the counter.

Mr. Libby glances toward me before adding, "Think about it," in a hushed voice. "Well, I'll let you two get to work."

When he disappears, Noah devotes his attention to our handout again.

Well.

I guess I'll have to take the lead on this lab.

No problem there.

The first step is to trace the rectangle on one of the papers, and then we draw a dashed line straight down the middle to indicate the normal. I don't exactly need Noah's help for that.

The silence, though, is unsettling as I trace the glass, plexiglass, and rectangular tub.

I hunch over, long hair falling in my face. "So, uh, how's your STEM project coming along? We only have a couple more weeks to finish up, and I've got something spectacular in the works."

He eyes me uncertainly. "I don't know anymore."

I scoff. "Well, you're not going to beat me, Noah Barton. My project is monumental—at the very least."

Amusement tugs at his chapped lips. "Is that a fact?"

"I never lie."

Except apparently to Mama.

"To put me off my game?" He snatches up the laser, ready for the next step, but I'm still drawing the lines. "You would do anything to win first prize this year. We both know that."

I scowl. "Not anything."

"Fine, you wouldn't cheat, but you'd certainly play mind games." He laughs as he clicks the laser on and off, thankfully pointing it into the deep sink. "What are you working on?"

My hand quivers, upsetting the protractor. "Microorganisms." I readjust the angle—back to ninety degrees—and narrow my eyes. "Why? What are you working on?"

His fingers drum on the countertop. "It's a computer program."

"Really?" I pause to look at him. "Don't you usually do something a little more hands-on? More interesting?"

He shrugs. "It's...important." His eyes are glassy, unfocused.

God, why is he so weird?

"When should we get together to write up the report?" I try to smile—not sure I'm successful—when he looks at me. "I have most evenings free this week, but obviously, I need to devote as much time as possible to the STEM project."

Noah offers me a grim smile. "Actually, I was hoping we could meet at your house this time. If that's alright."

I gape at him. "I don't know…"

"It wouldn't take long. I mean, we're both capable, right?" He's almost pleading. "Surely, we can get along for an hour or two."

Mama would hate it. There's no way she'd allow me to have a boy over, even for a joint assignment. It's not possible.

But Noah's eyes, still glassy, beg me to agree.

"I guess we could."

A genuine smile tugs at his lips. "Great."

"Come over Thursday after school."

Mama will be gone till late Thursday. They won't have to interact. She won't even have to know he was there.

"Edie, he's going to be here tomorrow. Why are you running around like a maniac?"

I pause in the middle of my organization to glare at her. "I am not a maniac, Tins. This is serious."

She rolls her eyes.

"Do you have any idea how many boys have seen my bedroom? Zero!"

Tinsley sits up and pushes aside her *Cosmo*. "Well, duh. But he didn't ask to see your bedroom, did he?"

I return my attention to sorting the papers on my desk. "Of course not."

"Your mom isn't going to be here. Why would you bring him to your bedroom?"

"I don't know." I tear open the drawer and shove the stack of papers inside, plus an assortment of pens. "What if Mama gets home early? I haven't told her he's coming over. Can you imagine what she would do if she found me with a boy in the house without having told her?"

She scoffs. "Can you imagine what she would do if she found you with a boy in your bedroom?"

I pause.

I hadn't thought of that.

I hadn't considered what it might look like with the two

of us studying on my bed. But it'd be easier to hide him in my room—I could shove him in my closet or under the bed, and she'd be none the wiser. She wouldn't know I'm keeping a secret.

God, Mama's gonna flip if she ever finds out about this.

Tinsley sighs. "Why don't you tell her you're having someone over for a partner project?"

"She'll want to chaperone."

"What's wrong with that?"

"He's a boy."

"A cute boy?"

I freeze. "What?"

Tinsley, a devious grin on her painted lips, closes her magazine. "I'm just saying, your mom wouldn't be keen on finding you with a cute boy in your bedroom when you're practically engaged to that Colton guy."

"I'm not engaged to anyone." But I shift uncomfortably at the words. We haven't spent as much time together—I haven't had time to tell her anything about the Trustee Weekend, and she'd probably tell me I'm overreacting if I tried to tell her how icky my encounter Colton made me feel. "I don't know if I'll ever get married. There is far too much to do with my life."

She laughs. "But you don't argue that Noah's cute?"

I open my mouth but stop. I've never considered whether Noah Barton is attractive. It doesn't matter. He's just Noah Barton.

But Tinsley cackles in victory. "It's okay if you do. Everyone thinks Noah is cute in that adorably shy, bookish way. I mean, he's not my type, but I think he's cute."

I clear my throat. "I hadn't considered it."

"But you're considering it now."

Who wouldn't?

"Hell, you're going to bring him to your bedroom while your mom's away. You must think he's cute on some level."

I scoff. "That has nothing to do with this, and you know it, Tins. Don't try to make this into something it isn't."

"I have no idea what you're talking about, Edie."

My hand tightens into a fist atop the desk. "You know exactly what I mean. Stop it."

Tinsley shrugs—an unsuccessful attempt to appear nonchalant. Laughter bubbles in her throat, and irritating as it is, I'm glad she's in a better mood tonight. More chipper. More like her regular self.

CHAPTER 21

NOAH

EDEN LETS ME INTO THE HOUSE WITH AN AWKWARD smile. She's pleasant enough, even though she doesn't want me here.

Of course, she doesn't. It wasn't her idea.

This is the first time I've been inside the Prince household. It's decidedly smaller than my own but still nice. Their family is well-known throughout town since Ronald Prince was Tourmaline's mayor for a long time—before he got sick. Mrs. Prince has taken care of Eden since, and their budget was drastically cut.

Eden nods me toward the stairs, and I follow. "Let's get to work."

Upstairs, she settles on her purple comforter, and I sit a few feet away and pull my papers from my backpack. She already has her laptop and notes spread across the mattress. She probably already outlined the entire report—or wrote half of it like last time.

I flip to my notes. "Okay, index of refraction. Where do you want to begin?"

She types in her passcode, and the laptop loads. "I typically start with the procedure since that's straightforward. Do you want to…?"

I shrug, my eyes flitting around the space. "I mean, it's your laptop."

This house is oddly uncomfortable. Not that I'm comfortable anywhere. And not that she seems more comfortable than me.

In fact, she seems less comfortable. She taps her finger lightly against the keyboard, careful not to make a stroke, and she nibbles her lower lip. Her eyes dart toward the closed door, then the window, then back to her laptop regularly.

Is this really that stressful? Or is she as worried about showing me her house as I was about showing her mine?

When she doesn't speak, I adjust my position. "Where's your mom? Working?"

Eden nods. "Yeah, she's pretty busy. Shouldn't be home for hours."

I shift, suddenly nervous. As much as I didn't want her to spend more time around my dad, I didn't expect us to be alone. Is she okay with this?

She stretches forward to retrieve her open textbook from behind the laptop, and my eyes gravitate toward her butt, accentuated by the pleated skirt, and her smooth fawn-colored thighs.

My gaze jolts to my notes when she pulls back. "So, um, the procedure?"

Her fingers brush mine as she grabs the assignment from my hand. "I usually type up the instructions, then add in details from my notes. There's a lot to add between the steps."

"Right. Mr. Libby likes his reports as detailed as possible." I lean close as she types everything up. "So is this normal?"

"What?" She doesn't look at me, and her typing doesn't slow.

"Your mom being gone. Are you normally alone like this?"

She shrugs, her fingers typing away. "Mama works constantly."

"What about your dad? Was he—I mean, before he got sick—did he…?"

That does make her pause. "I'd prefer not to talk about that, thanks."

A number of questions tug at my lips, but I refuse to let them pass. She deserves her privacy as much as anyone else. As much as I do.

But despite her previous words, she adds, "We've known each other since we were seven, and you don't know any of this? I figured everyone in town knows what the Asians are up to."

I frown. "I never really thought of you like that."

"Hmm?" Her typing is back to normal. She's already halfway through the instructions, typing at a ridiculously fast pace. No wonder she wants to be in charge. Her speed is stunning.

"You've always been Eden Prince to me." I shrug, trying not to say too much. "You're an insufferable know-it-all, intelligent and ridiculously dedicated. Your ethnicity never mattered."

A frown tugs at her lips. "Well, it matters to me."

"I didn't mean that it was…unimportant. It's obviously, you know, part of who you are, but I…" I heave a sigh. "I'm never going to say this right, am I?"

She almost laughs. "No, but I get what you're trying to say." Then, she pauses and turns to me with solemn eyes. "Thank you for not…you know."

I nod. "Right."

"Most people look at me and see a Vietnamese girl—or worse, an Asian girl because nobody around here knows the difference. They don't see me."

I almost laugh. "You never gave me the chance to see you as anything other than you. I've always rather admired your abilities, you know. It's hard to picture you as a stereotype when you're so incredibly…you." I shrug, but an uncomfortable heat rises to my cheeks.

She offers me the lab instructions. "Will you read the rest to me?"

I clear my throat as I take the stapled papers. "Sure."

"We don't have a lot of food," Eden says as she slips inside the bedroom again, carrying a plate of julienned veggies. "But you can have some of this if you like." She sets the plate on the bed between us and settles into her spot.

I shrug. "You didn't have to feed me."

She doesn't respond—she's already wrapped up in the report again.

"This is better than what I eat most of the time anyway,"

I say, taking a piece of carrot. I pop the carrot in my mouth and immediately cringe—it's sharp, tart, and the unexpected taste of vinegar overwhelms my mouth. "What is this?"

Eden looks up with a chuckle. "I should've warned you. They're pickled. Mama makes do chua as a snack all the time. Carrots, cucumber, daikon, sprouts, and jalapeños in water, vinegar, sugar, and salt. Easy to make."

Now that I'm prepared, the second bite is much better. "Yeah, I wasn't expecting that. My parents just throw something premade into the oven. There's no real cooking. We never have anything like this."

She studies me a moment. "Even before your mom died?"

I shrug. "She cooked sometimes, but that required her to be home. I mean, she spent her last six months at the International Space Station."

"She's why you're so interested in astrophysics."

It's not a question, and I don't deny it. Mom is the reason I've always been interested in space and astrophysics.

"We used to sit on the roof and look at the stars. She loved it here because Maine doesn't have a lot of light pollution and the visibility is great. We'd study the constellations—Draco was her favorite, and we'd find it, slinking between Ursa Major and Minor—and pull out the telescope so she could point out where her next mission would be."

"That sounds nice."

"It was. Those are…my best memories." Yet, I couldn't manage to look at the stars when I tried.

"What about your dad?"

I frown. "What about him?"

"Are you close?"

My shrug is minuscule. "He wasn't prepared for me."

Eden cocks her head.

I almost laugh. "You've met my brothers. Strong burly football players. I couldn't throw a football to save my life, even after calculating the exact way it needs thrown for optimal arc and distance. I've always had my sights on a telescope, and Dad has his on the football field. I'm a disappointment."

I'm not sure why I'm telling her this. We've never been friends before—but she also never asked before. "He doesn't know what to think of me. I defied all expectations. He didn't know what to do with a boy who identified more with Mom than him. I'm quiet, reserved, analytical, pensive. Dad is none of those."

Outside, gravel crunches, and I frown. We've been working for nearly two hours, but Eden made it sound like her mom wouldn't be home for longer than that.

"Oh." There's a sharp uncertainty to her voice as she rises from the bed to look through the lavender curtains. "Did you hear something?"

"Your mom here?" I turn back to the report—we only have a couple short sections left to finish, and we'll have completed a lab report together, as a team, exactly how Mr. Libby wants it.

"I don't know. I can't see where she parks from my window, but I heard a car."

I look up at her anxious tone. "What's the big deal?"

Eden bites her lip before stumbling toward the door and pressing her ear against the wood. She stays there for a long moment, and all I can do is stare. Has she gone insane? What does it matter if her mom got home early? We're just working on a report.

I clear my throat. "Eden?"

A shiver runs down her spine, but finally, she retreats from the door. "I guess it was my imagination." She crawls onto the bed again, settling next to me and the food, and pulls the laptop back onto her knees—but her eyes continue to flash toward the door and back.

I lean closer. "What's going on?"

She sighs. "Nothing." She clears her throat, then says, "Do you think you'll look at the stars with anyone else?"

My brow furrows as I try to process the sudden change.

Honestly, I hadn't considered it one way or the other. I'm not sure I've come to terms with Mom being gone, so the idea of doing something we did together with someone else hasn't crossed my mind.

"Someday, maybe."

She turns her attention back to the laptop. "Well, if you ever need company…I mean, it wouldn't be difficult to get away."

I glance toward the door.

No, I bet it wouldn't. She's probably as lonely as I am.

"Yeah," I say, "that'd be nice."

Outside, a car door slams.

Eden slides the laptop and plate of veggies away and pushes me down against the mattress, eyes wide. "You have to hide. Now. She can't find you here."

For a long moment, I lie under her, her face inches from mine, as the panic in her eyes grows, then fades. As her frenzied breath settles, I process Eden's body firmly against mine, her boobs spilling from the scoop-neck tee, her fingers clenched tight on my shoulders, her legs straddling my hips. In a position that can't be construed as anything other than sexy.

"Eden," I say slowly, silently begging my voice not to betray my thoughts, "covering me with your afghan won't hide me from your mother. Tell me what's going on."

She sighs, relaxing against me. "Sorry, I didn't mean to startle you. I just, um, forgot to mention you were coming over to work on the report?"

I raise an eyebrow. "'Forgot'?"

She wets her lips—I can no longer take my eyes off her mouth—and rolls to the side. "Yes, fine, I chose not to tell her. She's not supposed to be back until late, but maybe she changed her plans. She probably knows. She can read the guilt on my face."

I miss her touch immediately, but at least her side presses against mine, still close, still touching. "What's there to feel guilty about?"

"Mama's very old-fashioned," she says slowly, avoiding eye contact. "As far as she's concerned, it's inappropriate for me to spend time alone with a man, unless we're in a serious relationship—practically engaged."

"Oh."

"She already has someone in mind."

I twist to face her. "The guy from New Year's Eve?"

She gives a short nod.

"What about you, Eden? What and who do you have in mind for your future?"

A little smile tugs at her full pink lips. "You know better than anyone what I would do to get into Archer Collins. I don't have any other plans."

"Right."

But her rich brown eyes study my face, and her breath brushes my lips. For the first time, she doesn't mind the short distance—and she closes what little remains as she lays a hand on my shoulder, leaning in.

My eyes flutter shut, waiting, hoping, for her mouth to touch mine.

Another car door slams shut.

Eden jumps, pulling back, her grip on my shoulder impressively firm.

Then, another.

I release a long sigh as I open my eyes and push up into a sitting position, then slip off the mattress.

The window doesn't provide a good view of the driveway—I can't see Eden's white Prius—but I can see the neighbors piling out of their minivan.

"Just the neighbors, Eden."

On the bed, she breathes a sigh of relief.

When I look back, she's still pressed against the headboard, struggling to relax.

And I should be helping, not putting more pressure on her, unintentional though it may be.

"Come on," I say, nodding her up into a sitting position. "Let's finish this so I can get out of your hair."

CHAPTER 22

EDEN

Mama knocks on my open door, a bright smile on her wrinkled face. "Good, Thien, you're awake."

I roll my eyes beneath a layer of black hair. Of course I'm awake—it's nearly 6 p.m., and this afternoon, the email came. I was one of fifteen students chosen to receive the Trustee Scholarship, and they're giving me twenty thousand dollars annually, provided I keep at least a 3.5 GPA while there.

How in the world could I sleep?

I open my mouth, eager to tell her, but she's on a mission—I can see it in her warm brown eyes.

"I have a surprise for you tonight."

My stomach drops. She says it like it's something exciting and amazing and wonderful.

Surprises are never good.

"What is it, Mama?"

Her smile doesn't ease my discomfort. "We're having ca kho to for dinner…"

That's hardly a surprise. It's a normal family meal, but we rarely have those now that it's just the two of us.

"And we have a dinner guest tonight."

There it is.

"Who?"

Mama's smile widens, her eyes sparkling with excitement. "Colton is in town for his spring break. I thought you'd enjoy seeing him again. You were so happy to visit him when you were at Archer Collins."

Right.

Of course he's in town. Archer Collins has their spring break during the second full week of March, so there's no overlap with ours, which starts in six days. I'll spend the entire vacation working on my presentation for the New England STEM Fair now that the project's complete.

I push up into a sitting position. "When will he be here?"

She nods toward my closet. "You need to get dressed now, Thien. A skirt or dress."

Great. He's probably about to walk in our front door.

In the middle of the table, Mama's ca kho to sits inside our large clay pot. Per usual, the caramelized fish fillet is delicious—sweet and salty with the perfect amount of umami.

Colton, however, isn't sure how to eat it.

He watches as I pile rice onto my plate, then top it with a large helping of the fillet while Mama passes out cups of canh ca chua. The two sweet and savory dishes are perfectly matched.

After observing for a minute, Colton accepts the serving spoon and places a small serving of each on his plate. He's not sure about the food—and I'm not surprised. Even this simple Vietnamese family dish is strange to the residents of tiny Tourmaline.

I clear my throat. "So Colton, how were your midterms?"

He flashes me a smile. "They're always difficult, but this is my final semester. It's hard not to be excited, no matter how I did. I'm so close to graduating."

I have the urge to roll my eyes, but with Mama present, that's a terrible idea.

But seriously? I don't understand that perspective. I'm about to graduate as well, but there's no way I could be blasé about my performance.

Across from us, Mama smiles. "I understand completely."

I can barely eat my food with my queasy stomach, but this is my role. This is what I'm supposed to do. I'm supposed to laugh and smile and be the perfect daughter—and marry the uninteresting man beside me.

Is Colton interested in getting married? He's only twenty-two. Does he realize that's where my mother is leading this strange relationship? Does he see that, in her eyes, we're practically betrothed?

"What about you, Eden?"

Eyes wide, I turn to him. "What about me?"

Colton grins. "How are your classes going? Are you ready for graduation? You've only got a couple months left too."

I take a deep breath—at least it's a topic I'm interested in—and lay down my chopsticks. "I'm not worried about most of my classes. They're not much more difficult than last year. What I'm focusing on is my project for the STEM fair in Portland next month. I've spent the last ten months breeding microorganisms—"

"Thien," Mama chides, "I'm sure Colton isn't interested in whatever you're breeding for your little project."

But beside me, he shrugs. "Actually, that sounds pretty cool. Maybe you could tell me about it after dinner?"

I have to swallow down the discomfort and pick up my chopsticks again. "Maybe. How long are you staying in town?"

"Through the end of the week," Colton says. "My parents get really excited whenever I come to town, especially since I'm staying in Pennsylvania after I graduate. I hate to disappoint them, but I'm not a big fan of Maine weather."

Mama leans forward with an eager smile. "Are you staying in the same city?"

Colton bobs his head from side to side uncertainly. "Archer Collins is on the outskirts of Bethlehem, but I'm considering a few places in the area. It wouldn't be more than an hour away."

"Thien—Eden—have you heard anything about the Trustee Scholarship?" The question is directed at me, but her eyes don't leave him. "You know, if she wins the Trustee Scholarship, she might attend Archer Collins. We haven't made a final decision, but if you think it's a good school, maybe…"

Part of me can't believe my ears.

Mostly because Mama really is trying to marry me off before I've graduated high school, but also because my ill-conceived ploy to fake interest in Colton may actually pay off. She'd let me attend Archer Collins?

I bite my lip. "Actually, Mama, I got the email this afternoon. They're offering me twenty thousand to attend."

Across from me, she grins and finally meets my eyes. "That's wonderful, Thien." But again, her attention quickly returns to Colton. "What do you think? Is the school good enough for my daughter?"

It's the first time my mother has ever complimented my intelligence, my education, my mental capabilities. It's the first time she's cared about my test scores or my IQ.

But there is too much I want to do to marry Colton Danvers, to devote so much of my life to someone I don't care about, even to make Mama happy.

After dinner, Colton presses a kiss to my knuckles and says goodnight to Mama. Only when the door closes and his car backs out of our driveway can I relax.

"It's nice to see you two get along so well, Thien." Mama wraps an arm around my shoulders and squeezes. It's as close to a hug as she gives, but it carries no comfort.

"Yeah, get along," I murmur.

The moment she releases me, I make for the stairs.

In my bedroom, I lock the door and collapse on the bed, trying to settle the icky feeling coursing through my body.

Mama thinks she's doing what's best for me, I know that. That's why I let her, why I don't know how to tell her no. But how can she not see I have no interest in what she wants for me? That I am uncomfortable with the idea of marriage? That I only go through these awkward situations to make her happy?

I sigh.

Then again, like Tinsley says, I can't expect Mama to understand things I don't explain.

Tears prick my eyes, but I blink them away.

Tinsley.

I need to talk to Tinsley.

My phone is somewhere in the mass of covers, and I tug it free.

She picks up after the second ring. "Hey, girl, I'm glad you called. I want to touch base about the art show—"

I release a shaky sigh. "Mama invited Colton over for dinner as a surprise."

"What?" On the other end of the line, something bumps loudly, and it takes her a moment to come back. "Sorry, I dropped the phone."

Despite myself, I laugh.

"So you had a weird chaperoned date that your mom just kind of…sprung on you?"

"Exactly."

"What the fuck?"

The laughter bubbles out no matter how anxious I am, and I'm grateful for it—for her. "I don't know how to explain this to Mama. She's considering letting me attend Archer Collins, and I know I don't even like Colton, but Archer Collins is so important—"

"No, Edie. Don't you dare consider sacrificing part of yourself and your freedom just to attend college."

I'm not sure how to explain this to Tinsley either, though. She doesn't care about academics the way I do. She doesn't have a preference for her college, and she doesn't understand why Archer Collins matters so much. She doesn't see I would do anything to attend Archer Collins.

"There are other ways," Tinsley says. "This STEM fair. If you get into the international fair, they award prizes for all kinds of things. You could get a decent amount of money. Especially if you win the whole damn thing. You can get to Archer Collins on your own, understand?"

I chuckle through the tears. "I don't know. Can I?"

"Of course you can. You're Eden fucking Prince, and you are the smartest, most capable woman in the world, you understand me? You've told me about your plastic-eating bacteria, and it's amazing. You are a badass, and you can win that first prize."

My chest feels lighter with her blind support. No matter what, no matter how much distance we've had over the last couple weeks, she believes in me, and I am so grateful for our friendship.

"You always have another option, okay?"

I nod, though she can't see me. "Okay."

"Besides, you can't let Noah Barton attend Archer Collins without you."

I stifle a laugh. "I'm not sure Noah will go to Archer Collins."

Tinsley chuckles—like I'm telling a joke. "No way. Noah's wanted to go there since we were kids. That's where his mother went."

I hesitate, but I can't keep secrets from her. "I overheard him and Mr. Libby talking last week. Noah's dad wouldn't let him go to the Trustee Weekend—that's why he wasn't there—but he told me he wanted to get a head start on his STEM project. He lied to me."

For a minute, Tinsley doesn't say anything. "Edie, you sound upset."

How am I supposed to respond to that?

Of course I'm upset. Tonight has been a mess of awkwardness and discomfort. At least, my tears have slowed.

"I mean upset about Noah."

"Oh." I frown. "I don't know. It's weird he might not attend Archer Collins, you know? Like you said, it's been his dream for years, but his dad doesn't want him to go."

"You know," Tinsley says slowly, "you sound like you might actually care about Noah Barton."

"What?"

"You have a crush on him, don't you?"

My mouth drops open. My eyes clamp shut. "How could you possibly think that, Tins? I don't—I don't have time for a crush. I have a project to present in less than a month, and we're about to graduate, and I cannot believe you think I have feelings for Noah Barton. What a completely ridiculous notion."

But she laughs. "Not really, Edie. I've gotten that impression for a while."

I wet my lips, but I don't know what to say. "I don't like him, Tins."

Well, I don't know what to say that would make her believe me.

CHAPTER 23

NOAH

I saw her at lunch for half a second, but she disappeared. We haven't had an experiment in almost two weeks, but writing that last lab report was an intensely strange experience.

She smiled at me. Like we might be friends.

And unless it was my imagination, she was about to kiss me. I might have been about to kiss her.

I don't know.

It must've been my imagination. It was nothing. Definitely nothing. It doesn't mean anything. I'm not nervous or anxious about seeing her. And she definitely hasn't haunted my thoughts.

"Noah?"

I nearly drop my tray.

"Jeez, Noah, what the hell?"

When I look up, Tinsley Edwards offers me a

smile—my stomach sinks. "Uh, hey, Tinsley. Anything I can help you with?"

Why am I disappointed? Did I really expect it to be Eden? I've blatantly avoided her for the last week. Even she should've noticed how awkward I've been, but I doubt she has. Eden was never good with social cues. And frankly, neither am I.

Tinsley chuckles. "Why are you so jittery?"

"I just, um, you know, nerves?"

She looks unimpressed. "That's cute. Who are you looking for?"

"What do you mean?"

"You've been looking around the cafeteria for the last five minutes. I figured I should figure out what's going on before you walk into someone."

"Oh. Yeah, it's been a weird couple days."

"Anything I should know about?"

I cock my head. "Not really." What could she possibly help with?

Tinsley raises an eyebrow. "Anything to do with Edie?"

"Eden?"

She nods.

"Of course not." I laugh nervously. "Why would I think about her? Why would you say that?"

Tinsley snorts. "She thinks about you all the time."

My jaw drops. "She does?"

She chuckles. "You have no idea how often she complains about your academic achievements—especially when you beat her. She's worried about the STEM fair and this final semester, you know? If she doesn't get Valedictorian, she's gonna flip."

"Oh, right." I nod, but it's forced. "Why else would she talk about me?"

Tinsley watches me curiously, a hint of a smile on her fuchsia-colored mouth. "You sure there's nothing I can help with? You seem really out of it."

I swallow down any remaining uncertainty and step around her. "I'm alright. Thanks, um, for the offer, though."

"No problem." She watches as I head to my table.

God, could that have been more awkward? She knows. She must realize. I was instantly more nervous the moment she brought Eden up.

I should never play poker.

And then, there she is.

My eyes follow Tinsley to her lunch table, where Eden waits, her box lunch open and neatly organized. Her face lights up when Tinsley sits, and after a moment of chatting, Eden's brown eyes seek me out.

I avert my gaze.

Great. Definitely want to be caught staring.

Heat rises to my cheeks, and I turn to my lunch and my book. Not that the bland beef ravioli, salad, and roll are anything to write home about. But this is what I need to focus on.

This is what's important.

Planning my presentation for the STEM fair.

Not Eden.

When I get home, Dad's Chevy Equinox is parked in the garage. I stow my bike inside, and the garage door whirs loudly as it closes behind me.

Inside, Dad's in the living room watching a grilling show. Not that he knows how to grill—there must not be any sports he likes on.

Even so, I don't want to say hello.

He's never home this early, and his presence doesn't bode well. He must have some plan, and whatever it is, I'm not sticking around to find out. Today has not been a good day.

I make for the kitchen.

He turns off the TV as I pass. "Where are you going?"

"I'm hungry," I call out, not pausing.

In the kitchen, I grab a bag of Doritos from the pantry and tear it open. It's not much, but it'll be enough while I work on homework.

"Of course you're hungry—it's almost six o'clock. School got out hours ago. Where have you been?" His voice quivers with anger. "You cannot disappear for three hours, Noah."

I glance over my shoulder. "I went to visit Mom. Like I always do."

The muscle in Dad's neck trembles, but his anger abates.

Perhaps because he hasn't been to Mom's memorial since the ceremony in November. He can't even muster the effort to visit her.

"At least have the decency to text me next time."

I bite my tongue as the frustration rises in my throat.

What would that achieve? He's never here this early, so why text him every day in case he came home at a normal time for once? This is a complete overreaction.

I swallow down my irritation and keep my voice steady, calm. "I'm almost eighteen, Dad."

His eyes narrow, his vein throbs. "You're not an adult yet. You are my child, and as long as you're under my roof, you go by my rules. I need to know where you are at all times. Either you're in school or you come home. That's how this works."

My hands clench around the Doritos bag. The chips crunch between my fingers, but what can I say? He's technically correct, even if he's completely insane. "What about Mom?"

"Your mother is not a tree, Noah. She's dead." He shakes his head, breaking eye contact. "It's time you came to terms with that. You can't keep crying over her forever."

I scoff and push past him out of the room.

If I stay, I might say something I'll regret.

Dad—and Ethan and Cliff—continually show me I'm the only one who cares Mom is gone. They laugh and work and behave like complete morons. Like her death, like her absence, is meaningless. Like they don't have a giant hole in their heart because she went away.

At least I have emotions. At least one of us does.

When my bedroom door slams shut, I bolt it in place and throw myself on the bed. I will never understand him.

CHAPTER 24

EDEN

I CLEAR MY THROAT AND READ THE HANDOUT WHILE Noah takes the lead: "'When placed in an external magnetic field, a current-carrying wire experiences a force due to the magnetic field. This experiment explores the direction of that magnetic force, its magnitude, and the parameters affecting that force.'"

"Right," Noah says as he places the horseshoe magnets on the scale.

"Newton's Third Law of Motion says, 'For every action, there is an equal and opposite reaction,' so here, the magnet creates a force on the wire, but the wire has an equal but opposite force on the magnet." I nudge a few strands of hair behind my ear, but my eyes gravitate toward Noah again.

Basically, force comes in pairs.

In every interaction, there is a pair of forces acting on

the two objects in question. The size of the force on the first object is equal to that of the force on the second, and the direction of the force on the first object is opposite to the direction of the force on the second.

Perhaps that's the real reason Mr. Libby switched our lab partners. Noah and I interact with equal and opposite force.

Noah flushes when our eyes meet. "Uh, right, so next we need to clamp the dowels onto the crossbar."

Then again, we've found a strange rhythm.

I don't know how that happened, but oddly, I don't mind. We still argue, but in between, Noah looks at me like he doesn't know what to make of me—and frankly, I don't know what to make of him either. It never occurred to me we could become friends. Is that what we are now?

"How's everything going?" Mr. Libby pauses by our lab station, a grin on his face. "Any questions about the experiment?"

I scoff. "Of course not, Mr. Libby. Your handout is a perfectly capable explanation."

He raises an eyebrow but turns to Noah. "What about you?"

Noah offers him a soft smile. "It's magnetic force and batteries. It is pretty straightforward."

Mr. Libby chuckles. "Have you found the direction of the magnetic force on the wire?"

Across from me, Noah is only now hooking in the complete series circuit.

I roll my eyes. "We haven't finished the apparatus. What do you think?"

"I'm surprised at you," Mr. Libby says, meeting my gaze

with serious eyes. "Harmony and Kevin have already finished their apparatus, you know."

I stifle a gasp and push up for a better view of our ex-partners' station at the other end of the lab.

Fortunately, Harmony and Kevin are still struggling to put it together.

I turn back to Mr. Libby with a scowl. "That's a nasty trick, you know."

"Maybe," he says with a blasé shrug, "you should show a little respect to your superiors, Eden. You are incredibly smart, but you're also incredibly rude."

Arms crossed, I hunch over the counter, and my lips twist into an irritated scowl, even after Mr. Libby departs. "Well, he's incredibly rude too," I murmur to myself.

"Huh?"

My eyes locate Noah again, and I snatch up the handout. "You're almost done, right?"

He clears his throat. "Yeah. What's next?"

"We have to determine the direction of the magnetic field with a compass." My eyes scan the handout, and I read aloud: "'How does the direction of the magnetic force on a current-carrying wire relate to the direction of the magnetic field and the direction of the electrical current?' We already weighed the magnets, right?"

He pauses. "I don't have it in my notes. Do you?"

I haven't written anything, but I'm pretty sure we did it. A frown tugs at my mouth. "Did you forget to write it down?"

He shrugs. "Sorry, I've been...it's been a long week."

I heave a sigh—because I have to weigh the magnets again, but also because I can relate. The sudden and incredibly awkward dinner with Colton. Trying to figure out how to pay the rest of Archer Collins' tuition. Plus, Tinsley's ridiculous accusation. It all adds up to an increase in my cortisol levels.

After weighing the magnets, I mark the mass in my notes and return them to the apparatus, and Noah reattaches everything.

He glances at me with a hesitant smile, cheeks tinged pink. "Ready to turn it on?"

All I can do is stare.

Because Noah Barton increases my cortisol levels more than anything or anyone else. He stresses me out, he irritates me, he drives me insane—also, he blushes every time he looks at me. When did that happen?

We had a moment while working on that last lab report. I don't know what came over me, what I was thinking, but there was something about being close to him that confused my brain. If I didn't know any better…

Well, I almost kissed him.

My lips quirk to one side. "Are we friends now?"

His brow furrows. "What?"

"Have we become friends? Is that why we fight less?"

"I don't know." His fingers flatten across his notes, but he twitches. "Do you want to be friends?" The flush on his cheeks is more apparent now.

Honestly, I never considered it. What would that entail? How would that effect…well, everything?

We've been rivals, enemies, for ten years, and that rivalry has become a mainstay in my life. If our rivalry is suddenly moot, what else changes? Do I want it to change?

Or am I reading too much into this?

I take a steadying breath. "Next, we turn it on and slowly increase the current…"

Noah proceeds according to the directions. We are officially moving on.

This is the first experiment where Noah has taken the lead—well, where I've allowed Noah to take the lead. Oddly, he doesn't gloat about my relinquishing the reins.

He follows my instructions to the letter, though slowly. "When are we getting together for the lab report? I'm free whenever now that our STEM projects are finished, and the report's not due till after spring break."

I pause in the middle of reading the next step. "I was hoping we could get together at your house this time."

Last time was a mistake. I spent the whole time internally—and for a short period of time, externally— panicking that Mama would walk in and accuse me of… well, I don't know what.

Colton and I aren't even dating, so why does it matter if I spend time with a different guy?

More importantly, I don't want to risk the urge to kiss Noah. There was no follow-through before, but that wasn't due to self-restraint. That was circumstantial.

"Yeah, we can do that." Noah's voice quivers, as does his hand. "How's Friday night?"

Well, it's not like I have other plans.

"Sounds great."

Tinsley meets me outside my final block classroom with an excited smile. "It's officially spring break!" she announces at the top of her lungs, then links her arm through mine and leads the way toward her locker.

I wait while she puts away her textbooks and stuffs everything she'll need over break into her backpack. "I don't know why this is such a big deal. They assign more homework over the break because we have extra time."

She shoots me a glare. "Don't ruin my joy, Edie."

"I'm just being realistic."

"You're only ever realistic. Sometimes, you need to be excited and passionate about something." She slams her locker shut and latches the lock.

I frown as we turn down the hallway toward my locker. "I'm passionate about things, you know."

"Of course you are." Tinsley heaves a sigh. "I didn't mean it like that."

How else was I supposed to take it? How else could she have meant it?

"Speaking of having more free time," she says, tugging on my arm to draw my attention. "Next Friday is the regional art show, remember?"

I cock my head. Already?

"I've only been talking about it for months, you know. I have four pieces in the show, and you know, I might actually win something this year. You're coming with me."

Unease settles in my stomach. "When is it?"

"Friday at six. My mom and I can pick you up around five—it's only an hour drive this time. It's located in Credence this year."

I bite my lip. "Noah and I just made plans to work on our lab report that day—"

"Edie!"

We stop at my locker, and I turn to her with pursed lips. "I'll talk to him. Make sure we're meeting early enough in the day to get things done before five o'clock."

"Before four thirty," she corrects, nodding toward my locker. "You have to have time to get dressed up. Unless you're planning to wear a pretty dress for Noah and want us to pick you up there?"

I ignore the heat that rises to my cheeks. "Don't be ridiculous, Tins." Finally, I turn to my locker and open the padlock. "Why would I get dressed up for Noah Barton?"

She starts to speak, but I shoot her a dangerous look, and she zips her mouth shut.

I know exactly what she's going to say already.

She'll say I'd dress up because I have a crush on him. Because I want him to notice me, to pay attention to me. Because I want to impress him.

And that's not true. Not even remotely true.

CHAPTER 25

NOAH

"You included our graphs, right?"

I lie on my bed, stomach pressed to the mattress, typing up the last of our report, while Eden furiously flips through her notes, her back against the headboard. This is Eden, so she needs to make sure we've included literally everything.

To be fair, the lab was intricate compared to our previous experiments this semester.

I frown as I pull back. "What do you think?"

Eden pushes the notebook aside and crawls toward the foot of the bed to join me. Her arm brushes mine as she settles beside me, her eyes flitting over my conclusion. "It's good. This wording here is a little weird." She points to the first sentence in the final paragraph. "Maybe shorten it?"

"Alright." But my eyes are focused on her warm shoulder pressing against me.

"So as long as you included the graphs, great." She

flashes me a smile.

I raise an eyebrow and clear my throat in an attempt to gather my thoughts. "Does it meet Eden Prince's approval? I didn't think that possible."

She nudges me with her elbow. "I mean, I could've done it better, but you did pretty well on your own."

"Right, like I did it on my own. This is a partner project for a reason, Eden." I snicker. "You want to read over it one more time before we turn it in, don't you?"

The smile she dons is hesitant, nervous. "Maybe twice?"

I push up from the bed with a laugh. "You're worse than I am."

She shoots a scowl in my direction. "If by *worse* you mean *better*, then yes."

Laughter bubbles from my lips, and I shake my head in amusement. But I'm glad for any reason to extend this meeting.

I don't know why she requested we work earlier in the day, but if it means we spend more time together, I am very okay with that decision. It's only four thirty, and I don't want her to go yet.

"I'm gonna grab a drink," I say. "You want anything? We have soda, juice, water. We might have some milk."

"Coke?" She doesn't look up. She's too busy scrolling to the top of the document.

"Sure."

Downstairs, the house is already somewhat dark. The sun doesn't officially set until five thirty this time of year, but the big orange ball is already closing in on the horizon.

It doesn't help that Eden insisted we turn off the lights we weren't using for the sake of the environment. I laughed—mostly at the way she badgered me about it—but complied without question or complaint. There's no point leaving them on anyway.

I flip on the kitchen light and grab a couple Cokes from the fridge, then pause and go back for a couple bottles of water. She'll have to be happy with the fact that we recycle. I flip off the light again before heading back upstairs.

The stairwell is particularly dark—the only window is the one leading up to the roof and Mom's telescope.

If she were here, we'd be prepping to study the stars once it got dark. We'd put together snacks and grab some blankets and climb out there. We'd watch the sun set and enjoy the twilight and the stars slowly sparkling into view. Then, finally, we would look through the telescope, and she'd test my memory, my skills.

It's easily two hours till we can get a good look through the telescope, but I want to share this experience, this memory.

"Hey, I've got an idea." I keep my voice quiet as I enter the bedroom, but Eden doesn't look up.

She shakes her head—already denying me. "I'm almost done with my first read-through. Don't interrupt."

I roll my eyes.

She's an incredibly fast reader, but she's also the most pigheaded person I've ever met.

"Do you want to look at the stars with me?"

Eden lifts her head slowly, her eyes meeting mine.

"Really?"

I shrug, but my chest tightens and thrums with anxiety. "Sunset's in an hour, but we could, I dunno, throw together a few snacks and go up to the roof to watch." I hold out my quivering hand to her.

A smile spreads across her rose-colored lips, and she closes the laptop. "I'd love to." She takes my proffered hand and lets me lead her from the bed.

Eden burrows into the blankets next to me and tugs the platter of crackers, cheese, and deli meats closer. It's not much, but it's good enough considering how last minute this idea was.

I stretch across to grab a cracker—she's hoarding them for herself.

In the distance, the orange globe hovers above the horizon, slowly sinking from view. Official sunset is in ten minutes, but the hills and trees shroud the sun in shadow, giving a false positive.

"Thank you for this," Eden murmurs, and she grabs a cracker and a slice of capicola. "I don't often relax enough to enjoy things like this."

I chuckle. "You're not the only one."

She hesitates. "And thank you for letting us work on the report here instead of my house. I just…"

"Your mom," I say with a nod. "I get it. My dad is the reason I didn't want to work here either. He was, you know, completely embarrassing last time."

Laughter bubbles from her perfect lips. "Insinuating we

were going to have sex? Loudly offering you condoms? No, that's not embarrassing at all."

But 'insinuating' isn't the right word. He was far more direct than that.

"Right," I say, despite the heat rising to my cheeks. "What a ridiculous idea, huh?"

She nods, but the smile fades. "Yeah, that would never happen."

I try to relax beside her, but there's a chill in the air, and I pull some of the blankets over my chest.

Beside me, Eden shoots me a glare and scoots closer. "I didn't realize we were sharing."

A little smile plays on my lips. "You have three blankets. Yes, we're sharing."

She shrugs, unapologetic. "So once night falls, what are the first stars we'll see?"

I quirk my mouth to the side. "Usually, the first stars are actually the planets because they're so close, but only Mars is visible at dusk right now. None of the others show up till after midnight."

Her laughter lights up her eyes. "I don't think I can stay that long."

"Other than that," I continue slowly, trying not to consider that possibility, "the brightest stars are Betelgeuse, Vega, Sirius, Arcturus, Rigel, depending on the time of year. You'll probably notice Orion and Sirius the Dog-Star first."

Eden's eyes dart around the sky, but the lovely hues of sunset are only just beginning—delicate lavenders, faint pinks, and a startling orange near the lowering sun. "Anywhere in particular I should look?"

"Not yet."

She stretches toward the platter to grab another slice of capicola. "I feel I should apologize about my behavior during our last lab report. God, I must've seemed crazy—"

I shoot her an irritated glance. "You don't have to apologize for anything, Eden. You explained everything perfectly at the time."

But she bites her lip. Obviously, she doesn't agree.

"I just…" I take a deep breath before venturing further. "I wish your mom had more faith in your abilities and your judgment. You're one of the most responsible people I know. You obviously have your best interests at heart, and she should trust you to make those decisions on your own."

A small smile twists to one side of her mouth. "I wish she did too. Ever since Papa got sick, we didn't have much of a choice. She's done everything she can to take care of me, and as much as I disagree with her methods, she wants to make sure I'm safe, that I'm provided for."

I frown. "You can care for yourself."

Eden laughs. "She doesn't think so. At least, not yet."

"Dating an older guy doesn't guarantee your safety or security. He doesn't have a serious job. He hasn't even graduated college yet."

She eyes me curiously. "And who would you propose I date?"

A flush rises to my cheeks, and I look away. "No one. You said you weren't interested in anyone."

"I didn't say that."

I turn to her sharply.

She meets my gaze with a steady, controlled eye. "I said I don't have plans to date anyone, for a relationship. I never said I wasn't interested."

"Oh."

Eden raises an eyebrow. "You're not going to ask?"

I frown. "Is it really any of my business?"

"No, but aren't you curious?"

One short glance tells her everything: I'm desperately curious but too nervous, too scared to admit it.

A smile tugs at her perfect mouth, but instead of answering the unspoken question, she leans her head on my shoulder and faces the setting sun. "It's beautiful."

I nod, but I can't take my eyes off her—not the sunset.

"Papa and I were really close when I was little. He was the one who encouraged me to pursue science. He taught me about the environment—he helped make so many protection laws and programs while he was mayor. But when he got sick, all I had was Mama. She went straight into survival mode, trying to piece together our lives from what little remained. We were never that close, we never connected." She releases a quiet sigh, trying to hide the tremble in her voice. "I'm pretty sure she thinks I've abandoned our heritage. I know she's glad we're here—we have so many more opportunities in the U.S., and even after Papa got sick, we don't live in poverty like she did. But part of her hates how utterly...American I am."

Hesitant, I slide an arm around her back. "Well, I think you're perfect just the way you are," I murmur.

Eden pulls back.

My cheeks flush.

I hoped she wouldn't hear that.

Soft fingertips stroke my jaw, tilting my head to face her, and she presses forward to lay her lips on mine. But before I can react, she retreats, pink dusting her cheek-bones, her eyes downcast, and lays her head on my shoulder again, relaxing against my side.

Well.

That happened.

The sun has officially set now, and dusk slowly sets in. The moon is still up, round and nearly full, and it casts a shimmering white glow on much of the world around us. Still, as the light fades, several stars slowly come into view.

"There," I say, pointing just above the horizon where the sun set minutes previously, "you see that bright red-orange star?"

She nods.

"That's Mars. That's why we can see it so well." I pause, glancing around the darkening sky. "And do you see that sideways *W* to the north?"

She shifts to look. "Maybe?"

"It's still a little faint, sorry." I release a nervous chuckle. "That's Cassiopeia. When it gets darker, you can see it better." Next, I point toward the south. "Just over that ridge of trees, do you see the really bright star?"

"Yeah…"

"That's Sirius the Dog-Star; it's the nose of Canus Major, Orion's dog. And pretty soon, we should be able to see Orion."

Almost exactly in front of us, I can barely discern the three stars that form Orion's Belt. Rigel and Betelgeuse, located at opposite ends of Orion, are the easiest to see, being the brightest stars in the constellation. None of the others are visible yet.

"When can you show me Draco?" she asks in a tiny

voice.

"We have to wait a little longer. It's not very bright, and it's pretty close to the horizon in the north. It wraps around the North Star."

"That's your mom's favorite constellation, right? What's yours?"

I glance toward the Schmidt-Cassegrain telescope a few feet to our right, but it's not dark enough to warrant its use. "The Seven Sisters. We can't see them yet." I scratch the back of my neck uncertainly. "And it's not a constellation; it's just a bunch of stars clumped together."

"I haven't heard of that."

"The Pleiades," I add, "or M45." I point toward Taurus, but Mars is overwhelmingly brighter than the blurry spot that marks the bull's shoulder. "It's easiest to see in November, but when it gets darker, I can show you."

"There are seven?"

I laugh. "Not exactly. On a moonless night, you can see eleven or twelve with really good eyesight. With a telescope, there are a lot more—maybe twenty, maybe more."

She relaxes against me again, resting her head on my shoulder instead of examining the darkening sky, and I close my eyes to relish the closeness.

I don't know the last time I was this physically close to someone.

I don't know the last time I wanted to be this physically close to someone.

Generally, I prefer my own space, and I don't appreciate having to share. But this is different. This is Eden.

When my eyes flutter open a few minutes later, more stars are visible in the gray-violet sky.

I nudge Eden, and she pulls away so I can scoot closer to the telescope. She follows, bringing the blankets with her, and when I ready everything to look through the eyepiece, she drapes one of the blankets on my shoulders.

The first thing I find is the small cluster of stars in Taurus. With this light, I can only pinpoint six or seven stars, but I nod her close and lean back so she can look through the telescope.

"Wow." A smile spreads across her lips. "It amazes me how much people achieved by using the stars for navigation."

I tug the blanket tight, enjoying her warmth and smell on the thick material. "Well, the name—Pleiades— is Greek, meaning 'to sail.' The day the cluster first appeared before sunrise was the beginning of the ancient Mediterranean navigation season."

"How far away are they?" She shoots me a smirk. "I assume you know everything about them."

I try not to laugh, but her smirk widens into a smile, and I have to—because she's right. I know exactly how far away they are. "Four hundred thirty light-years away."

Finally, she scoots back, closer to me. "Thanks for showing me. I know it must be difficult. You know, to show this to someone."

I avoid her eyes. Last we talked about it, I knew I would have to find someone incredibly special to share this with. This place, this telescope, this moment is special. "It's what my mom would've wanted—for me to share this with someone like you."

"Hmm?"

"Someone who understands me." I shift away to adjust

the telescope again.

What should we look at now?

Polaris maybe, since she mentioned celestial navigation.

She lays her hand over mine, and I hesitate before turning to her. "Thanks for understanding me too." She shuffles closer, and this time, when she kisses me, she doesn't hesitate.

My eyes widen for a split second, then flutter shut, and I wrap my arms and blanket around her and relax into the embrace. Her hand reaches up, abandoning her own covers, and delves into my thick blond hair, and she presses close, banishing any remaining distance.

Never in my life did I expect this development, especially considering Eden always abhorred me more.

And hell, even if she didn't, Eden Prince is utterly out of my league.

But that doesn't bother her. She lays a palm against my heart and opens her mouth to me, slow and patient and intimate.

Like in everything she does, Eden is sure, confident, and commanding, and I am more than pliant to her demands. When her tongue traces my lips, I open for her, and she deepens the kiss without hesitation.

The crunch of gravel below signals a car pulling into the driveway, and I retreat.

Dad's home.

CHAPTER 26

EDEN

My cheeks ache from smiling, but Noah won't look at me as I pack up my laptop and notebooks. "I'll read over the report again and let you know if we missed anything," I say in a quiet voice.

Hovering by the door, Noah's cheeks are bright red.

And I can't blame him. I'm nervous too. How are we supposed to talk now? I didn't mean to kiss him—

Well, the first time.

The second time was definitely premeditated and intentional.

But still, I never anticipated anything to come from the strange quiet friendship we've developed.

"Right," he says. "That sounds good. So I'll see you Monday, right?"

"Exactly."

Knock, knock.

The door nudges open at the pressure—we didn't close it all the way—and Noah's dad sticks his head in.

"Yeah?"

"Oh, sorry to interrupt." His eyes gravitate toward me. "Eden, right?"

Near the door, Noah rolls his eyes, but I never expected Mr. Barton to remember my name.

"Yes, sir."

"Great to see you." He returns to Noah. "I'm home a little early tonight, so I thought we might go out to eat. Catch up. Want to eat at Virgil's for dinner—if the two of you are finished?" He pulls back, then hesitates. "Eden, you're welcome to come with us."

"Oh." I flush at the offer. "Thank you, sir. That's very kind. I'd love to."

Noah whips his head around, eyes wide.

But his dad nods in approval. "Wonderful. Be downstairs in five." And he disappears.

After a moment of uncomfortable silence, Noah swallows, his eyes falling to the floor. "You don't have to come with us. I mean, it'll just be me and my dad, and he's not... great company."

I shrug, but my smile returns without difficulty or hesitation. "I'm hungry. And your dad isn't the only person at this dinner, right?"

His blush returns full force. "Right."

I step closer, bridging the gap, but he won't look at me. "You know, I enjoy spending time with you, Noah. Not many people can keep up with my intelligence."

He rolls his eyes, but he's smiling. "Not many people can keep up with your ego, Eden. Let's not mince words."

When my laughter fades, I bite my lip and take another silent step toward him. "We have five minutes?"

Noah raises an eyebrow.

My backpack's packed and ready to go, we both have our shoes on, and I want to kiss him again.

He meets me halfway this time, and I wrap my arms around his neck, tugging him closer. His hand runs down my side to my hip, then back up to my shoulder, and I tilt my head for better access to his warm lips, parted just enough I can delve my tongue inside.

A shaky sigh escapes his nose, and when he pulls back, I follow, not ready to separate, not ready to sacrifice the warmth that spreads through my body from our lips.

"You guys ready to go yet?"

Mr. Barton's voice is quiet at this distance, but it's enough to pull Noah away from me.

I release an irritated sigh as he separates, a goofy grin on his shiny pink lips. Mine must be equally swollen.

"Let's go," he says in a quiet voice, nodding toward the open door.

"You like Italian food, right, Eden?"

My eyes flit to Mr. Barton's tan face, his dark-brown eyes assessing me, and I feel the need to reassure him. "I'll eat almost anything." But my eyes return to the menu to search for something that sounds appetizing.

Yes, I will eat almost anything, but I prefer a lighter palate. Italian food is so rich and I'm lactose intolerant, but thankfully, there are a number of soups and salads. That should do nicely.

"Don't worry about the price," he adds, scanning his menu. "Pick whatever you like. I've got the bill."

I smile, but it's forced. The fact that he's covering the bill is exactly the reason I would worry about the price. Thankfully, their house salad isn't expensive.

"What are you thinking?" Noah, beside me, already has his menu closed, his hands clasped on his lap. When our eyes meet, a flush rises to his cheeks.

A smile spreads across my face. "A Caesar salad sounds good. What are you getting?"

He shrugs. "Chicken Parmesan."

Opposite me, Mr. Barton closes his menu with a sigh. "Where is our waiter?" He strains to look around the room, but the server who attended to our drink orders has yet to return. Irritated, Mr. Barton rises from the table.

Leaving us alone.

I close my menu too and turn to Noah.

He clears his throat. "When are you heading to Portland?" His fingers play with the fork and butter knife, organizing and reorganizing them again.

It takes a second to realize what he's talking about.

Portland.

The New England STEM Fair.

It's less than two weeks away now. The first weekend of April.

Apparently, kissing him is a nice distraction from reality. I'd nearly forgotten.

"Probably right after school Friday." I sip my water. "Mama cleared her whole weekend so she could drive me and Tinsley like every year. What about you?"

Noah nods mechanically. "Probably Friday too. We haven't discussed the logistics yet." He shoots an irritated glance in his father's wake.

"Cutting it a little close, isn't it?"

A scowl mars his face. "Something like that."

Apparently, this is a sore subject.

I lay my fingers over his fidgeting hand and offer him a reassuring smile. "You'll do great. I'm sure of it."

He squeezes me back, but a little smirk plays on his lips. "I thought you were going to beat me this year?"

My eyes narrow, and I pull away, but his fingers lace with mine. "Of course I'm going to beat you, Noah Barton. There is no doubt in my mind that I will win first place in the regional—maybe in the international fair too."

Noah smiles.

"You can still do great, though." I shrug. "Second place is pretty great with the number of applicants, and that would send us both to the international fair."

He chuckles. "Placing at all is pretty great with the number of applicants."

"At last!"

Mr. Barton's back—along with the server, an agitated college student with a partially filled-in mustache and a tray of drinks.

I pull my hand away, and Noah releases me without hesitation. Hopefully, his dad didn't notice.

The server distributes the drinks—Noah got a soda and Mr. Barton ordered a rye whiskey—then pulls out his notebook. "What can I get you folks to eat?"

After he returns to the kitchen to put our order in, Mr. Barton turns his attention to us.

He takes a sip of his whiskey and swills the liquid in his mouth before swallowing. "So what were you two working on this time?" His scruffy eyebrows quirk upward in the middle.

I glance at Noah, but he's tugging at the edge of the tablecloth, so I turn to his father. "We just finished up a lab report on magnetic force."

Mr. Barton nods. "You're lab partners in Physics?"

"Yes, sir."

He laughs, waving away my words. "No need to be so formal, Eden. We're rather relaxed in this family."

But in the chair next to me, Noah looks anything but relaxed. He won't look at his dad—he barely acknowledges the conversation.

Under the table, I lay my hand atop his—as discreetly as possible—and he shoots me a curious glance as our fingers entwine.

It seems he's about as skilled at talking to his dad as I am at talking to Mama.

CHAPTER 27

NOAH

THE CHICKEN PARMESAN IS A LITTLE DRY THIS TIME. NOT that we eat out often, especially since it's just me and Dad most of the time.

And when have we ever gotten along?

"Have you managed to catch up with your studies?"

Speaking of Dad.

"Since your, uh, break?"

I frown. What a stupid way to refer to my month away from school. I may not have attended classes, but that was anything but a "break."

Eden nudges my calf with her toe and sends my dad a charming smile. "He's doing great. Anyone else would've needed time to adjust, to get back into the swing of things, but not Noah."

Dad raises an eyebrow at me, and I shrug.

"You know," she says, carrying on as she picks at her

half-eaten salad, "he had to do a number of assignments to make up for his missed time last semester, but he caught up easily."

It helped that most of the teachers gave me a lot of slack when it came to last semester's assignments. There were several, but they were mind-numbingly easy. Everyone took pity on the boy who lost his mom.

"That's wonderful," Dad says, but his brow furrows as his eyes land on me again. "You'll graduate on time, then, right?"

I nod.

That's what he cares about. He wants me to graduate so I can stop being a burden.

"Of course," Eden says. "Noah doesn't back down in the face of adversity." She flashes me a devious smirk. "I'd know."

I snort into my Coke. "Yeah, you would," I add under my breath, then dig into my food again. The penne with the chicken is *al dente*—not my preference, but it's decent enough.

Dad finishes his food—he ordered spaghetti and meatballs with plenty of marinara—and pushes his empty pasta bowl toward the open chair. "So the two of you have been spending quite a bit of time together."

Not a question.

"I guess," I say before taking another bite.

Eden shifts in her seat, leaning back. "That's a requirement to complete our experiments and reports." There's almost a hint of her normal bitterness, but it fades. "It's been one big adventure this semester." Under the table, she clasps our fingers together again.

Heat rises to my cheeks, and I force myself to keep eating to hide the blush.

"Did everyone's lab partners change at the start of the new semester? Isn't it the same class as the fall?"

I bite down wrong and cough into my paper napkin.

As established, Eden is the one who answers: "No, Mr. Libby thought we would…do better together than apart."

"Mr. Libby?" Dad shoots a skeptical look my way. "He's your favorite teacher, right? The gay one?"

"Dad," I snap, glancing around the restaurant to make sure no one heard. "Don't say things like that. Mr. Libby isn't gay."

But Dad purses his lips, unconvinced.

"You met him once," I say after a heavy sigh. "Sophomore year. Parents' night. That was his first year as a full teacher. He taught our Bio class."

He nods, then turns to Eden, which is probably the smartest idea. "And you, Eden…what are your plans after graduation? You always compete in those science fairs. I assume you're attending college. Have you decided what to study?"

I almost laugh. No one calls them "science fairs" once you pass third grade.

Eden sits up, her perfect posture emphasizing the soft curve of her butt—I have a particularly nice view. "Right now, my plan is to study Biology and Ecology at Archer Collins. Environmental sciences, you know? I want to study climate change, pollution, the effects our air quality has on asthma and allergies, ocean acidification…that sort of thing."

"Archer Collins, huh?" His question is directed to her,

but his eyes are on me.

I shift uncomfortably and nudge my plate away. I lost interest in eating a while ago.

"It is the best science and engineering school on the East Coast," she says.

He diverts his attention back to her. "That's quite a laundry list of things you want to explore. Do you have time for everything?"

Eden's brown eyes study the remnants of her Caesar salad, and creases spoil her smooth forehead. "I don't know. I don't know how much time I have for what I want."

I run my thumb along her palm, drawing her gaze, and quirk my head to the side. "You okay?"

She smiles, but it doesn't reach her eyes. "Of course."

I squeeze her hand to reassure her, and she leans into the touch.

Dad clears his throat. "I think we're about done here, don't you?" He glances around the room and raises his hand to signal the server. "I'll pay, and we can head back to the house."

Reluctantly, I release Eden's hand and scoot my chair out. "I'm going to wash up then. Be right back."

"We'll meet you at the entrance, Noah," Dad calls out as I head toward the restrooms in the back of the small restaurant.

I splash some water on my face and stare at my reflection. Per usual, I'm pale and scrawny and completely out of place.

Being out of place, feeling alone—that's been my whole

life.

I've always been the one who didn't fit. My head was in the clouds, chasing after Mom and her lofty aspirations.

But Dad.

Ethan.

Cliff.

The three of them have always been grounded in the grass, the dirt, the earth beneath our feet. They've always been part of this world; instead, I strive to be anywhere but here.

I run a damp hand through my tangled, dirty-blond hair with a shaky sigh.

For the first time, I want to be part of this bodily world. I want to experience the day-to-day events. I want to feel the grass between my toes, the dirt underfoot. Maybe being pushed back down to Earth isn't so bad.

To an extent, I have Mom to thank for that. Her death, rather. As much as I want to be like her, that part can wait.

Really, it's all thanks to Eden.

No matter how much hostility existed between us, there was always something intriguing about her. We always understood each other on an unspoken level. We always had a connection.

And now?

I feel more connected to her than ever before. Especially after that kiss.

Well, those kisses.

There isn't much more "bodily" than losing yourself in a lip-lock with Eden Prince, holding her close, hoping it never has to end.

But what about us?

Are we dating? Are we thinking about dating? Are we friends who occasionally kiss? Are we even friends at this point? That's never been fully established.

All I can do is hope.

CHAPTER 28

EDEN

I HOVER BY THE RESTAURANT ENTRANCE, GLANCING toward the back, where the restrooms are. Where Noah is.

But Mr. Barton pushes open the door and holds it for me. "We can wait out here. The weather's pretty nice."

I follow him out, biting my lip.

Outside the small Italian restaurant, there's a bench on either side of the main door. A planter, blooming pink and yellow tulips and lavender hyacinth spilling over the edges, stands near the bench on the right, and I sit beside the brightly colored flowers.

"I'm glad to get you alone," Mr. Barton says.

The cool breeze blows right through my long-sleeve shirt, but I didn't bring a jacket.

"What do you mean?"

Mr. Barton, looming in front of me, levels me with a determined gaze—one I've seen often on Noah's face.

"What are your intentions with my son?"

I gape. "My 'intentions'? What are you talking about?"

His face doesn't soften or relax, and he doesn't hesitate. "Are you the reason he's so determined to attend Archer Collins? To be with you? Are you sleeping together?"

My eyes widen. "No—"

"Don't think I'm stupid just because you're the smartest in your grade. You two have hardly kept your hands to yourselves all night, and you keep sending each other bedroom eyes. I've been married for nearly thirty years—I know what it looks like."

I avert my eyes, trying to figure out how to salvage this conversation. "Then you should realize we're not sleeping together. We've never had sex." But irritation—at the accusation, at being found out, at the embarrassment—swells in my chest. "Not that it's any of your business. If we do, that is our time together, and we don't owe an explanation to anyone else. You don't get a say in what happens between us."

Mr. Barton clenches his jaw, then his fist. "Noah isn't like most—"

"I know he isn't." I push up onto my feet to meet him toe to toe. "Noah is good and kind and brilliant. I don't understand how you could have possibly raised someone so wonderful."

He shoots me a glare. "He's sensitive. You can't string him along like this."

I nearly falter. Nearly. "I'm not stringing anyone along."

"What happens when you go off to Archer Collins and he doesn't?"

Okay, I admit…that does make me falter.

I wet my lips and cock my head. "Why wouldn't Noah go to Archer Collins? He's wanted to go there for as long as I can remember. It's your wife's alma mater."

Mr. Barton shoots me a scowl as he pulls his keys from his pocket. "Sometimes, we don't get a choice." He turns and marches toward the car, parked one row over.

Behind me, the door opens, and I glance back as Noah stumbles into the breezy spring air. His face is bright, excited to see me, and with his dad already walking away, he has no qualms slipping his hand in mine and leading the way toward the car.

I trail slowly.

Noah leans close, brow furrowed. "You alright?" His thumb rubs a long line back and forth on my knuckles.

I pull him to a stop.

His dad is in the car now, the engine running, the head-lights glaring against the two-hour parking sign in front.

"What's going on?" Noah asks, his voice quiet. "Did something happen?"

Instead of answering, I thread my free hand through his hair and stand on my tiptoes to press my lips to his. Right in the middle of the parking lot.

There's something oddly freeing about kissing him in public.

He pulls me tight and responds without restraint, and I'm grateful for that. It was a reckless decision, but I want to be reckless with him.

For once in my life, I want to do something for me. Something I want to do instead of what I'm supposed to do. Instead of sacrificing my desires for the good of the family. I know Mama just wants to look out for me, but the only person I want looking out for me is me.

I don't want to be trapped.

When I kiss him, and when he kisses me, I don't feel stuck. I don't feel trapped. I don't feel caught up between what I want and what I need to do.

I want to kiss him again and again, and I don't want to stop.

After a long moment, Noah pulls away, leaning his forehead against mine, his fingers tracing my hairline down to my jaw. "Come on." He nods toward the car behind us. "We should head out."

I lean forward to press one final kiss to his crimson lips, then allow him to lead me by the hand toward his dad's awaiting Chevy Equinox.

We sit together in the back seat just like on the way to the restaurant. This time, Noah openly holds my hand on the leather seat between us.

It takes a long moment to settle my beating heart from our make-out session, and in the wake of our public affection, Noah's face is beet red. Could he be more obvious?

Although, Mr. Barton's face in the rear-view mirror says he saw the whole thing.

I shouldn't be surprised, and I suppose I'm not. Making out in the middle of a parking lot in the nice area of Tourmaline is practically inviting onlookers.

How long till Mama knows?

Or was Mr. Barton the only one to spot our PDA?

The drive is short, but I pull my phone from my purse

to distract myself. There's a palpable awkwardness in the air.

I have six missed calls. Two voicemail. Five text messages.

The texts are from Tinsley. I'd wager the calls and voicemail are too.

One glance through our conversation, and it's obvious why:

Where are you? You're not home yet.

Are you still finishing up the lab report with Noah? Should we pick you up there?

Edie, where are you?

We have to go. Are you coming or not?

Then, there's a long break between messages, and the final text is only an hour old.

I lost track of how many times I called you, but this is seriously bullshit. You promised you'd come. We're at the show for the next two hours. If you can make it, that'd be great. If not, goodnight.

Shit, the art show.

How could I have forgotten?

The car pulls into the Bartons' driveway, and I clutch the phone to my chest as we climb out. The stars are out in full force now, and beside the car, Noah tugs at my wrist, nodding toward the roof.

"I have to make a call first, okay?"

"I'll be inside," he says before following his father in the front door.

I wait until they're gone and the door closes behind them before pulling up Tinsley in my contacts.

It's officially after eight, and they're probably heading back. I missed the whole thing.

She answers on the third ring. "You're alive."

I force an awkward chuckle. "Uh, yeah, I'm sorry. I got hung up with the lab report, and then Noah's dad showed up, and it was just this whole big thing." I heave a sigh. "Anyway, I'm sorry I missed the show."

Tinsley's voice isn't angry, but the words fall flat. "Nah, it's not a big deal. I'll see you at school on Monday."

Then, the call ends.

And that's it.

No anger, no rage, no frustration. It would even be justifiable. But instead, she had her emotions eerily under control.

Uneasily, I return the phone to my clutch and head inside Noah's house. His dad is watching TV in the living room, but the stairwell light is on—and we definitely turned that off when we left earlier.

Noah's in his room.

"Sorry," I say as I drop onto his bed. "I had to call Tinsley back. But that's out of the way now, so what's going on?"

"Well," he says, glancing over from his desk chair, "you probably need to head home, right? I figured you'd want your stuff." His desktop slowly boots up.

Yes, my backpack still sits at the end of his bed.

"Right."

But a small smile spreads across his face. "Why? Did you have something else in mind?"

I snicker and lie back on the bed to stare at the ceiling, covered in glow-in-the-dark planets and stars, probably from his childhood. The array is captivating, though juvenile.

Noah joins me on the bed, lying down in the open space beside me, and suddenly, he's quiet again. "I've never kissed anyone like that before." His tone is no longer joking. "I've never kissed anyone before actually."

I twist to face him and nudge his side. "Neither have I."

He faces me too. "Not even Colton?"

"Never."

A smile tugs at his lips. "Oh. Well, that's kind of nice."

I roll my eyes and pull him into a kiss. Yes, I need to go home—it's after eight—and yes, the door's wide open and his dad downstairs, but I don't care. Right now, I want to be close to him for a few quiet moments.

CHAPTER 29

NOAH

"HEY, MOM..."

I trace my fingers over the letters of your name. The stone they're etched into is worn and faded now, but your name is still black, firm, strong, ever present. You're not going anywhere, yet you already have.

It's been three days since I was last able to visit.

Dad has kept a tight leash. My STEM project is done, and all I ever do is work on schoolwork, prepare for graduation and college, and spend time with Eden.

To be fair, time spent with Eden is usually time spent on schoolwork. At least part of the time.

I tug my hoody zipper all the way up to block the cool breeze. It's April now, the New England STEM Fair is this weekend, but the weather hasn't improved much.

Since Dad didn't let me attend the Trustee Weekend in February, the STEM fair has become even more important.

The top three participants can head to New York City for the REGen International Science and Engineering Talent Search as officially sponsored finalists. Every year, the REGen Talent Search gathers somewhere around two thousand finalists from smaller fairs like the New England fair and awards nearly five million dollars to the top talents.

Even a small portion of that could help me attend Archer Collins.

I run a hand through my hair. "I don't know if it's worth it, honestly. I don't know if I'll become a finalist, but what other options are there?" I frown. "Is that still what you want?"

Or rather, is that still what I want?

I don't know what I want anymore. I don't know that what I want matters all that much. Even the largest prize wouldn't fund an Ivy League school for four years. What would I do when I run out of funds halfway through my tenure at Archer Collins?

A summer or evening job won't exactly cover that.

I'm running out of options.

Dad won't help. He doesn't want me to go. He doesn't care. He never has, and that's become increasingly apparent since you left.

But Eden does.

I'm not sure when or how—let alone why—but there's a large part of me that feels warm and light and inspired by that notion. By her.

We were never supposed to be more than friends.

Hell, we were never supposed to be more than rivals.

But she smiles at me and kisses me, and I don't want her to stop.

A heavy sigh escapes my lips.

When you died, all I felt was pain. I was numb from the shock, from the grief, from the discomfort. Everyone stared—they still do. They treat me differently, yet no one wants me to act differently. No one wants me to feel.

Maybe it's easier that way. Not feeling the pain.

Eden, though, doesn't treat me differently. She doesn't look at me like I'm broken. She doesn't expect me to get over your death in one night.

I don't feel lost or hopeless with her.

I feel like myself again.

But we haven't talked about what any of this means—the playful smiles, the addictive kisses, the silent touches. We haven't talked about what happens when we graduate, when we head to college, if we attend Archer Collins together, if we attend separate schools. And we haven't told anyone what's happened—well, I'm sure Dad spotted our make-out session in the Virgil's parking lot—and I don't know if we have any intention to spill the beans.

I stretch forward to graze my hand up the sapling's small trunk.

Mom, I miss you more than I thought I could miss anyone.

Tell me what happens next. I don't know what to do now. Show me the way.

The drive to Portland isn't long or difficult, but making the trip with no one but Dad to talk to isn't my idea of fun. He's silent most of the drive, not interested in even smalltalk.

Portland is the biggest city in Maine—the area contains more than a third of the state's total population. Which certainly explains why Tourmaline is so tiny.

The New England STEM Fair is located in the Oxford Waterfront Suites—the same place it's been for the last decade. It's a large building with fantastic views of the municipal ferries, fishing boats, and cruise ships.

Not that I'll notice the view.

I'll spend the entire time in the convention hall, explaining my project to people who probably don't have any idea what I'm talking about and trying to convince the panel of judges that I deserve to go to the REGen Talent Search.

Dad stops the car under the awning, and I follow him inside to check in to the STEM fair while he checks in to the hotel. Unfortunately, we have to share a room.

Inside, Dad heads for the main desk, and I wander the area.

The convention hall is on the second floor, and it's an easy ride up the escalator to find the enclave.

Two women, badges on their shirts, sit at a fold-out table with clipboards and name tags spread across the table.

I clear my throat. "Noah Barton checking in."

After they locate my name on the list of participants, one of them hands me my name badge and a map of the area and highlights my table. "You're free to set up any time between now and tomorrow morning. We'll only have the convention hall open till ten tonight. The fair starts promptly at 8 a.m., so I'd get to work if I were you."

I hang my badge around my neck and head back toward the front. We have to grab all my gear from the car anyway.

Dad is still talking to the main desk.

When I join them, the clerk hands him a small envelope with two key cards. "Have a wonderful stay. Thank you for choosing the Oxford."

Dad doesn't say a word as we return to the car.

Despite his silence, Dad is a hard worker. We carry in the first batch of boxes and bins together, but then, he leaves me in the convention hall to set up while he makes two more trips without complaint.

I roll out my diagrams and graphs and pin them to the barrier between my row and the next, then display the short description I wrote up for those who aren't technically inclined. That hangs in the most easily accessible location in large font—big enough to read from several feet away.

But the real showpiece is on the laptop, which displays the actual computer program.

I set the laptop on the table, atop a large fan designed to keep it cool for the hours it will sit here during the day and a half of presentations.

"Setting up, I see."

I glance over my shoulder and smile. "Mr. Libby, what are you doing here already?"

His eyes focus on the description, but he nods. "I left right after school released. I'm a volunteer this year." He flashes me a smile before returning his attention to my written words. "It's the first chance I've had to help out the fair since starting the job in Tourmaline because of the distance."

"Cool."

I return to the laptop and flip it open. Not turning it on right now—it won't stay here overnight—but I need to make sure everything looks right before tomorrow morning. I won't have time to tweak the setup because I'll have to spend all my prep time making sure the program demos are running smoothly.

Yes, I have a backup laptop in case this one decides to crap out on me. I'm taking no chances.

"That's an interesting project, Noah," Mr. Libby says in a quiet voice. "Did you decide on it before or after…?"

I bite my lip, not looking up. "Before, but it…took on new meaning afterward."

"I hope I'll be able to see your presentation tomorrow." His footsteps start toward the convention hall exit, then he pauses. "By chance, is your brother joining you this weekend?"

This time, I twist to look at him. "Ethan?"

He gives a tight nod.

"He didn't want to use his time off for something that happens every year," I say, mildly irritated but not surprised. "He said he'd rather see me graduate, and you know, when you don't have much time to spare…" I shrug—perhaps he did have a point.

"Ah." Mr. Libby smiles again, then turns away. "Good luck, Noah."

I frown at his receding figure.

"Something the matter?"

Dad's deep voice behind me makes me jump, and I spin round to face him. "Where'd you come from?"

He shrugs. "You were talking to your teacher, so I walked around the room. Found Eden and her mother around the corner."

"Oh." I strain to peek through the gaps, but I can't see anyone who looks remotely like Eden, Tinsley, or her mother.

We haven't spoken much the last couple days. Eden didn't want any distractions from her last-minute preparations for the fair, and I'm definitely a distraction. Besides, now that we're here, in the same convention hall as all the previous years, we're competing for three potential spots to REGen.

Neither of us wants to lose.

CHAPTER 30

EDEN

My fingers clench around Tinsley's as we take our seats outside the convention hall. Mama stands behind us, stern and solid and silent.

The weekend has been one long torture. First, because having to repeat myself over and over to groups of people who don't understand microorganisms or water pollution is exhausting. Second, because seeing Noah from afar and not being able to talk to him is one of the most difficult things I've done.

Even now, he sits a mere twenty feet away, his eyes constantly seeking me out, but all I can do is smile at him.

Mama cannot know.

And hell, I don't have the gall to tell Tinsley about us. I don't have the gall to bring up that night at all—I don't want to draw attention to my missing her art show, to distract her from the subject at hand.

Besides, my focus belongs on the STEM fair, not Noah. And the same is true for him. We both want to place here so we can move on to REGen...and compete against each other again.

The three weeks between this and REGen, though, will give us enough time to relax and enjoy each other's company.

Well, maybe.

We have to complete our finals and graduate from Tourmaline High, then immediately head to REGen.

Dr. Bhavana Singh, the head of the New England Science and Engineering Association and the fair's opening speaker, takes the stage. She clears her throat near the mic and begins: "Thank you for joining us at the annual New England STEM Fair at the Oxford."

The convention hall falls silent. All attention is on her words.

"As always, we're pleased the Oxford Waterfront Suites could host this event again. Thank you for all the hard work the staff has put in to help our STEM fair." She waves an ochre hand toward the nearby staff members laying out another tray of tapas. "And thank you to all of you who have attended our event, especially those of you who participated in the annual competition."

A couple more NESEA members join her on stage, one carrying a box of medals.

"There are three primary division classes: novice, advanced, and expert. We will begin the awards with the novice category..."

I have no interest in this division.

Tinsley offers me a tense smile. She's trying to be

encouraging, but we've barely spoken since I missed the art show. Not that we'd been talking much prior to my misstep.

Thankfully, it doesn't take long for Dr. Singh to reach the expert division.

Each year, they give out awards to the top ten projects in each division, but the expert division is highly competitive. Noah and I have placed in the top ten every year, but Noah only made it to REGen once, during our sophomore year. He didn't place there, but I'm still jealous I missed out on the experience.

"In tenth place…" Dr. Singh says, glancing down at her notes.

The crowd cheers as she reads the names, and one by one, the finalists head to the front for their awards.

Ninth.

Eighth.

Seventh.

My fingers clench tight around Tinsley's.

Only the top three placements get the honor of attending the REGen Talent Search and presenting their findings during the week-long event.

Sixth.

Fifth.

"Everything will be okay," Tinsley murmurs—I'm probably squishing her hand into oblivion.

Fourth.

So close.

"In third place," Dr. Singh continues, "Katherine Elliott for her presentation on substance abuse rehabilitation…"

I bite my lip. That was a really good project. What little I saw of it.

Which leaves only two spots left.

"In second place," the doctor says, "Eden Thien Hoang Prince for her project on plastic-eating microorganisms."

My body feels light as I rise on shaky legs, and Tinsley gives me a nudge toward the makeshift stage.

I got second.

That's fantastic. Amazing.

On the stage, one of the NESEA members hangs the medal around my neck. Another hands me a small envelope. I shake hands with both of them and Dr. Singh, and they signal me to remain onstage. I step toward the back, where Katherine Elliott too waits.

How could I only get second?

"Finally," Dr. Singh says, pausing to release a soft sigh into the mic, "our first place winner: Noah Barton for developing software to plot space travel using gravitational pull…"

My eyes locate him in the crowd.

He stands slowly, wide-eyed, and stumbles toward the stage to receive his medal and envelope. He can't even make it up here without falling all over himself.

Three of us stand center stage while Dr. Singh concludes her remarks:

"Thank you to all the participants in this year's New England STEM Fair. Thank you for making this a successful and enlightening experience for all. Thank you to the folks from NESEA for sponsoring our event, and of course, thank you to the Oxford for housing us yet again. It's been a pleasure."

She pauses, turning slightly to get a good look at the three of us. "Now, everyone, please give a round of applause for our three finalists. In three short weeks, we're sending them to New York City for the REGen International Science and Engineering Talent Search. Wish them luck!"

Noah catches my gaze and grins, clapping along with the rest of the room, and I soon join in. We're going to New York City, and the folks at NESEA will pay our travel fees. What could go wrong?

When we're released from the stage, I follow close behind Noah and trail my fingers up the back of his arm—as discreetly as possible—to garner his attention.

He glances back, eyebrow raised.

"Meet me around back in two minutes," I murmur, and he nods.

Two minutes later, the hallway bustles with movement, but I'm safely around the back, out of the way. Near a janitor's closet, actually.

I tap my foot. Noah's late.

But then, I see the top of his wavy blond hair pop around the corner, and his face comes into view as he hurries toward me, an excited grin on his delicate features.

"Can you believe it?" he says as he stumbles to a stop. "We got in."

"Of course we did," I say with a wave of my hand. "How could we not?"

He chuckles. "I wish I had your confidence."

"You should." I lay my hand over his chest, then curl my fingers into the tight fabric and tug him closer. "You won first place."

His laughter reverberates against my mouth when I pull

him into a heated kiss. His arms wrap around my waist, but I spin us round, press him against the wall, and delve my tongue inside his mouth.

I am addicted to his taste, to his vocal reactions, to his hands on my body. And there's nothing I want more than to ride out the high of this win with him.

Noah breaks away with a chuckle. "And I thought for sure you'd be pissed at me for beating you."

A smirk tugs at my lips. "Trust me, I will be." I pull him into another kiss, smothering his smug laughter.

Right now, I am too excited about REGen to care. Too happy in his embrace to be bothered.

CHAPTER 31

NOAH

Mr. Libby divides his stack of papers into sections to pass down each row. "Remember, this was our last chapter. Next week is finals for our seniors—congratulations, everyone—but the rest of you will remain in class with me and complete your finals the following week."

When the final two papers reach my seat, I pass the second to Leah behind me and skim the page. It's a study sheet for the final, going over everything we covered in this semester: thermodynamics, light and sound, reflection and refraction, electric circuits, magnetism, quantum physics.

The bell rings, and my eyes gravitate toward Eden on the other side of the classroom.

"Alright, see everyone on Friday," Mr. Libby calls as students stuff the study sheets into their binders and head for their next classes.

Eden gathers her things but waits for me before

standing. "When are we studying for the final?"

Not even a legitimate greeting.

I shoot her an amused look. "As soon as possible. The longer we wait, the more likely my brothers will be in town for graduation. I don't want to subject you to that."

She leads me to the hallway, pausing to flash a smile over her shoulder. "That's an overreaction, don't you think, Barton?"

"Don't you remember how annoying they were at New Year's Eve? You haven't seen them since."

She slows once we're in the crowded hallway, letting me catch up. "Then tell them not to be assholes."

"I tried that. It didn't get me anywhere."

"This weekend? Your house?"

"That works." I sigh. "I don't expect them to show up before finals are over anyway. Cliff has his own finals after all."

"What about your dad?"

A scowl twists my lips. "We might just have to deal with him. God, I swear, he didn't used to be this overbearing. Six months ago, he wouldn't have cared. I'll be eighteen in four days, and now, he decides to start parenting."

Eden stumbles. "Wait, your birthday?"

I pause beside her. "I guess."

She chews the inside of her cheek. "Do you want to do something this weekend? Go out to celebrate?"

I shrug and start walking again. "We never celebrate birthdays. It's not a big deal. I don't expect anything, trust me."

She assesses me as we walk, her beautiful brown eyes studying me from top to bottom. "I'll take your word for it."

I breathe a sigh of relief.

The last thing I need is Eden deciding to throw together a birthday party or give me a present on a whim. We're still getting to know each other. I mean, we've never discussed the nature of our relationship. Right now, it feels like we're friends who enjoy kissing. A lot.

"Do you want a ride home after class?"

I shoot her a frown. "What?"

"After class, do you want me to drive you home?" Her smile is small and innocent, but there's a twinkle in her eyes that makes me uncertain. "It's raining, and you only have your bike. And you know, we could hang out for a little while."

"Right, raining." I shrug. "Yeah, that'd be nice. Biking in the rain sucks."

We pause outside her final class, leaning against the lockers nearby.

"Yeah, it does," she says, inclining her head toward me. "Which is why I offered."

"You don't have loads of finals to study for after school?"

She steps closer. "I have a little—that doesn't mean I don't have a few hours to spend with you. Especially since your dad doesn't like you staying out late after school."

I'd argue a couple hours isn't particularly "late," but Dad…has grown paranoid.

"That'd be great." My eyes dart toward the hallway, where most of the students have disappeared inside their own classrooms. "Meet you out front?"

"Oh, there's Tinsley!"

Eden steps away from the lockers, grinning at her best friend, but Tinsley marches past her into the classroom.

Not a word or a glance.

Defeated, Eden slumps against the lockers. "I don't know what's going on. She's been really distant."

I force a smile. "It'll be alright. You two will have plenty of time to talk in a couple weeks, you know." I squeeze her hand—no kissing inside the school. "We'll meet out front, right?"

She's distracted, but she nods before trudging inside her classroom.

I hurry toward my own class, but the tardy bell rings after a few steps. I'm late.

By the time the release bell rings, the rain has slowed, but outside still looks gloomy.

I stop at my locker to pull on my hoody and grab my backpack. Finals are only a few days away now, and I have a lot to study. Can't mess up my GPA this close to graduation, right?

"That's all you have?"

I glance up as I zip my backpack, now full of textbooks, notebooks, and my binder.

Eden leans against the locker beside me, wearing a lime-green raincoat, a closed black umbrella with green polka dots dangling from two fingers. "Do you not have a rain jacket?"

"Oh." I pull my backpack over my shoulder and close the locker. "Not today, no."

She flashes me a smile, and we start, side by side, step for step, toward the front of the school. "I saw you and figured we might as well meet here, you know?" Her fingers brush mine as we walk, but she doesn't reach for me.

We decided not to be openly affectionate on school grounds, difficult as that may be. A squeeze here or there isn't bad, but no actual hand holding.

"Do you want to grab something to eat on the way?" She pushes through the glass doors at the main entrance, and we pause in the foyer, not ready to dive into the rain. "I'm starving, and I'd prefer not to have to leave early because I need to eat."

I raise an eyebrow. "Won't your mom worry about where you are?"

Eden smiles, shaking her head. "Not at all. I'm usually left to my own devices till she gets home between five and six."

That sounds uncomfortably familiar.

"Yeah, food would be alright." I divert my attention outside and pull up my hood, pause.

There's a black Lexus parked in front of the main entrance, flashers on, and two men hover close under one navy-blue umbrella. One of them is Mr. Libby, his bag of papers and schoolwork to grade tucked under one arm.

The other is my brother.

CHAPTER 32

EDEN

Noah pushes open the door and rushes down the stairs, his hand sliding along the wet railing, and I follow close behind, pausing to open my umbrella. Only when he closes in on the couple do I realize why he ran off.

"Ethan?" Noah stumbles to a stop several feet away from them. "What are you doing here?"

His oldest brother steps back, smile fading. "There you are, String Bean. I've been waiting for you." He nods to me, and his mouth twists into a smirk. "Why, Eden Prince, I thought I'd see you while in town, but so soon?"

I come to a stop beside Noah and allow my umbrella to cover him, even if he doesn't notice.

"Why are you here so early? Graduation's over a week away." Noah's voice quivers.

Ethan shrugs. "Figured I could spend a little extra time in town this trip." His gaze drifts to the other person under his umbrella.

I stifle a gasp. "Mr. Libby?"

At last, Mr. Libby faces us with an awkward smile. "Eden, Noah." He clears his throat. "Mr. Barton here was telling me—"

Noah's brother turns on him. "Ethan," he corrects. "You should call me Ethan, don't you think?"

Is Mr. Libby blushing?

Then, Ethan turns to us. "Figured I'd take you out to eat." He nods toward the Lexus behind him. "I don't know about you, but I'm starving. You can come too if you want, Eden."

I study Noah.

He takes a moment to answer. "How long are you staying?"

Ethan shrugs. "I'll head back after your fancy science fair. Cliff too—he'll be here right before graduation." He reaches deep into his pocket and pulls out the car keys. "You coming or not?"

Hesitant, Noah steps toward the car, then pauses to look at me. "That alright?"

"I guess."

It ruins my plans for getting him alone, but I don't mind spending a little time with him and his brother.

I follow him toward the car, but Ethan turns his attention back to Mr. Libby:

"Come with us."

Mr. Libby frowns. "Thank you for the offer, Mr. Barton, but that would be inappropriate."

Noah opens the back passenger-side door and nods me inside. I close my umbrella and slide along the seat, making room for him too, but I don't miss Ethan Barton's response:

"Who said anything about being appropriate?"

Noah closes the door behind us.

I wet my lips. "Well, that was unexpected."

"Yeah." He heaves a sigh and finally meets my eyes. "Sorry about that. I never thought Ethan would…"

"Right." I lean down to get a glimpse out the window, but it's difficult to see through the tinted glass.

What are they talking about still?

"You upset?" His voice quivers, but I can't tell whether it's from concern or his own irritation.

"Not at all." I scoot closer to him—we haven't bothered with the seat belts yet—and lay my hand on his shoulder. "Might as well enjoy our alone time…" I lean closer to press my lips to his cheek, but he turns to me.

The kiss is slow, gentle, and I give in to the affection without hesitation. He cups my cheek and runs his fingers through my hair, and his tongue, soft and silent, slides along my lower lip until I open my mouth with a quiet moan.

The driver's door opens.

I tear away, shifting back into my own seat, and buckle myself in.

Ethan slides inside. "Ready to go?"

At the far end of Pearl's Diner, two large booths are occupied by the high school cheerleaders, no longer in uniform but wearing their hair in two ponytails, adorned in ribbons of Tourmaline High's gold and black.

Thankfully, Ethan Barton chooses a booth at the opposite end, and he slumps into one side, stretching a leg across the seat with a heavy sigh, forcing me and Noah to share the opposite side.

Not that I'm complaining.

He slides in first, and I sit beside him, careful to put enough distance between us to remain inconspicuous.

Well, as inconspicuous as we can be.

"When did the two of you become friends?" Ethan asks, motioning between us.

Noah's eyes dart to me, then to the stack of menus on the table, and he grabs one. "I dunno. Being forced to spend time together was bound to make us more amicable, right?"

Ethan raises a skeptical eyebrow. "That makes me dislike people more."

"You usually dislike people."

I survey the rest of the restaurant—where is our server? This is awkward, and I need a glass of water. And a slice of Pearl's famous blueberry pie.

"Anything to add, Eden?"

I twist back toward him, but all I can do is bite my lip and shake my head.

"Really? But you're usually so opinionated." Ethan shoots me a challenging smirk.

But I won't rise to the debate.

"How is this any of your business?"

Ethan chuckles, relaxing against the wall.

Okay, maybe I will rise to the debate.

I heave a sigh and tug a menu close. "What about you? When did you befriend Mr. Libby?" I already know what I want, but I need something to do during this conversation.

Noah hums in agreement.

"Just now." Ethan shrugs. "What can I say? He made an impression."

Noah closes his menu and slides it back to the center of the table. "What sort of—?"

"Sorry about the wait, kids. We're a little short-staffed right now. What can I get you?"

We turn toward the server, an older woman with curly white hair and distinct smile wrinkles. Pearl, the owner.

Ethan points to something on the front of the top menu. "You remember my regular, right, Pearl?"

She snickers. "Of course, dear."

Noah and I order next, and she runs off to put in the order.

When we're alone again, Ethan straightens and faces us, hands clasped atop the table. "So are you two officially an item? Because you're not particularly discreet."

I glance at Noah, but he only glares at his brother. "Well," I begin slowly, "we're officially lab partners."

He looks unamused. "I'll take that as a no." A soft laugh escapes his thick lips. "I'd recommend not making out in the back seat of a car parked at your school then—even one with tinted windows."

I swallow, allowing the irritation to wash over me, then fade, but beside me, Noah flushes pink. "Why do you care? What we do in our spare time is none of your business."

Ethan shrugs. "No, it isn't. Just figured I'd offer a little friendly advice."

Noah's foot brushes mine, and his lips purse. "And what advice is that?"

His brother shrugs again. "If you think this is a secret

relationship, you're fooling yourselves. Anyone who's seen you two interact knows what's going on."

My brow creases, and I divert my eyes to the speckled gray tabletop.

How could "anyone" know what's going on between us? I don't know, and I'm one of the participants. Besides, who said we're in a relationship? Between REGen and graduation, how could I possibly have time for a relationship? We're not dating.

"What's that supposed to mean?" Noah asks, eyebrows knitted together. "We're not—"

"Stupid?" Ethan offers. "You two may be super smart or whatever, but you're incredibly dumb when it comes to people."

I wet my lips.

Mama can't know.

She cannot find out.

As far as she's concerned, I'm already in a relationship, and I should devote myself wholly to Colton. She has expectations, and while an increasingly large part of me wants to throw those expectations out the window, I don't know what Mama would do if I did. She's the only family I have, and I don't want to lose her.

A small plate slaps down on the table in front of me.

"Here you go, folks." Pearl distributes the food to each of us.

But worry eats at my stomach, rendering the typically delicious-looking blueberry pie a la mode unappetizing.

I don't know how to make Mama happy anymore. Not while also making myself happy.

CHAPTER 33

NOAH

"No, no, no...what the hell are you doing?" Dad releases an angry groan. "Don't go that way, you moron."

Ethan, beer in hand, sits on the edge of the couch beside him, eyes intent on the television.

Apparently, it's the NBA playoffs.

Not that I would know anything about that. I barely understand the concept of basketball, let alone how the NBA works.

But this is a bonding moment for father and son, right?

I pull out my phone, but I don't have any new texts or emails. Instead, I log in to my Archer Collins account.

It's the first of May, but they're already prepping for the new semester. I need to fill out a form to match me with a roommate, but how can I do that when I still don't know whether I can attend? Financial aid will only go so far on Dad's salary.

When Dad starts yelling again, I heave a sigh and close my phone.

There has to be something more interesting than this on TV. Somewhere. Anywhere.

On the couch, Ethan chuckles at Dad's gesticulations, but I don't share in amusement. This is an annoyance at best.

I clear my throat once Dad settles. "When is Cliff getting into town?"

Ethan glances my way. "Sometime before your graduation."

I roll my eyes. "Graduation is eleven days away. That's not helpful, is it?"

"Shush!" Dad swats his hand in my general direction, not taking his eyes off the television, completely immersed.

I scoff and rise from my chair, pocketing my phone, before heading toward the stairs.

I don't know if Dad's pissed at me or just doesn't care, but we've barely spoken since we got back from Portland last weekend. Frankly, at this point, I don't know why I should care. He doesn't care about my life, my goals, my dreams. Why should I make an effort?

Halfway up the stairs, I pause, and instead of continuing to my room, I push open the window in the stairwell and climb out.

The sun hasn't set yet, but the quiet solitude on the rooftop is refreshing, and I lie back and stare at the cloudless sky.

It's Friday afternoon, only an hour after the school week ended, and I should be spending every waking minute studying for my finals week. I need top marks for Archer Collins—but if I don't know whether I can pay for it, why bother? Why do grades matter if having good grades doesn't help me?

Not that I can say that to Eden.

My eyes flutter shut, and I breathe deep the outdoor air. Eden.

We're supposed to study tomorrow, but I'm not keen on the idea of studying here with Ethan and my dad hanging about, spying and prying. We're private people, but my family is not. They don't have boundaries when it comes to barging into my room for no reason. They're curious. Well, more nosy than curious.

"What're you doing up here, String Bean?"

My eyes open as Ethan climbs atop the roof and scoots close. "I was hoping to enjoy a little privacy."

Ethan chuckles as he settles into the space. "That wasn't very realistic, was it?"

I frown. Apparently not.

"This is nice," he says, glancing around, pausing on the telescope under its black tarp. "I haven't been up here in years."

"I wouldn't imagine so."

Ethan shoots me a glance, his mouth twisting into a frown, then turns his attention upward like me. "You know, sometimes, it almost seems like she's still up there, you know?"

My mouth goes dry. "I know."

"It's pretty surreal." He releases a quiet sigh, then settles into silence for a long moment.

I don't know what to say. I never expected him to bring

Mom up, let alone admit something like that, subtle as it is. Does he miss her?

"She really likes you, you know."

I freeze. "Huh?"

"Eden Prince." Ethan chuckles, but the sound is unsteady, uneven. "Really, String Bean, I'd expect you to figure that out by now."

Well, so much for that conversation.

But this too is something that eats at my very core.

"I don't know what we're doing." My eyes wander toward his silent form.

As much as I want to ask the question, I don't want to give him fodder. Unfortunately, I don't know who else to ask.

"Hey, Ethan…"

"Yeah?"

"How do you know if you're in a relationship?"

He snorts. "Having a conversation about it usually clears that up, String Bean. Talk to her, not me. I'm just here to enjoy the show—definitely not to participate."

I slowly push myself into a sitting position. "What about, uh—" I bite my lip. "I mean, all we've really done is kiss, but I get the impression she…"

Eyebrow cocked, Ethan rises on his elbows. "Get the impression what? That's a pretty damn open-ended statement."

Heat rises to my cheeks, but I ignore it. "That she wants more."

"Sex?"

"I don't…I don't know anything about it."

Instead of sitting up like I expected, Ethan collapses

back and clasps his hands over his chest. "What do you want to know?"

I clear my throat. "Don't get me wrong, I know how to research. I understand the anatomy and how it fits together, but what about the emotional component? How do you know someone actually wants to do it?"

"When they tell you." Ethan's words are firm, unwavering, leaving no room for argument. "If you're not sure, ask them. Don't screw someone if you can't confirm they want to be there as much as you do."

I swallow. "What if I don't, you know, last very long?"

He shrugs. "You'll do better next time." He opens an eye and stares me down. "But that doesn't mean you should ignore her needs. Always make sure the other person's enjoying themself."

"But I don't—"

"Research female sexual pleasure. There are a lot of things you can do to make a girl feel good, but if you're unsure, ask her for help. Sex works a lot better when both parties communicate. Trust me."

I nod slowly, but he's shut his eyes again.

I'm not particularly good at communication, but I also don't see anything this extreme happening between us. At least not now. Not yet.

Luckily, I'm saved from responding by my pocket vibrating.

The text is from Eden:

My mom is working all day tomorrow. Do you want to meet at my house instead? We wouldn't have to worry about our studies being interrupted.

A small smile graces my lips.

Yes, that's exactly what I want. Silence, privacy, quiet. The ability to think inside my own head instead of going insane. And Eden is exactly the person I want to share that silence and privacy with.

CHAPTER 34

EDEN

Noah reclines on the mattress, and I curl up beside him, my physics notes on my thighs, completely at ease with him close. At ease with the two of us alone.

"Should we talk about waves and particles next?" I nudge his cheek with my mechanical pencil. "Or should we do the differences between Newtonian and quantum physics?"

Noah, though, doesn't do more than shrug. "Whatever you think is best."

I heave a sigh as I push away my notes and roll to face him. "What's wrong? You've been out of it the last few days. Having your brother here can't be this difficult."

He sends me an amused glance. "Says the person who loathes them both with a passion."

I shrug a shoulder. "Ethan is less annoying than I initially thought, honestly."

"That's good to know."

"But it's not what's bothering you?"

He rolls to face me as well, putting us closer together than I anticipated.

My eyes gravitate toward his mouth. We haven't kissed since I picked him up a couple hours ago, and while I appreciate the devotion to our studies, part of the beauty of being alone is that we can kiss.

"It's part of it." His words are followed by an irritated sigh. "Mostly, it's my dad. He's…been really distant the past couple weeks, and I don't know if he's mad or what. I know I shouldn't care—it wouldn't be the first time he's been pissed at me for something stupid—but he's not usually so quiet or reserved about these sort of things. I don't understand him." He scoffs. "And I doubt there's any way I can."

A long sigh escapes my lips. "Mama doesn't want me to go to college."

He cocks his head. "What do you mean? You're the smartest person I know."

A blush rises to my cheeks. "She knows, and she doesn't care. She wants to make sure I'm safe, taken care of. That's what Colton brings to the table. Security, I guess. He's intelligent, graduating from Archer Collins, pre-law, but he's so boring."

"Isn't the age difference kind of creepy?"

"She was eighteen when she married my dad."

He bites his lip. "Do you like him?"

I almost laugh. "Not even remotely."

He hesitates then, a question on his tongue.

But I need to hear him say it.

"Yeah?"

"Do you like someone else?"

"Like who?"

His eyes dart to mine, then down, settling on the crumpled sheets between us. "Do you like me?"

Laughter escapes my lips, and I lean forward to press my mouth to his. I shouldn't have to answer that question.

He responds immediately, his fingers entwining in my hair. I lay a hand on his shoulder, scooting closer, and relax against him. His kiss is slow but steady, his lips hesitant but eager, and I'm impatient to feel more of him.

My fingers tug at his button-up shirt, pushing it up to locate the skin underneath. I trace along his ribs—he inhales sharply—and trail a line down his back. He shivers under my touch, releasing my hair in favor of caressing my sides.

And I know I want him to feel me, to hold me, to touch parts of me I never considered letting anyone touch.

Instead, he retracts, eyes shut, breath short. "We're supposed to be studying."

When his eyes flash open, I bridge the distance, climbing atop his lap and stifling any arguments with my mouth. He returns the kiss without complaint or hesitation, his hands clamped around my hips, and opens to me, allowing our tongues to mingle in a quiet duet.

We've kissed enough—in these glorious secret moments—I'm no longer enthralled by just his mouth. My fingers, wavering with anticipation, tug at the top button of his shirt, and his breath hitches.

He breaks the kiss again, but my lips trail down his neck to suck at tender flesh as I tear open the first button, then the second.

"Eden…"

My name comes out throaty and deep, and a flash of heat pools in my body.

I pull back to look him in the eye. "Yeah?"

Panting, Noah is a mess of tousled hair and glistening lips. "This is a little uneven, isn't it?"

I nod as I undo the final button. "You're right."

His eyes widen when I lean back and yank my shirt off—then immediately wrench his button-up down his arms. He gasps when I run a hand down his chest, but he kisses me with renewed fervor, and his hands trail up to toy with my white bra strap.

I rest my cheek on his shoulder, laying soft kisses along his collarbone. "You can take off my bra, you know."

Without a word, his hands reach around to tug at the clasp. The elastic pinches as he struggles, but finally, the clasp releases. I shrug the bra onto the floor.

Then, Noah slows.

His touch turns gentle. His hands caress my back and along my ribs, taking a slow, meandering route to my chest.

Finally, he cups my breasts.

A sigh escapes my lips. "Can you believe we're both finalists?"

He chuckles. "That's what you want to talk about?"

I can only nod.

He presses a kiss to my neck. "Think we have any chance of winning?"

"Of course"—pause for breath—"though I'm not sure the judges will agree with the regional assessment. You only beat me in Portland because your mother's dead."

He squeezes, harder than before.

I bury my face in the crook of his neck, muffling a moan against his skin. "That was rude, wasn't it?"

"You've never had a way with words, Eden."

But when he pulls me into another kiss, there's no malice or irritation. His lips are chapped but soft, and his hands cup my breasts like they're precious and perfect. And that's exactly how he makes me feel. Precious, wanted, beautiful, sexy.

I melt into the embrace, giving in to the desire building within me.

My hands trail down his soft bare chest to the waist of his shorts, and my fingers clamp around the hem.

His eyes widen. "We don't have to—"

"I'm not ready," I say, shaking my head, but my trembling fingers undo the button and slide the zipper down. "But I want to see you."

I slip off his lap and lie beside him, and he lifts his hips as I drag the shorts down. The bulge in his boxers is obvious now, and his body convulses when I graze him. He pulls me down for another kiss, and I slip my hand under the elastic hem.

He's firm and solid and thick when I wrap my hand around him. I don't know what I expected, but his smooth skin makes me pause. I pull back to look, and whimpering, Noah buries his face in my chest. "Eden…"

I squeeze him again, experimenting with the appropriate amount of force, and he demands another kiss. His hand, hesitant but unyielding, envelops mine and begins a steady rhythm.

I said I'm not ready, and I meant it.

But an eager, primal part of me needs to feel him. It's the heat spreading through my body. It's the shiver running down my spine. It's the moan on my lips. It's the wetness between my legs—and for the first time, I wouldn't mind some help with my little problem.

I pull away long enough to tug his boxers down—he doesn't have an extra pair—and trade them for my abandoned shirt, which he twists around our hands. I press another kiss to his mouth and let him guide me as his even pace devolves into an increasingly haphazard tempo.

He gasps against my lips when he finishes, and the rhythm slows, then stops.

I kiss him slowly, enjoying the happy, dazed way he responds.

But I have needs too.

"This is a little uneven," I murmur against his lips.

Noah's eyes flash open, and he deepens the kiss, only to break away. He sits up by my hip, pausing to finish cleaning, and chucks my messy shirt to the floor. With both hands free, he undoes the waist and slides the short shorts and underwear down and off my legs.

At last, nothing separates us.

He leans close, slowly and systematically examining my every inch, but when he finally touches me, I cannot breathe or think.

I yank on his arm, pulling him back to my side. "Touch me…"

His blue eyes, darkened despite the bright light in my bedroom, meet mine, and he presses a gentle kiss to my lips. "Show me."

Trembling, I grasp his hand and guide him through the

motions, starting slow but firm until I need fast. I do the work, but Noah's touch sets me on fire. His kisses keep me calm and quiet, even as I stumble over the edge, head first.

Afterward, he lies beside me, an arm draped over my hip, and I burrow into his side, relishing the closeness in a way I've never felt before. I don't want to move. I don't want to get dressed. I want to stay in his arms for hours. Eternity, if I could.

Knock, knock.

"Thien…"

The door squeaks open.

I bolt upright, yanking my afghan to cover us—

Mama freezes in the doorway, mouth agape.

My eyes scan the room—no clothing in reach—before returning to her. "Why didn't you knock?"

Beside me, Noah searches too, but all he can reach are his boxers, deep under the blanket.

Which makes it all the more apparent we're naked.

"Mama?"

She hasn't stopped staring. She hasn't spoken. She's in shock.

But instead of speaking, she stumbles backward out of the room, shutting the door behind her. Heavy footsteps descend the stairs.

I collapse against the pillow. "What the hell is she doing here? She shouldn't be back for hours."

Noah meets my gaze with wide eyes. "What do we do?"

A shaky sigh escapes my lips. "You should go home. I have to talk to her."

CHAPTER 35

NOAH

I CLEAR MY THROAT, TRYING TO REMAIN CALM. "OKAY, the barbarian's power comes from their fury, generated from fighting enemies and using your abilities."

Ethan scowls as he fiddles with the controller. "What about you?"

"Hmm?"

"Where do your monk powers come from? Jesus?" He snorts.

I roll my eyes. "From my spirit. I can deflect arrows and resist damage."

Ethan shrugs. "I guess that could be pretty cool."

"And I do martial arts."

"Sure you do, String Bean. I could whip you in two seconds, and you know it." He nudges me with his elbow to signal his callous words are in jest.

But right now, I am immune.

"You were trained by the Marines, Ethan. I don't think that makes it a fair fight."

He snickers. "How do I grab that health potion?"

I release a shaky sigh. "It's automatic. You just walk close to it, like the gold."

"Right."

Ethan's eyes focus on the screen, his mouth hardens into a straight line. This isn't his normal type of game, and he's struggling to figure it out.

But I'm struggling with my conscience.

I shouldn't have left her there. She shouldn't have to deal with that alone. I abandoned her. She must hate me. I know she told me to go, but I should have stayed, if only for support. I should have stayed.

The game pauses.

Ethan sets his controller on the coffee table. "Talk. You've been weird since you got home. What's going on?"

I blink a couple times before turning to him. "What are you talking about?"

"Don't play dumb."

"Ethan, nothing is—"

"Did something happen with your girlfriend? You were with her all afternoon, right?"

He's far too perceptive for how idiotically he behaves. But how can I explain what happened without sounding like a complete asshole?

"Talk to me, Noah."

My eyes close so I can focus. "Her mom was supposed to work all day, but she came home early. Eden never told her I would be there."

"What's the big deal? Is she not allowed to have guests?"

Ethan's voice quivers with skepticism.

"Not guys." I hesitate. "And definitely not a guy naked in her daughter's bed."

He cackles—not even remotely appropriate. "Damn, String Bean, that was fast. Way to close the deal."

I scoff. "We didn't have sex."

"Oh, did she interrupt partway through? Ouch."

An irritated sigh escapes my lips. "She didn't interrupt anything like that. We'd just…gotten to know each other."

Ethan chuckles, and there's a smirk in place when I glance his way. "So what happened?"

I frown. "Nothing. Her mom just walked out of the room, and Eden told me to leave. I don't know. I bailed on her."

He shakes his head. "She knows how to talk to her mom better than you do. Plus, you know, it would probably be more difficult for them to have an open conversation with you there. Leaving was the right thing."

"You sure?"

"Positive." He plucks up his controller and says, "Come on, let's keep going." He presses play, but I trail behind.

No matter what he says, I'm not sure that coincides with what I know is right. Because it wasn't right to abandon her like that.

"What the fuck are you two playing?"

I pause the game.

I know that voice.

"Cliff!" Ethan jumps up from the couch and pulls our brother into a short man-hug. "Wondering when you'd get in, man. Looking good."

Cliff does look particularly nice in his gray Polo shirt

and khakis; he's even clean-shaven. "Figured I should look good when I get into town. You know, in case I meet somebody." He shoots us a wink.

Typical Cliff.

Ethan sends me a glance. "Break time?" He leads the way into the kitchen to grab a snack.

I follow slowly.

In the kitchen, Cliff snags a beer from the fridge and tosses another to Ethan—I shake my head when offered—and the two of them pop their tabs simultaneously, amusement playing on their faces. Ethan grabs a bag of popcorn from the cupboard and starts the microwave.

I wait.

"How was the trip, man?"

Cliff shrugs and takes another slurp of his beer. "Boring. You guys could've picked me up at the airport, you know."

Ethan sends him a smirk. "Wouldn't that ruin your image? You know, in case you meet somebody."

I frown. "Who would you meet in Tourmaline? This town is tiny."

Cliff nods in agreement.

"I don't think you're allowed to talk, shrimp." Ethan sends me a challenging look, but he doesn't push further.

"Wait a minute, wait a minute!" Cliff shoots me a little smirk. "What's going on?"

"Nothing," I insist.

But Ethan only has to say two words: "Eden Prince."

Glancing between us, Cliff howls with laughter. "Really? You're tapping that? She's way too hot for you."

I roll my eyes, but heat rises to my cheeks. "There's no 'tapping' going on. We're just…lab partners."

Cliff snorts. "Sure you are."

But it would seem Ethan takes pity on me. Instead of continuing this ridiculous conversation, he slams his can on the counter and slings an arm around my shoulders. "Cliff, have you heard about his science project? It's pretty exciting actually."

Cliff raises an eyebrow. "What is it?"

For a minute, I'm caught off guard, but Ethan apparently knows me better than I know him—because I can't resist talking about my STEM project, even with my brain on Eden and her mom.

"Uh, I designed software to locate interplanetary superhighways formed by gravitational pull." I clear my throat. "Basically, I found a way to make space missions easier, and I designed a program that can do it better than the one currently used by NASA."

Cliff's eyebrows shoot up. "You realize you're eighteen, right?"

"I'm well aware of how old I am."

But he shakes his head. "That's insane, String Bean."

Ethan squeezes me closer. "Pretty badass, huh?"

"What's badass?"

We turn toward the doorway, where Dad's standing with a little smile, and Ethan releases me at last.

Cliff gives him the nod. "Hey, Dad."

Ethan nudges me. "We were talking about String Bean's science project. Has he told you about it?"

Dad shrugs and goes to riffle through the fridge. Not interested, like always.

"Did you realize how much he knows about computer science?" Ethan asks over the noise of the fridge. "Where did you learn it from?"

I spent months alone in my room while they watched football and baseball and basketball and wrestling together, while Mom was working. Learning about computers and astrophysics was easy in my room with a computer.

"Yeah, maybe this year you'll win at REGen," Cliff adds.

Dad pulls back from the fridge with a scoff, empty-handed. "Well, you've done this every year since sixth grade, and this is only the second time you've managed to make it to the international fair." He shakes his head. "I don't know why you bother with this ridiculous affair."

I frown.

Despite their previously kind words, Ethan and Cliff fall silent. Per usual.

"This is what I've always wanted to do," I say, stepping forward. "This is what I love."

He turns away and heads for the sink. "It's what your mother loved too." He runs the hot water and soaps up his hands and forearms, suds forming over calloused skin. "Astrophysics didn't get her anywhere."

"That's not true." My hands clench into fists, but I'm shaking. "She was an astronaut for NASA. She got to see the stars. She explored the solar system, traveled in a Space Shuttle, worked in the International Space Station. I would give anything to do what she did."

Dad's soapy hands clamp around the counter edge, hot water steaming. "Would you die for it?"

"Yes, I would."

For a minute, Dad doesn't move or speak.

Nor does anyone else.

I don't know what else to say. He never listens to me

anyway. He doesn't care.

"That's not an option." Dad's voice is firm but quiet, and he finishes rinsing. "The New York trip is off."

My stomach drops. "What are you talking about? NESEA is paying for us to go, for me to go. It's a week and a half away. I worked on this for a year." I can barely breathe. "This isn't what Mom would've wanted. Why can't you see that? If you ever cared about her, that would matter."

He whacks the faucet off and tears a paper towel from the roll. "This isn't a discussion anymore, Noah. The trip is off. You've left me no other choice."

Dad pushes away from the counter and marches out of the kitchen, crumpling the paper towel between his large fingers. In the distance, his footsteps ascend the stairs.

In his wake, Ethan and Cliff stare in silence.

Finally, Ethan taps a finger against the island counter. "Sorry, String Bean."

"Yeah," Cliff agrees. "That sucks."

I scoff. "Thanks for backing me up."

"You know Dad…"

But the words are meaningless. Ethan and Cliff have never backed me up for exactly that reason. Our father is single-minded and determined. When he makes a decision, it is not up for debate. Not that they ever tried.

"Whatever."

I don't want to hear their excuses anymore.

Eden is the only person who has ever believed in me as much as Mom, and after this afternoon, I don't know if I have her support or trust anymore.

CHAPTER 36

EDEN

WHEN AT LAST I VENTURE DOWNSTAIRS, MAMA SITS ON the green armchair in the living room, staring at a distant corner, a mug of lukewarm tea in her hands.

Noah is nowhere to be found.

Which is good.

It means he made it out alive.

I take a moment to get a glass of water from the kitchen, then sit on the couch nearest her, but she doesn't look at me. She doesn't say a word. She doesn't acknowledge me at all.

"Mama?"

She releases a shaky breath.

"Mama, we need to talk about this." When she doesn't speak, I continue: "Mama, I'm eighteen years old. I'm graduating high school in less than two weeks. I'm old enough to—"

"No."

I blink.

The words are firm and strong, but she still doesn't look at me. "You are not old enough to understand what you've done. You are a child."

"I'm the same age you were when you married Papa," I say in a quiet voice.

"Marrying your papa was the smartest decision I could have made, Thien. It was not hasty." Her lips flatten into a thin line. "And we grew to love each other."

I swallow down the bile in my throat.

I don't want to grow to love someone, to learn to love my future partner. I still don't know whether I want to be in love or get married, but I'm supposed to sacrifice everything I want because she knows better than me?

"Noah is a good person. He would never hurt me."

But Mama shakes her head. "You don't understand. He has already hurt you. Your best feature, your greatest advantage is your innocence, don't you see that? Now, you've given it away to some ridiculous boy who could never take care of you."

My mouth is dry.

"Why would Colton want you now?"

I feel sick.

"And he was going to surprise you at the international fair." Mama releases a deep sigh and takes a long drink of her tea.

Finally, I find my voice: "Mama, Noah and I didn't have sex. We haven't."

She shoots me a skeptical glance—the first direct look since she discovered us in my bed. "Oh, Thien…"

She doesn't believe me.

"What am I supposed to tell your papa?" she whispers, more to herself than to me. "I failed you. I was supposed to protect you, and I failed you."

My chest aches at the words, and I blink back tears. No matter how different we are, no matter how much I disagree with her, no matter how much I struggle to understand her, she cannot take the blame for my actions.

I inch closer, barely out of reach. "Tell him I made a mistake. Mistakes can be learned from. Mistakes can be fixed."

"How can we fix this?"

I allow my eyes to flutter shut in a poor attempt to keep the tears inside. "Tell Colton I look forward to seeing him at the REGen Talent Search. We can discuss our future."

A hand touches my knee, and I open my eyes to meet Mama's. "Thien." A pale smile spreads across her lips. "You didn't…?"

"No. I'm still…innocent."

The word leaves a sick taste in my mouth.

My fingers shake as I pull Tinsley up in my contacts. She's the only person I can talk to. She's the only person who understands.

The phone rings a long time before going to voicemail.

The second call ends the same way.

The third only rings twice before asking me to leave a message.

The fourth rings once.

Finally, on the fifth call, she answers. "Yeah?"

"Hey." Even my voice trembles. "Can we talk?"

For a moment, Tinsley hesitates. "What's going on?"

I swallow to wet my dry throat, but it doesn't ease my discomfort. "I, um, need to tell you something. You see, Noah and I, we—"

"I already know, Eden."

I freeze. She stopped calling me anything but *Edie* years ago. "Know what?"

Her sigh crackles the phone. "You're dating Noah. I saw you two kissing in Portland."

"Oh."

Tinsley scoffs. "'Oh'? That's all you have to say?"

"I don't know what to say, Tins."

"You could apologize for leaving me out of the loop. You could explain why you kept it a secret, even from me." A frustrated sigh echoes through the earpiece. "Hell, you could actually suck it up and tell me he's the reason you bailed on my art show. You stayed with him instead of joining me for one of the most important nights of my life, didn't you? Did you know I got first place in two categories?"

"No." The word is a whisper.

"Of course you didn't. You never saw it. You probably wouldn't even remember the paintings if I told you which ones medaled."

My fingers clench around the phone, but words fail me.

"You know what?" she snaps. "I'm glad you called. Glad you admitted it. Now, I can say congratulations. And good luck. I wish you two all the happiness in the world at your perfect Archer Collins, and I'm sure you'll live happily ever after."

"Tinsley, we're not—"

"You won't miss me. We've barely spoken in the last month, and you didn't notice. You had no reaction whatsoever." She pauses for a second. "And why would you? You've spent every year since sixth grade obsessing about your stupid STEM fairs and trying to beat Noah. Do you know what's going on in my life? Do you even care what I'm dealing with? Because all you talk or think about is yourself."

"I'm sorry," I murmur.

"Sorry isn't good enough, Eden." She releases a shaky sigh. "You bailed on me and ignored me every time I needed you. You're a shitty friend, and I'm done."

When the call ends, I clutch the phone as the hot tears wet my fingers and spill onto the screen.

Tinsley, who has been my closest friend, staunchest ally, and firmest supporter for nine years, doesn't want to talk to me. She wouldn't give me a chance to explain. She doesn't want to be my friend anymore.

Who am I supposed to talk to now?

CHAPTER 37

NOAH

DAD, ETHAN, AND CLIFF ARE SOMEWHERE IN THE CROWD, but the auditorium is such a mess they're impossible to find.

Still, I would rather have my eyes searching the crowd than locating what they really want to seek.

Midway down the long column, Eden sits on the edge of her white fold-out chair, her long shiny hair braided to one side. A small stalk of flowering white gladiolus, entwined in the plait, accents the smooth curve of her cheek and neck.

She hasn't spoken to me since I left her house two weeks ago, and my attempts to talk at school were useless—to be fair, we had finals to focus on. She never gave me an explanation. She never told me what happened with her mother after I left.

I heave a sigh, but the row finally starts to move. I

follow the student to my right along the aisle of chairs, forming a line behind the previous row.

I shouldn't complain. *Barton* is at the beginning of the alphabet, so I can get this over with long before most students. Long before Eden will even rise from her seat.

When we line up alongside the bleachers, I have a better view of the other side of the auditorium, though it's slightly farther away. Ethan is easy to spot now—he has a particular way of carrying himself, even while relaxing—and Dad and Cliff sit on either side of him.

The line moves quickly.

Even when Liliana Bailey turns to me with an anxious smile. "Are you nervous?" She tucks a strand of honey-brown hair behind her ear, but the bob is too short to stay in place. "I'm nervous."

I shrug. "We just have to grab the fake diploma and shake Mr. Woodard's hand."

A smile tugs at her lips. "You're so coolheaded."

My eyes wander toward Eden, who remains in her seat, not looking at anything specific, and despite myself, a sigh escapes my mouth.

"Did you two break up?"

A flush rises to my cheeks when I turn back to Liliana. "Who? What are you talking about?"

Her smile turns into silent laughter that lights up her eyes. "You and Eden. You two have been inseparable for the last month or so, then out of nowhere, you avoid each other like the plague."

"That's not true."

She's the one avoiding me.

"Plus," Liliana adds, "you get this mopey, wistful look

in your eyes when you stare at her. Were you even listening to her Valedictorian speech? Because you were definitely making that face."

I frown.

Am I that obvious? Were we? Did everyone know while we were pretending it was a secret?

Because it's not like I see Liliana Bailey outside of our English Literature class—obviously no longer a factor. Eden wasn't even in that class.

Were we really that obvious?

The line makes another large jump forward, and we press into a quiet nook where the bleachers meet the wall by the stage. There are only a few people between me and freedom—plus our principal Mr. Woodard and the other administrative helpers.

Liliana climbs the steep stairs, and I grip the railing as I follow.

"Kellie Aspin."

Liliana and I move up again, and once Kellie has takes her first step off stage, the announcer continues.

"Liliana Bailey."

She shoots a final anxious smile over her shoulder before crossing toward the table to receive her ceremonial diploma, and I climb the final two steps. Then, she too is returning to her seat.

"Noah Barton."

Halfway to grabbing my diploma, the obnoxious blare of an air horn echoes through the gymnasium. I don't need to look to know.

God, they're an embarrassment.

I grab my fake diploma and move on, only to pause by

Principal Woodard.

His thick umber hand grasps mine in a firm shake, and we pause, turning toward the camera for the signature photo. "Congratulations, Noah," he says, but when I start to separate, he continues. "You'll do wonders at Archer Collins. We're all very proud of you."

"Thanks," I say, withdrawing my hand from his, and stumble down the steps.

In the safety of my fold-out chair, I breathe a weighted sigh of a relief.

I almost thought those stupid sad looks had faded. That people had returned to forgetting who I am. I much prefer the anonymity.

But apparently not Mr. Woodard.

A glance toward my family reveals a security officer confiscating Ethan and Cliff's air horn. They were banned from the ceremony for a reason, idiots.

Yep, definitely no anonymity.

Beside the pair of complete morons, Dad leans back in his chair, arms crossed, mouth tight, amused but refraining from commenting. They're both adults. How much say does he have in what they do?

I take a shaky breath.

I'm an adult now too. Only eighteen for a couple weeks, but legally, I'm an adult. How much say does Dad have in what I do either?

The air releases slowly through my nose.

Oh, fuck it.

I'm going to New York City. The ticket and hotel are covered by NESEA. I just have to find a way to get to the Portland airport. Hell, I can probably convince Ethan to drive me in his rental car.

And Dad can't complain. I'm an adult. And now a high school graduate.

What does he think he can do?

"Something wrong, Barton?"

I twist round to find the fervent olive-green eyes of Tinsley Edwards, irritation curling the sides of her mouth. "What?"

"I'm sure your girlfriend will make you feel better once the ceremony's over." She, along with the rest of her row, rises from their seats, but they don't move yet. "What do you have to worry about?"

My eyes dart toward Eden, but I force myself to focus. "You don't know?"

Tinsley scoffs. "Know what?"

"Eden and I haven't spoken in two weeks." I swallow before continuing. "We had an awkward run-in with her mom, and well, I don't know what happened afterward. She hasn't…"

The row starts to move toward the stage, joining the line of remaining students from mine.

"What are you talking about?" Tinsley asks, now a couple feet away. "She never talks about anything else. She's head over heels." Concern slips into her voice, then she hardens her features. "You have no idea how annoying it is."

I frown. "When was the last time you spoke to her?"

Tinsley's brow creases, but she doesn't answer.

Her line moves again, and she's out of range—we're not going to yell at each other in the middle of the graduation ceremony.

I turn back toward the stage and run a hand through

my loose blond hair.

She can't even talk to Tinsley about it—no wonder her speech sounded particularly mechanical. She's functioning on autopilot.

I have to talk to her.

CHAPTER 38

EDEN

THE CAFETERIA, TYPICALLY FILLED WITH LONG RECTANgular tables with attached benches and smaller circular tables near the food lines, instead teems with people. Recent graduates in brilliant golden-yellow robes and their families mingle in the otherwise empty hall.

Mama said she would meet me outside the front office, but now that we've finally been released from the gymnasium, reaching her will be a difficult feat.

I hold my cap atop my head and dive into the crowd, slipping and pushing through the masses to reach the opposite side. At least then I could follow the wall toward the main office, have something to ground myself to.

"Eden!"

I freeze momentarily as Noah's voice echoes over the din—then walk faster.

It's been two weeks, and we do not need to have this

talk in the middle of a crowd. I don't need to explain myself to him. And I don't need to make excuses for something that won't change.

Fingers wrap around my wrist, and he tugs me into his arms, my back pressed against his chest. "Eden, we need to talk," he says, his loud voice sounding quiet, inconspicuous in the middle of the crowd. "You can't keep avoiding me."

"You can't tell me what to do."

He lays a hand, gentle and slow, near my waist. "Eden, please."

I twist to face him. "I can't."

Noah's sad eyes meet mine. "Why not?"

Irritation wells in my chest. "We can't screw around and expect nothing bad to happen. I have obligations, responsibilities." A frustrated sigh escapes my lips. "We're not lab partners anymore. We don't have to pretend to enjoy each other's company."

His blue eyes narrow at the words before softening again.

"Noah, Eden…"

Mr. Libby stops near us, but I don't look away. Neither does Noah.

"I hate to interrupt," our teachers says, his voice dripping with discomfort. "I wanted to congratulate the two of you."

"What about your obligation to yourself?" Noah's hand still holds me in place, keeping me close. "Your obligation to be true to you?"

I shake my head, stepping back, and he releases me reluctantly. "I can't."

Mr. Libby clears his throat. "I'll just, um, be…over

there." He makes his retreat, leaving us alone again.

Well, as alone as you can be in a packed high school cafeteria.

"I'm sorry," I say, taking another step away. "I have to go."

Mama is waiting for me.

I turn on my heel and head toward the front of the building, stumbling over my painful, black stilettos.

But when I reach the front of the building, Mama isn't standing by the front office. She isn't standing in the foyer, by the floor-to-ceiling glass doors, or outside them. Where did she go?

I push my way through the glass doors and stand on the top step, searching the area.

Families make their way down the stairs and through the parking lot, but there's no sign of Mama. I don't even know where she parked the car. She dropped me off at the front door since we were running late.

The doors push open beside me, and I step aside to make room.

"Yeah, well, where the hell did Ethan go? He was right behind us."

Shit.

I turn away, casting my gaze toward the far end of the parking lot, hoping the Bartons won't notice me.

"I'm sure your brother has a perfectly good reason to get distracted," Mr. Barton says, his thick voice firm and unforgiving.

"To disappear," Noah adds in a quiet voice. "I guess the Raider training is paying off. He ghosted out of there."

"In the middle of a crowd," his brother Cliff says,

unimpressed. "Not that hard."

Their voices fade, and I chance a glance after the group as they make their way down the large staircase.

"He disappeared right before we walked out the doors," Noah snaps. "Not that many people hovering there, Cliff."

Mr. Barton turns on them quickly. "Stop. We'll see him at the house. We came in two cars anyway."

Then, his gaze falls on me.

He tugs his key ring from his pocket and shoves it into Cliff's hands. "I'll meet you at the car in a couple minutes."

"Dad—"

"Go."

Shoulders slumped, Noah follows Cliff to the bottom, then they turn to the right and head for where I imagine their car is parked.

Mr. Barton, however, climbs a few stairs to reach me. He stands five steps below, facing me, giving me the high ground.

Only I'm not sure I hold the high ground.

"You didn't listen to me." His deep voice is even, accusatory. "You ignored everything I said only to—"

"Mr. Barton, please."

He pauses, eyebrow cocked as if daring me to disagree.

My voice falters. "I never meant to hurt Noah."

"That doesn't change the facts." His gaze on me is steady, unyielding. He doesn't even glance toward his sons, who now trail across the far side of the parking lot. "That only makes you irresponsible for not considering the consequences of your actions."

"I am not responsible for Noah's feelings. I'm sorry he got hurt, but I have obligations to my family. Surely you would understand that. That's why you're talking to me, isn't it?"

"You might not be responsible for his feelings, but you are responsible for your actions. Part of that responsibility is taking into account how others will react to your decisions."

I wet my lips, struggling to think. "He's overly sensitive."

"That's really none of your business anymore, is it, Eden? You may not owe me an explanation, but you certainly owe him one. Don't you think he deserves that?"

Yes, of course he does, but...

"Sometimes, we don't get a choice," I say, shaking my head.

Finally, Mr. Barton's gaze shifts to the parking lot. Noah and Cliff have reached the car, unlocked the doors, and are sitting inside, waiting. Probably impatiently.

"Bullshit." He turns back. "You always have a choice."

Silently, he spins on his heel and marches down the remaining steps, and I lean against the concrete wall, resting my head atop my hand, and watch him traverse the messy parking lot.

You always have a choice.

But I'm not sure I do.

Not if I want to attend Archer Collins, and that is the most important thing—not because of the school itself but because of what it represents. Archer Collins is what I've wanted for so many years, what I've strived to reach. Archer Collins is freedom.

I release a soft sigh as Mr. Barton reaches the Chevy Equinox and climbs into the driver seat. With the engine already running, it only takes a couple seconds before the white reverse lights come on, and they back out of the parking spot.

Mr. Barton doesn't understand.

Not that that surprises me.

Mama doesn't either. Her entire outlook is based on survival. Even years after she immigrated to this country, she's still trying to keep herself alive. To keep me alive.

But there are more important things than mere survival.

"Aren't you done here yet?"

I glance over my shoulder, but the speaker isn't talking to me. They probably haven't even noticed me.

Mr. Libby, his back to me, heaves a sigh. "No, I have to—"

"Meet me after." Ethan Barton steps closer to him—a little too close for a professional setting. "I'm only in town a couple more days. We're flying to New York on Monday."

"I thought your father decided your family wasn't going to the Talent Search."

Ethan catches my gaze as he shakes his head—I turn away. "You think Noah would let anything stop him from going to that stupid science fair?" He chuckles. "Meet me when you're done."

"Mr. Barton, I don't—"

"Ethan."

"Ethan," Mr. Libby corrects himself, his voice softer this time. "I don't think it's a good idea."

"I'm not your student, and the only hint of a conflict of interest literally just graduated."

Mr. Libby hesitates. "Your individual training starts when you head back. And after that, how many months at a time will you be deployed? How often can we see each other?"

Ethan hums in amusement. "Worried you'll miss me?"

"Ethan…"

"Let me give you a reason to wait for me."

I tap my finger against the concrete. A decent amount of the cars are gone now, but there's still no sign of Mama. My eyes search the parking lot anyway—anything to pretend I'm not privy to this private conversation.

"I have to get back."

"Meet me when you're done."

Mr. Libby sighs. "Three o'clock?"

"I'll be there."

For a long minute, there's silence, and I glance back to find Mr. Libby disappearing through the glass doors.

And Ethan Barton is smirking at me.

I turn away again.

"You're pretty nosy, huh, Eden Prince?" He joins me, resting his elbows atop the wall. "What are you doing hanging out here?"

I avoid his eyes. "Not trying to eavesdrop."

"Didn't say you were." He pauses. "But considering you're the most opinionated person I've ever met, surely you have something to say."

"It's none of my business."

"Oh, come on, Eden."

I swallow and finally turn. "Did your father really say Noah can't go to the international fair? He won first place at the regional. Doesn't that mean anything?"

Ethan winces. "Dad's just…he didn't handle things with Mom very well. He's a little lost right now."

"He shouldn't take that out on Noah. Noah never did

anything wrong."

"If you feel that strongly, why'd you dump him?"

I frown. "What makes you think we were in a relationship? We never—"

"Maybe it wasn't official, I don't know. Either way, Noah is the one being punished for your problems. Not sure you can sit on your high horse right now."

"You think I'm not being punished too?"

Ethan shrugs, not concerned. "Who can tell? You refuse to talk to anyone. Do you even know what you want?"

I bite my lip, considering, but the problem is, I want too many things. How am I supposed to determine what's most important? How can I—?

"Thien!" Mama holds open the glass door, one arm on her hip. "Where were you?"

"I—"

"Let's go home."

"Of course."

She releases the handle and starts her march down the staircase, completely ignoring Ethan.

I turn to him with a tight smile. "I guess I have to say goodbye, then."

But Ethan scoffs. "Do you?"

Instead of answering, I trail after Mama, who's already at the bottom of the stairs.

CHAPTER 39

NOAH

Dad is in the living room, flipping through TV channels, an impatient scowl on his face, when I get home from Mom's memorial.

I pause—he's rarely home this early on a weekday—but don't bother stopping.

Today is the day, and I don't have time to get into an argument. I have to get to Portland. To the airport. To New York City and the REGen Talent Search.

Screw whatever consequences he puts into place.

Dad casts a bored glance in my direction as I head for the stairs, but he returns to the television without speaking.

Strange.

Surely he knows what today is.

The upstairs is equally as quiet and unassuming. Both Ethan and Cliff's rooms are open, dark, and silent, and that's not good. It would seem Ethan and his rental car are my only real shot getting to the Portland International Airport. But how can I ask him if he isn't here? What other options do I have?

Now that I think about it, Ethan's rental wasn't in the driveway either. Just Dad's Equinox.

Shit.

I push open my door and flip on the light—and nearly knock into the wall beside me.

Ethan and Cliff are inside, Ethan at my desk chair with his legs crossed in an imposing manner, Cliff reclining on my bed next to my packed duffel bag. My rolled-up sketches and diagrams sit inside a box atop my desk, nestled behind Ethan.

"What the hell?"

Ethan scowls. "What's taking you so long?"

My brow furrows. "What are you talking about?"

On my bed, Cliff snorts. "Thought you were smarter than this, String Bean."

"How can you put this off till the last minute?" Ethan plants his foot on the floor and leans forward, elbows on his knees. "What if I had plans today? What if I couldn't drive your sorry ass to the airport?"

I swallow and nudge my bedroom door shut. "Who says I was going to ask you anything?"

"Don't BS me, String Bean." He shakes his head. "Just say the words."

Instead of responding, I cross to my bed and tug my bag closer to double-check the contents. I can't forget anything. Plenty of clothing and hygiene supplies, but more importantly, my laptop and backups are securely in place. My presentation is in tact and ready to go.

"Obviously, you already packed," Ethan says from behind me.

I glance over my shoulder. "Obviously."

He offers me a small smirk. "Aren't you going to ask?"

A deep sigh slides from my lips as I zip the bag closed. "Where's your rental car?"

Ethan grunts. "That's not the question."

"How can I ask you to drive me to Portland if your rental car isn't here?"

"Just ask, Noah."

At last, I turn to him, lips tight in uncertainty. "Will you drive me to the airport so I can go to the international fair? I don't know how else to get there."

Ethan's hint of a smile expands into a huge grin. "You know, I would, but unfortunately, I just returned my rental car this afternoon."

I gape at him. "What? How are you going to get back to base? How will you get around in the meantime? You guys fly out next Sunday—that's a week away."

But he taps his foot against the carpet thoughtfully. "What time do you have to check in?"

I frown. "For REGen? Any time before 7 p.m."

Cliff pushes up into a sitting position. "And there are tickets for all of us, right? On the flight?"

"Yeah." My eyes dart between them. "What's going on?"

Finally, Ethan rises from the chair and claps his hands. "We're already packed. We just have to the load the car."

I follow him to the door, trying to process everything. "Wait, we're stealing—"

Cliff laughs. "We're not stealing anything, String Bean."

I scowl. "Fine, borrowing—the meaning is the same in

this instance."

Cliff elbows me in the side as he pushes past me to the door. "You have so little faith in us."

Well, yeah.

What have they ever done that would make me believe in them?

"The flight's at three, right?" Ethan calls over his shoulder as he marches down the dark hallway. "We've got plenty of time to get there."

"Three ten," I correct, hovering in my open doorway as they disappear inside their respective rooms. Not that it makes a difference.

What the hell is going on?

Not long later, they emerge, bags in hand, and head toward the stairs. And like an idiot, all I can do is watch.

Ethan raises an eyebrow as he passes. "Aren't you coming with us?"

Unable to speak, I grab my duffel bag and the box of diagrams from my room and follow them downstairs.

In the living room, the TV is off.

Dad has his keys in hand. His gaze moves right past me to Ethan, who leans against the wall, his bag on the floor by his feet. "Is this everything?"

Ethan gives him the nod.

"Okay," Dad says, his hands clamping tight around the key ring, "let's go."

The flight from Portland International Airport to JFK is only an hour and twenty minutes, but being crammed between Ethan and Cliff makes it almost unbearable. Dad sits in the seat behind us next to an elderly couple, and he doesn't speak the entire flight.

I don't know what I'd expect him to say.

I don't know what could have changed his mind.

When the plane lands, we take the subway to Hell's Kitchen, and while Dad and Cliff head to the Sheraton to check in to our hotel, Ethan and I walk the couple blocks to the Javits Center.

I've been here once before, but the glass convention center is an overwhelming and formidable structure. Ethan, though, remains unfazed by the massive building as he leads the way inside.

It's nearly six o'clock, and I need to check in with the Talent Search and get everything set up before the morning. The five-day international fair starts at 9 a.m., and I have to be ready right away.

Once inside, Ethan lets me take the lead. We head straight for several fold-out tables set up near the main staircase. Two people sit at each table, checking in finalists, and a woman with her deep-red hair in a loose bun stands closest, giving instructions and directions to anyone who asks.

She turns her vibrant hazel eyes on us as we approach and offers me a tight smile. "Location of origin?" She taps her pen against the thick plastic clipboard in her hand.

"Uh, Maine. Tourmaline High School."

She double-checks her list, then nods us toward the nearest table. "You'll check in with Amanda in the first chair."

I head over, but Ethan hovers near her and begins to

ask questions.

Five people are ahead of me, but the line doesn't take long.

"Noah Barton," I say when I reach the table. "Tourmaline High School, Maine."

Amanda, a woman in her twenties with big hoop earrings and a pixie cut, flips through the pages of her list of names before finding mine. "Alright, Noah, you're officially checked in," she says as she runs a green highlighter along my name.

Beside her, a guy not much older than me—probably an intern—scrambles to find my name badge from a big box labeled *A thru F.*

"Here you go," he says as he finally tugs it free. A flustered smile crosses his face as I take it, and he leans forward to grab a couple sheets of informative papers for me. He snags one of the highlighters to mark the map. "Your table is here—it's also on your name tag. Make sure to wear that at all times."

"Thanks."

But he's already moving on to locating the next finalist's badge.

"Where now?" Ethan asks when I join him again.

I force a smile. "Want to help me get everything ready for opening day?"

CHAPTER 40

EDEN

My eyes scan the Javits Center, teeming with people.

The Talent Search has been going for three days now, and we've presented our projects to a vast number of parents, students, professors, sponsors, college reps, and over a thousand judges. Yesterday, we were open to the general public—and that was the most exhausting day so far.

A lot of the finalists might be overwhelmed by all the people or plagued by the idea of losing. But me?

Not for a second.

This is my arena, my happy place. And I know my presentation is solid. My project is monumental. My display is interesting and aesthetically pleasing. I'm not at all concerned I might lose.

"Eden?"

I turn to Colton with a reserved smile. "Sorry, distracted."

He nods. "You sure your mom is okay by herself?"

"She'll be fine for a few minutes," I say with a shrug and turn away from the presentations. "I need a restroom break."

I wind my way toward the restrooms and hurry into the ladies' room, leaving Colton behind.

In the privacy of my stall, I allow myself a long moment to relax. Even if it's just for thirty seconds. I don't mind presenting my project to large masses of people, but it would be far less stressful if Colton didn't hang around the whole time. He didn't arrive till Tuesday afternoon, but he's been at my side ever since—encouraged by Mama, of course, who has been more than happy to give us uncomfortable moments of privacy.

At least I have the luxury of being able to ignore him in favor of interacting with the judges and college reps. It's not rude if it's the reason we're here in the first place, right?

When I finish, Colton leans against the wall outside. His lips pull up into a smile when I join him. "Wanna grab a coffee on the way back? You know they've got a Starbucks here."

I nod, and he leads me through the crowd by the small of my back.

We stop at the end of the line, and Colton eyes the menu. "You know what you want?"

I glance at the menu before allowing my eyes to study the nearest presentations. "Just a Caffe Americano."

He sends me a frown. "Not a latte or Frappuccino?"

"I'm lactose intolerant."

One of the nearest projects is advertised as a miniature superconductor. Damn.

I quirk my lips to the side. I haven't had the chance to look at any of the projects except those nearest to me, but what I've seen has been overwhelmingly good—and that's bad.

The line moves slightly closer.

"See any cool projects?" Colton asks, lazily glancing around. "What about the New England finalists? Did you know either of them?"

My gaze falls to the floor.

I haven't seen Noah or the other finalist sponsored by NESEA. There are over two thousand students here to present their findings, and we haven't run into each other. I did, however, catch a glimpse of the other Barton brothers last night.

"Not yet," I say in a quiet voice.

We move forward.

It's better this way. I don't think I'm prepared to see Noah. We haven't spoken since that uncomfortable conversation after graduation, and the whole point of that conversation was that I was ignoring him. Which I still am. Or I would be if I saw him.

What could I possibly say to him now?

Colton reaches the register, orders our drinks, and hands the cashier a twenty-dollar bill. We wait at the pickup location, farther down the counter.

"You're really in your element here," he says close to my ear. "It's nice to see you enjoy yourself."

"Thanks." I glance behind the counter. How long until our drinks are done? I want to get back. Relieve Mama of her duties and hope she didn't do irreparable damage with her abrasive behavior and poor speaking skills.

The barista sets the drinks on the counter, and we grab them.

"Come on," I say, nodding toward my display, "we need to head back."

Colton follows close behind as I weave through the presentations, careful not to spill my hot drink. I definitely don't want to leave Mama by herself for—

"...as conceived by Martin Lo."

I stumble to a stop.

That's Noah's voice.

"Most space missions are now designed to take advantage of the gravitational pull of planets and the Moon, and Lo's software was the first designed to use the Sun's gravitational pull on the planets or a planet's pull on its moons."

"What makes your software different than what's already used by NASA?"

A small crowd is gathered around Noah, including a couple judges. He looks nervous.

I nudge closer, but not close enough to draw attention to myself, and Colton, curious, follows at my heels.

"The program currently used by NASA is Martin Lo's LTool. It's not actually a computer program—it's what's called a Problem Solving Environment with a 3D visualization, among other things, and it is then integrated with a common software environment." He takes a deep breath, and his eyes scan the crowd—I try to make myself smaller—before returning to the judges. "What I've done is use computer science to solve an astrophysics problem. This is actual computer software that can plot and navigate a spacecraft's journey through our solar system—and beyond. Also, it's faster."

One judge chuckles, and a smile tugs at my mouth as well.

"Basically," Noah continues, "this software will better use gravitational pull to travel along these interplanetary superhighways in order to move faster and use less fuel."

One of the judges—her name tag says Teri—nods toward the display. "What was your inspiration for this project, Noah? What made you want to explore interplanetary superhighways?"

Noah opens his mouth, then closes it again, his blue eyes struggling to focus. "I, um…my mother." He clears his throat. "She was an astronaut aboard the Space Shuttle *Endurance* when it…was destroyed during reentry in October."

Her face falls.

But he doesn't stop: "She's been my inspiration since I was little, and I've done everything I can to make her proud."

The judge steps forward with a small smile. "I'm sure your mother would be very proud of you, Noah. This is a remarkable project."

He smiles back, but his squinted eyes glisten with tears. "Thank you."

The presentation, it would seem, is over. The judges move on, and the crowd shifts, switching places to examine new projects. Noah quickly starts talking about the project again with a new set of viewers, but not far behind him, Mr. Barton has a tight grip on his own chin, his mouth taut. He blinks and blinks again, but it doesn't prevent a droplet or two from sliding down his cheek.

I wasn't sure they made it till I saw Ethan and Cliff the other night. I wasn't sure Noah managed to make it after his father denied him.

But I'm glad he did. I'm glad he's here and he has a chance.

Hell, who knows? There are a number of college reps, even a couple for Archer Collins. Anything could happen.

Colton lays a hand on my shoulder. "Eden? Come on. I thought we were going back."

I nod, and we start moving again.

"Who was that?"

I bite my lip. "Noah's another NESEA finalist. We go to the same high school." I hesitate. "Went."

Colton nods. "Well, sounded like a cool project, huh?"

A small part of me wants to laugh at the awkwardness, but nothing about this situation is particularly funny.

CHAPTER 41

NOAH

CLIFF SLAMS THE EMPTY PINT GLASS ON THE BAR BEFORE signaling for another. That's his third in the last hour, and I doubt he'll stop.

Ethan, at least, has been slightly less embarrassing. He only just finished his second beer.

I take a sip of my ice water.

"We brought you down here to loosen up, String Bean." Ethan claps me on the shoulder, and I wince under the pressure. "You're still all anxious and jittery."

I shoot him a glare. "Well, it's not like I can drink beer."

On my other side, Cliff smirks. "I thought you didn't need alcohol to have a good time, nerd?"

My mouth twists into a scowl. Cliff has a better memory than I give him credit for.

The bartender slides a new pint to Cliff, then offers a third to Ethan—who agrees, because apparently, the goal is for them to get trashed tonight, and that will somehow help me relax.

Unlikely.

"How am I supposed to get the two of you upstairs later?"

Ethan snickers. "There's an elevator for a reason."

"Yeah, I have to drag you to the elevator in the first place." I glance toward the hotel lobby, but the elevator is easily thirty feet away from our location. "You realize you're over two hundred pounds of muscle, right?"

"You realize you're a spoilsport, right?" Cliff counters, pointing one thick finger in my face. "Relax."

But I'm not sure how.

This STEM fair decides my entire future. Whether I can attend Archer Collins. Whether I can become an astronaut. That's a lot of pressure.

"There are over two thousand other finalists." My fingers drum an unsteady beat on the bar. "Only five can receive one of the large cash prizes, then the first-in-category finalists receive a small prize."

"Aren't there unofficial prizes?" Ethan asks—still sober enough to follow the conversation.

"Most of them are category specific. There are only a couple sponsors who would consider my project, and even then, who knows if they'll choose me." I take another sip of water, but it doesn't make me feel better.

Cliff nudges my side. "You're starting to panic. Just relax."

"I'm not panicking," I snap. I clasp my hands around my glass of water and breathe into it so the glass fogs up. "I'm confused."

"About?"

I glance between them.

Is it better to ask when they're sober or when they're drunk? How open do I want them to be?

"Why did Dad bring me here?"

Ethan cocks an eyebrow. "For your fancy science fair."

I roll my eyes at the inaccurate label—it's not even worth correcting anymore. "Why did he change his mind? He never…"

But for the life of me, I don't know how to phrase the words. I don't know how to ask the question without uprooting a more difficult topic.

Once Dad makes up his mind, he doesn't change. No matter how ridiculous or stupid it is, he will not bend to anyone's will but his own.

You could say he's stubborn, blame it on that.

But the truth is, Dad doesn't care about anyone else enough to meet them halfway.

That's what I can't wrap my head around. How is this different? What happened to convince him this wasn't the worst idea in the world? Who?

Ethan and Cliff are conveniently silent, though it's difficult to tell if that's due to my questions or their current state of inebriation—

Or the fact that Eden Prince was just escorted into the restaurant by her date from New Year's Eve. Colton, she said. That's great.

I shift back to my brothers, but Cliff is too busy finishing off his fourth drink.

And Ethan?

He's grinning at his phone like an idiot.

Yeah, they're drunk. Did they even hear my questions? Or did they get distracted before coming up with an answer.

I heave a sigh and finish off my ice water. "I don't know why I bother."

Cliff slides his pint glass toward the other side of the bar, making space for his massive arm to rest there instead. "Bother with what?"

I shrug. "Trying to have a conversation while you two are drunk for starters. Ethan hasn't had that much, but his phone is more interesting than anything else."

At last, Ethan looks up, blinking rapidly to adjust to the dim light. "Huh?"

"Who are you texting?" I ask.

A giant grin spreads across his face. "Wouldn't you like to know."

"That is why I asked." I release an irritated scoff. "Fine, don't tell me."

Ethan chuckles a little too loudly. "If you insist. His name's Michael. We've been on one date."

Despite the quiet classy atmosphere, Cliff lets off a raucous whoop.

"If you can call it a date," Ethan adds, then follows it with a smug smirk that makes me gag.

"That's disgusting," I snap.

But Cliff leans closer, curiosity etched on his otherwise expressionless face. "Wait, Michael what? What's his last name?"

"And when did you have time for a date?"

Ethan's phone lights up again, and he pulls it close to read the new message. "You really want to know?" His eyes dart toward me before returning to the screen. He unlocks it and types a response right away. "He doesn't want to tell the whole world, you know."

I frown. "Who?"

"Libby," he says without looking up. "That's his last name. Michael Libby."

I blanch. "You're dating my teacher? How could you do this? That's inappropriate!"

Cliff laughs.

Ethan shoots me a skeptical glance. "He's not your teacher anymore, and our date was after your graduation, thanks. Not like it matters."

"'Not like it matters'?" I shake my head. "Of course it matters. I can't believe you're dating my teacher."

He shrugs. "Well, you may have to get used to it. Though not till I'm done with ITC."

I frown. "Doesn't your individual training take nine months or something?"

He nods. "So you've got nine months to adjust to the idea."

With a sigh, I run a hand through my wavy hair and glance around again.

Eden and her date are cozied up in a booth. His arm's wrapped around her lower back, and he leans close while they talk.

Awesome.

"Whatcha looking at, String Bean?" Ethan asks, but he falls silent when he follows my gaze. Instead, he lays a hand on my shoulder and squeezes.

I know I should, but I can't look away.

Like watching a car crash. No matter how horrible or

painful it is to look, you look anyway. You back up traffic in a lane that wasn't otherwise affected just to see the damage.

Eden's eyes find mine across the expanse of the bar, but she immediately returns to her date.

"Hey," Ethan says in a hushed voice, "we can go if you want."

I nod, but instead of moving, I watch as that asshole presses his mouth to hers. Worse, she closes her eyes and lets him, even responds to the kiss.

Cliff stumbles from the stool. "Back to the room!"

Ethan stands next, pulling out a ten from his wallet and leaving it as a tip, and nods toward the exit. "Come on."

After one final glance, I slip from the stool and land on my feet.

CHAPTER 42

EDEN

"I GOT AN INTERNSHIP AT A MID-SIZED LAW FIRM IN Allentown." Colton swirls his glass, and the brown liquid sloshes from side to side. "That's only a twenty-minute drive from Archer Collins."

I nod, but my eyes focus on Noah and his brothers at the bar.

If I knew he was here, I would have insisted we go somewhere else. There are plenty of nearby restaurants we could have eaten at instead of at the hotel.

"You know," Colton says, tugging me closer, pulling my attention from Noah, "I'm glad you're attending Archer Collins. We'll have the opportunity to get to know each other better, you know?"

A smile spreads across my lips. "So you're going to live in Allentown or…?"

"I just signed a lease for an apartment on the south side

of town. You can visit any time you like." He pauses. "I'm still figuring out law school, so this internship is a great opportunity while I make a final decision."

"It'll be nice to have someone I know in the area."

Despite myself, my eyes return to Noah.

Will he be able to attend Archer Collins after all? His dad let him come to the international fair, so what about Archer Collins? If he wins a prize here to help, will he attend even if his father refuses?

I don't know much about his precarious situation.

I wish I knew more.

As if feeling my eyes on him, Noah shifts on his barstool and turns his gaze on me, and for the life of me, I cannot stop staring.

I wish I could talk to him again. I wish I could kiss him again. I wish everything were different.

But it's not.

I shift back to Colton—he's been talking for the last few minutes, rambling on about his internship, but I haven't listened to a single word.

"You're incredibly confusing, you know that?" His soft words are quickly followed by an amused smile.

"What do you mean?"

"I'm still trying to wrap my head around you, Eden." He tilts his head to the side, considering. "I know this isn't ideal, but family is important. It means a lot to my mom that you're willing to give this a try."

My brow furrows. "How does that make me confusing?"

Colton leans closer. "Maybe you're adjusting to the idea, I don't know, but if I'd been on this many dates with anyone else, we would've kissed by now."

"Oh."

"Do you mind if we try?"

For a moment, I hesitate.

Noah and his brothers are sitting only twenty feet away, and I'm not keen on the idea of kissing someone so publicly.

But I need to know.

I give a short nod.

He doesn't hesitate before pressing his mouth to mine, but he's slow and patient, waiting for my response before taking anything further.

I shut my eyes—shut out the rest of the world—and relax.

He threads his fingers through my hair and, with his other hand clutching my waist, deepens the kiss. I allow him to take the lead—he obviously wants it—and open to him. His tongue slips into my mouth.

Then, he pulls away.

I spend a moment, eyes closed, testing my breathing and heart rate.

"Well?"

I wet my lips and frown at his taste. "I don't know."

"Nothing?"

Finally, I open my eyes and meet his gaze. "Nothing."

Colton nods. "Yeah, that's what I thought."

I force a tight smile. "I'm sorry."

He shakes his head.

But my eyes are immediately drawn to the empty bar. Noah and his brothers left—was it because of that strange kiss?

Colton leans back, giving me some much desired space.

"So what now?"

My mouth is dry. "Mama won't let me attend Archer Collins without the pretense of doing so to be close to you. What about your parents?"

"This'll hit my mom pretty hard, but Dad can help her through it. He doesn't care either way," he says with a shrug. "Archer Collins… Are we doing this anyway, then?"

"I don't know." I bite my lip, trying to focus. "I'm not particularly good at feigning interest in something—even with so much of my future riding on it."

He takes a long drink from his tumbler, considering. "We can think about it a couple days."

"True."

"The awards ceremony is Sunday morning, right?" He shrugs. "We can talk again then, before I head back to Pennsylvania."

My lips purse in thought, but I don't have a better idea. I don't have a solution, and obviously, neither does he.

I can't fathom a solution that doesn't break Mama's heart.

"Yeah," I finally say. "We'll talk again that afternoon."

When I lie down on my mattress in the dark that night— Mama's already asleep in the other bed—I finally pull out my phone. I'm not going to fall asleep for a while. Not after that evening.

There's a text on the home screen, and I unlock the phone to read the message:

Can we talk?

I half expected a message from Noah after what he surely saw in the hotel restaurant, but it's not him.

It's Tinsley.

I bolt up from the bed and shut myself in the bathroom for privacy. The phone rings as I sit on the toilet lid.

She answers after a couple rings: "Hey." Her voice is soft, hesitant.

"Did I wake you?"

Quiet laughter jars the phone. "It's barely ten. I wasn't sleeping."

I nod, clutching the phone close, clinging to it. "I didn't think...I wasn't sure I'd hear from you."

"Technically, you called me, Edie."

Strangled laughter bubbles from my throat—it's good to hear her use that nickname. "How have you been? What have you been doing since graduation?"

"I'm pretty sure I should be the one asking you questions. You're at REGen for god's sake. This has been your dream for years." Tinsley pauses. "And I'm sorry I'm not there to share it with you like we always planned. I just... needed you to know that."

"I wish you were here too."

"So—" Her voice breaks, and she clears her throat and tries again. "Tell me everything. How have people reacted to your magical microorganisms? What's the competition like? What do you think your chances are?"

I heave a shaky sigh. "Honestly, Tins, there are over two thousand finalists. People have reacted well to my presentation, but I don't know how I could possibly win anything."

"What happened to your confidence, Edie? You made bacteria that eats fucking plastic. How could you not win?"

My cheeks ache from the smile—Tinsley is my stalwart companion, my rock. "I didn't actually make the bacteria," I remind her. "I only bred it in a way to enhance its plastic-eating ability."

"Same diff."

I laugh, and for a long minute, we sit in comfortable silence, even hundreds of miles apart. But there's so much we cannot leave unsaid.

"I'm sorry," I murmur into the phone. "I know I'm not always the best company, and I get really into the things I'm working on and dealing with, and I'm sorry that means you're relegated to second best. I'm sorry I don't listen to you."

"Oh, Edie." Her voice trembles. "Your determination is one of my favorite things about you, don't mistake that. But sometimes, you lose sight of everything else—of everyone else."

She pauses, and I want to speak, but I don't want to interrupt.

"I, um, I've been struggling a lot lately," she finally settles on. "My parents are getting a divorce."

"What?"

"My mom moved out in February."

Oh.

February.

It's the end of May.

She's kept this to herself for three or four months, and I never noticed. I was so focused on myself I never realized anything was wrong.

"I'm sorry. That...really sucks."

On the other line, Tinsley chuckles. "Yeah, it does. I

should have told you what was going on. It's just, with your dad, I didn't feel comfortable."

"Why not? Just because he's…you know—that doesn't mean we can't talk about family. I'm certainly not the only one allowed to have a messed-up home situation."

"I don't know how to bring up family stuff. You never talk about him, and I don't want to pry." She hesitates. "You should visit him. I know it's hard, but he deserves that. You both do."

I take a shaky breath. "Yeah. You're probably right."

With a deep sigh, I pull my feet up onto the toilet seat and rest my chin atop a knee. This isn't the most comfortable position, but there aren't a lot of options. And this is a conversation that should've happened months ago.

"You know," Tinsley says, her words tinged with snark and amusement, "Noah said something interesting at graduation."

"Oh?"

"He mentioned something about a run-in with your mom. Didn't go into more detail, but it didn't sound good." She shuffles on the other end of the line. "And you two stopped talking?"

I wet my lips, uncertain. "Mama found us in my room a couple weeks before graduation. She, um, wouldn't let me see him anymore. She was really upset."

"No offense, but your mom always overreacts when it comes to boys. Remember your boyfriend in sixth grade? She made him cry." She pauses to chuckle. "What were you two doing anyway? Studying alone? How terrible."

I fall silent, unable to put it into words.

"Wait, what were you two doing?"

"We were, uh, indisposed," I whisper. "We weren't…you know, but we were naked."

For a long moment, Tinsley doesn't speak.

Then, she bursts into laughter.

"Not funny, Tins," I snap. "It was embarrassing, and she was so upset, and I…caved. I know what you said before, but I couldn't see her that upset. And unless something drastic happens, even with the Trustee Scholarship, I can't afford Archer Collins."

"So you and Noah broke up."

"I guess." I pause, thinking back to my awkward date downstairs. "Colton Danvers is here, but he's having second thoughts. I have no idea what will happen next."

Tinsley hums thoughtfully. "Edie, you can't let your mom run your life forever. I know she's been struggling since your dad got sick, but that doesn't mean she gets to decide your future."

"I don't want to hurt her more."

"Sometimes, it's the right thing to do." She releases a solemn sigh. "It's your life. Don't you think it's time you took charge?"

CHAPTER 43

NOAH

ETHAN NUDGES MY SIDE. "YOU NERVOUS?"

I try to shrug him off, but he has a point. The awards ceremony is about to start, and I have no idea how my presentation will fare.

Talking to the judges is always the most difficult part—made worse by the fact that there were over a thousand milling about throughout the week.

But Thursday morning really threw me off.

I should've expected the inspiration question. I should've expected someone to ask eventually, even if it wasn't a judge. But I didn't.

I was caught completely off guard.

"Oh, God, you're really nervous."

On his other side, Cliff snorts. "Calm down, String Bean. This isn't your entire future, you know."

But he doesn't get it, doesn't understand.

This is my entire future. Placing in the top five would give me a decent prize, but placing in the top three? That would be phenomenal. That would enable me to attend Archer Collins. Like Mom did. This is the only way I can afford it.

Ethan elbows me again. "Breathe, Noah."

On my right, Dad sits in the folding metal chair in silence. The din of the finalists and their families, of the judges, of the reps, of the press, is overwhelming, but he sits there, eyes meandering the Javits Center, off in his own world.

He hasn't said much the whole week. The four of us share a room upstairs, and he consistently goes to bed right after dinner. When I finally dragged the drunk duo upstairs the other night, he wasn't pleased to be woken by their unruly stupidity.

Ezekiel Strange, the CEO of REGen, takes the stage. He taps the mic before starting his speech. The Javits Center falls eerily silent as all attention turns toward his dark-umber face and impressive hand gesticulations.

His speech is simple. He's not the one in charge of the Talent Search, after all, but it's customary for the CEO to give the opening speech since, you know, his tech company funds the event.

"No matter how the awards are distributed," he adds at the end, "we want to congratulate each and every one of you. Not many students can make it this far. You have all done tremendous work."

The crowd cheers, but the nausea in my stomach insists I disagree with his sentiment. I don't want to be placated.

At least, not till I lose.

"Now, without further ado, please welcome Dr. Vicki Long, Director of REGen's International Science and Engineering Talent Search. Give her a big round of applause for putting this together year after year…"

I clap halfheartedly.

Ethan leans close as the applause abates. "You okay?"

I shrug, trying to stay nonchalant.

"You look a little green."

I shake my head. "I'm not sick."

He stifles a laugh. "Just nervous. I didn't realize you were so competitive, String Bean."

Competitive?

Hardly.

But this is my future. How could I not be nervous?

Especially when this awards ceremony takes so damn long. We're going to sit here forever, waiting.

Instead of listening, I scan the crowd.

She's easy to find, her pretty black hair pulled into a tight bun, a yellow cardigan wrapped around her petite shoulders. They're only a few rows ahead of us. On her right, her mother sits, paying strict attention to the ceremony, and on her left is Colton.

I blink. I can still picture them kissing.

This is not helpful, but I can't take my eyes off them.

What happens if we both attend Archer Collins?

Sure, our majors would be different, but we'd both have to take physics and chemistry classes. She'd focus on biology or ecology, and I'd focus on physics, but we'd be at the same school, often studying in the same building. Maybe living in the same dormitory.

What happens then?

Especially if she's dating him. I never want to see a repeat of that kiss.

Worse, what happens if we don't attend Archer Collins together?

I've rather gotten used to Eden Prince in my life. I'm not ready for us to be far away, even if she dates Colton.

Not that my opinion holds much weight.

Eden made that clear. She moved on. She won't talk to me anymore.

"You know, you're supposed to be listening to the speech, not staring at your girlfriend."

I roll my eyes. "We're not dating."

Ethan smirks. "Then maybe you should ask her out instead of creeping on her."

Heat rises to my cheeks. "I'm not 'creeping' on her, and she obviously already has a boyfriend."

"A date and one kiss do not count."

Cliff snaps his fingers in front of us. "God, will you two shut up?" He shoots us a snarky grin and chuckles at his own joke.

Because there's no way in hell Cliff actually wants to listen to an extensive speech about the origins and importance of a company's own event.

The first section of awards are the category awards. Three students and their projects are chosen per category, plus one honorable mention. When I attended the Talent Search the summer after sophomore year, I won five hundred dollars for honorable mention in the Physics section.

A number of special prizes are also awarded by

third parties. The American Geosciences Institute, the National Institute of Drug Abuse, the American Institute of Aeronautics & Astronautics, the Air Force Research Laboratory, the Environmental Protection Agency, you name it. If it sounds sciencey and it's a big organization, they've probably sponsored an award.

Most of the prizes are a nice sum, but they're nothing compared to the grand prizes, which are only awarded to the top five projects.

It's no surprise when Eden wins first place in Environmental Microbiology, and when they finally make it down to the Physics and Astronomy section, Dr. Vicki Long calls out my name and my project for first place.

I grip Ethan's shoulder as I rise from my seat and glance between him and Cliff. "If you two idiots blow off an air horn again, I'll kill you myself."

Ethan levels me with a challenging gaze. "I would love to see you try."

Without another word, I head for the stage to receive the check and a few handshakes, but I only have eyes for Eden. She watches from the edge of her seat, a long crease marring her pretty forehead, as I take my prize and head back to my seat.

The special prizes come next—I garner a few more awards from several physics and astrophysics organizations, but I wait, impatiently tapping my foot against concrete floor, for the grand prize announcements.

"At long last," Dr. Long says, pausing to flash a smile. "I know you've all been waiting for this moment. We're finally to the grand prize winners." She pauses for dramatic effect. "The REGen Foundation awards these prizes based on the finalist's commitment to authentic research practices, innovation in tackling challenging scientific queries, and creating solutions to the world's problems of tomorrow."

Behind her, the projector shifts to showing the first award: the REGen Foundation's Curious Young Scientists.

"Two finalists, chosen from the group of Best in Category projects, will receive the REGen Foundation's Curious Young Scientist Award, including a twenty-five-thousand-dollar scholarship. This prize is awarded to the finalists who have demonstrated their curiosity, above all else, in the execution and production of their project." Her eyes dart down to her notes, then back to the crowd. "Now, for the twenty-five-thousand-dollar scholarship... In the category of Behavioral and Social Sciences, Santianna Walker from Manchester, England."

A section near the front erupts in rambunctious cheers as she saunters to the stage. She accepts the plaque with tears in her eyes, then pauses for a picture with Ezekiel Strange and Dr. Emmeline Bancroft, one of the other presenters.

"Don't worry so much, String Bean," Ethan murmurs.

Does he think that's helpful?

On stage, Dr. Long continues: "In the category of Physics and Astronomy—"

Ethan claps me on the back, and I hunch over, wincing.

"—Noah Barton from Tourmaline, Maine."

As I rise, Ethan jams two fingers in his mouth and whistles so loudly my ears ring, and on his other side, Cliff stands up for full mobility while clapping.

Like before, I stand near center stage to receive my plaque and take a photo before falling back beside Santianna.

"The REGen Foundation's Innovative Young Scientist Award, along with a fifty-thousand-dollar scholarship, is awarded to the two Best in Category finalists with the most pioneering and revolutionary projects. In the Robotics and Intelligent Machines category, Hunter Sheffield from Morro Bay, California."

Hunter, a particularly tall black guy from the far back, runs up the aisle to receive his plaque before joining us to Santianna's left.

"In the category of Microbiology," Dr. Long says, "Edien Thien Hoang Prince from Tourmaline, Maine."

My eyes zero in on her as she rises from her chair, grinning, and joins us. When she finishes with her photo, she stands beside me, clutching her new plaque to her chest.

"The Arthur E. Whittle Grand Prize Award was named for Arthur Whittle, cofounder of the REGen Corporation in…"

Eden shuffles close enough to rub elbows, her beautiful brown eyes finding mine, and she grins.

"…and the Arthur E. Whittle Grand Prize, with a seventy-five-thousand-dollar scholarship, goes to Aaradhya Mehta from Jaipur, India, in the category of Biomedical Engineering."

The crowd cheers, and I clap along, but I'm not smiling about Aaradhya's award or the prizes we've won. I'm smiling because I've missed seeing Eden happy.

CHAPTER 44

EDEN

Noah disappears in the crowd when the ceremony ends.

I have to see him. I have to talk to him. But I can't do that if he's nowhere in sight—not even with his dad and brothers, since they're looking for him too.

Plaque tucked under my arm, I march down the aisle right past Mama and Colton, waiting for me.

When I find him, he's sitting atop the concrete wall outside the front of the Javits Center, his legs dangling over the side, facing away.

"What are you doing out here?" he asks when I lean against the wall beside him.

I tug my canary-yellow cardigan closer—even in mid-May, the breeze is cold. "Congratulations are in order. Winning a grand prize is amazing in and of itself."

His eyes dart toward the plaque as I set it on the wall

before shifting toward the New York streets. "Not quite as amazing as yours. Congrats."

I shrug—not that he's paying attention. "Well, having good competition certainly helps. Honestly, I'm surprised I beat the kid who did his project to honor his dead national hero mother."

He tenses.

And I cringe. "I said something insensitive again, didn't I?" I heave a sigh and reach for his hand. "I'm sorry."

Finally, he turns to offer me a small smile. "Yeah, but I expect that." Despite the serious topic, he laughs. "Honestly, it's refreshing. You were the only person who still treated me like a regular person. I suppose I should thank you for that."

I try to shrug it off, but the intense look in his eyes draws a blush to my cheeks. "It doesn't mean there's something special about you. I can't pick up on social cues."

"I'm aware, Eden."

"Do you hate me?"

He raises an eyebrow.

I tug my fingers away from his—he wasn't holding me back. "After what happened, I wouldn't blame you. Besides, you've always considered me an annoying, insufferable know-it-all."

"Eden—"

"Let me finish." I cross my arms over my chest to conserve heat and allow my eyes to flutter shut. "When Mama and I talked that night, she was devastated, and I don't know, I said what I knew would calm her down and make her happy, even though it meant hurting you. Even though it meant hurting me."

"You kissed him." Noah's mouth contorts into a scowl as I open my eyes.

I release a shaky breath. "It didn't mean anything."

He shoots me a skeptical sidelong glance. "How?"

"We just...well, I needed to know."

"Know what?"

"That there was nothing there." I lay my arm beside the plaque—my name in all caps—and rest my chin atop my hand. "I shouldn't have to tell you the verdict. It was bland and boring, and he didn't feel anything either."

"Then why is he still here?"

"We agreed to make a decision today—whether we'll date to please our parents, despite our lack of chemistry—but I know what I want. Now, I have to figure out how to break it to Mama." I bite my lip. "Any idea what your verdict is?"

He cocks an eyebrow.

"College. Archer Collins. Can you go?"

Noah heaves a sigh. "Honestly, I don't know. It's not like I expected a better prize, but I don't see how this could be enough."

"You filled out the FAFSA. What about financial aid? Work study?"

He turns to me with a smug grin. "You must really want me to attend Archer Collins."

"Please be serious."

He chuckles then and scoots closer. "I am being serious, Eden. You've seen my house—the financial aid and student loans I'm eligible for aren't nearly enough to pay annual tuition." His hands clench into fists, and he clamps his eyes shut and murmurs, "I'm sorry, I failed, Mom."

"You're not a failure." I reach for him but hesitate. He wasn't welcoming the first time, so why would now be different? "I saw you present your project on Thursday. You were fantastic. Honestly, you should've beaten me." I glance at him, but his eyes are distant—he's staring across the street again. "You know, I think you made an impression on your family."

He snorts. "Yeah, right."

"I'm serious, Noah. Your dad looked...I dunno, emotional."

His mouth contorts into a scowl. "My dad doesn't get emotional. He doesn't have emotions. He didn't get upset when she died. Why would he get emotional about my 'science fair' presentation? It's illogical."

I heave a sigh.

And he's ready to change the subject: "So what are your plans now?"

Even if my perception is accurate, there's no way I can convince Noah his father cares. That's something he has to figure out on his own.

I shrug. "Between this, financial aid, and the Trustee Scholarship, I'm not worried. Right now, Mama says she'll cover anything else, but...well, I haven't talked to her about Colton yet. I doubt her offer will remain once I tell her we aren't interested in pursuing a relationship. God, I don't know if I can talk to her about this. Every time I try, it's a disaster."

He lays his hand over mine and squeezes. "But you need to, Eden. If you never tell her what you want, she'll never know."

I snicker. "That's what Tinsley always says."

"Good. The more people telling you, the more likely you'll listen."

I twist my hand so our fingers thread together. "You say that, but..."

Noah snorts. "But you don't listen to anyone but yourself, right?"

"So what's the verdict, Noah Barton?"

"Hmm?"

When I study his face, he watches me with quiet ice-blue eyes, and I struggle to word the question. "What's the verdict? Do you hate me?"

He chuckles. "I could never hate you. You know that."

Obviously, I don't.

"The truth is, I've liked you for a long time. A lot longer than I realized." His lips twist into an apprehensive smile. "I think I've always liked you."

A blush spreads across my cheeks. "We were never friends until a couple months ago. Why would you like me? I cannot fathom it."

He laughs. "Of course you can't."

"Is that supposed to be an insult, Noah Barton?"

"Perhaps a little bit." His eyes meet mine again, and he grins. "You were the one who kissed me, you know. You made the first move."

I look away. "That was spur of the moment. It didn't mean anything."

"The first time, sure. What about all the times after that? You could barely stop kissing me." A subtle smirk plays on his lips. "Besides, you are an insufferable know-it-all."

I scowl.

Noah twists around and slips off the wall to stand

beside me. When he lands, he's still holding my hand. "But you're also the smartest, most amazing person I know."

"Oh."

He squeezes me. "What?"

I allow myself to look at him again. "Most people don't have that much faith in my abilities. They think I'm irritating, bossy."

"Oh, you're certainly that, but it's cute."

My nose creases in distaste. "I'm not cute."

His eyes crinkle with amusement. "Endearing?"

I chuckle. "I suppose that's better."

"Glad to meet your approval."

A smile spreads across my face. "I wouldn't bet on it, Noah Barton." But I tug him against me and press my mouth to his.

The kiss is slow at first, and he holds me tight in his arms while I take the lead. I push my free hand through his soft hair, the loose blond strands twisting between my fingers, and close any remaining distance between our bodies.

He returns the affection with equal fervor, his arm hooking around my waist, and I do not want this moment to end.

Unfortunately, it has to.

Mostly so I can breathe.

"For the record," I say when I pull back, short of breath, "I don't care what anyone says or thinks."

"Even your mom?"

I shake my head. "I don't want to be with you because you're reliable or financially viable. That doesn't matter. You're the person I want to be with, the person I care about."

He nudges a loose strand of hair behind my ear, his finger pads pausing at my neck, a little smile on his face, and he leans in.

Yet again, I am lost in the kiss, in his arms, in the moment.

When he releases me, he rests his forehead against mine and exhales shakily. "What happens now?"

"Well," I say with a laugh, "we should probably pick up the information about our scholarships, right?"

He rolls his eyes. "I meant with us, Prince."

I lay a chaste kiss on his mouth. "We should start slow."

"We have less than three months till college. How slow?"

"Hmm, fair point." Then, I shrug. "At least give me time to figure out how to tell Mama I have a boyfriend."

Not the boyfriend she wants me to have.

We're barely eighteen, and Noah can't provide for me—and I wouldn't want him to. Because I'm going to make my own way through college, and if we're still together at that point, maybe we'll consider something more permanent.

His fingers trace my jaw, and he draws me into another slow and delicate kiss. "Don't keep me waiting too long, Eden."

For now, all I know is I want to be with him, and I'm ecstatic he wants to be with me too.

CHAPTER 45

NOAH

THE ELEVATOR DOOR CLOSES BEHIND US, AND EDEN presses me against the side of the car and covers my mouth with hers. My hands clutch her waist, gripping her tight. Cold fingers slip under my shirt to count the ribs up my side, and I breathe a shaky sigh through my nose.

No one else was awake yet, so we met for an early breakfast in the hotel restaurant. We weren't hungry. We just wanted time together.

Apparently, we need more privacy than the restaurant provides.

Eden grabs my wrist and guides me to her breast, and when I squeeze, she breaks away to roll her head back. My lips cover her exposed neck with a flurry of kisses.

I could kiss her forever.

The elevator beeps as it comes to a stop, and we tear apart to lean against the wall, side by side, as inconspicuously as possible, as the door slides open.

What floor are we at?

Oh, this is only three.

A small family, two parents, a toddler, and a baby, joins us in the elevator car, and as the door slides shut again, Eden slips her hand into mine and leans against my shoulder, eyes shut, for the rest of the ride.

Both our rooms—and Katherine Elliott's, as it was also booked by the NESEA—are on the same floor, though they're a hallway apart.

The family departs on the eighth floor, then we exit on the next, still holding hands.

I lead the way toward my family's room, as it's the nearest of the two, but she yanks me into another kiss only a few feet before we have to part ways. My fingers entwine in her silky hair, and she pushes up on her tiptoes and wraps her arms around my neck.

This only gets more and more fun as we practice.

She backs me up to the wall—my shoulders hit with a loud *thump*, knocking the air from my lungs, but she doesn't pause.

Not like I mind. I can't get enough of her enthusiasm.

I can't get enough of her.

"...that sound?"

Eden pulls back, and we turn toward the open door, where Ethan casts an inquisitive glance around the hallway before spotting us. Eden flashes him a sheepish smile as she untangles herself from my arms.

Silent, Ethan crosses his arms, and a smug grin spreads across his face.

Dammit.

"You can't say anything," I warn in a quiet voice. "Nobody knows."

"My mom doesn't know," Eden adds for emphasis— that's definitely the conversation we worry about most.

"Yeah, yeah, yeah," Ethan says, waving our concern away. "But you need to come pack, String Bean. Checkout's in less than an hour, and we have some planes to catch."

I heave a sigh but nod. As much as I don't want to part from her, it's necessary. I press a final kiss to her lips, and she relaxes at the open affection.

When we separate, she shoots me a final smile before sauntering down the hallway. Her hips sway with the movement, accentuated by her choice of lace short shorts.

I stare until she's out of view.

"Come on, loverboy." Ethan drags me inside the room by the arm.

The heavy door slams behind us.

Our room is a mess: bedsheets falling off, half the pillows piled by the window, a mass of papers spread across the desk, used towels stretched across one bed, partially packed bags laying in any open space, a random bunch of bananas sitting on the mini-fridge. Cliff is on his hands and knees, searching under the bed, and Ethan immediately returns to work, clearing out the remaining toiletries.

Dad's nowhere to be seen.

Most of my things are already packed. I just have to grab my toothbrush and tuck in my pajamas. My project supplies have been packed and ready since we cleaned up at the Javits Center last night.

Cliff rises from the floor with a victorious laugh, a white phone cord wrapped around his fingers. "Fucking finally."

I stifle a laugh. "Where's Dad?"

"Said he had a call to make," Ethan says, coming out of the bathroom with an armful of random hygiene products. He drops them on the nearest bed and glances between us. "Who do these belong to?"

Cliff chuckles and grabs a couple items. Followed by a couple more, then even more.

Ethan and I glance between each other and laugh.

Of the three of us, Cliff would be the one to use the most grooming products. How else would he impress his girlfriends?

I zip my bag shut, ready to go.

Ethan finishes next, and we watch in amusement as Cliff throws every product from the bathroom into his bag. Good thing he'll check his luggage on his flight back to Oklahoma.

We all have to separate ways at JFK International. Cliff is heading back to his apartment near school, and Ethan is leaving for his individual training, the location of which he cannot disclose—it's the last leg of his application to join the Marine Raiders. Dad and I will take the short plane ride back to Portland, then drive home. The Equinox waits for us in long-term parking at the Portland airport.

When Cliff finishes, I do one final sweep of the room—and grab the bananas—so we can meet Dad downstairs.

Like the drive down to the Portland International Airport, Dad is quiet, though now there's no Ethan or Cliff to fill the awkward silence. The radio plays Elton John as we take the three-hour drive up I-95 to Tourmaline. Neither of us likes Elton John, but neither do we make a move to change the station.

I fiddle with the plaque in my hands, focusing on REGen's company logo. *REGen Foundation Curious Young Scientist* is printed in all caps at the bottom.

The Elton John song comes to a close, but instead of following it with another tune, the deejay starts chatting about summer family vacations.

Dad stretches forward and turns off the radio.

Under my fingers, the cool acrylic front warms. I read it over and over, trying to distract myself from the uncomfortable atmosphere.

Not that I wanted to listen to the deejay, but Dad could've tried a different station instead of this silence.

We've made the drive to Portland for the New England STEM Fair alone many times, but it's never been this strained.

My phone vibrates, but I have it on silent. I tug it from my pocket to check the message—a text from Eden:

I told Tinsley. I'm sure you don't mind.

Just like Eden. Unapologetically upfront and honest, especially when it comes to her best friend.

I never would've expected otherwise, I text back and slide the phone into my pocket.

"Who are you talking to?"

I glance toward Dad, trying to decide how to answer the solemn question. Eden isn't ready to announce our relationship to the world. Not till she figures out how to tell her mom.

So what do I say to Dad?

I clear my throat. "Just a friend."

He doesn't say anything.

In my pocket, the phone vibrates again, but I hesitate to look at it.

"Your mother…" Dad's voice cracks.

I frown at my hands, folded atop the plaque.

"Your mother would be proud of you."

"Thanks."

He flips his blinker on to switch lanes and pass the car ahead of us. "The memorial at Arlington got approved yesterday."

My stomach clenches. I hadn't heard that yet.

"It'll be another month or two before they put everything together. We'll probably have the ceremony near the end of summer. You'll have time, right?"

I nod, emphatic.

Even if it takes longer, even if I've started my first college semester, I will do everything in my power to attend. I doubt Archer Collins—or any other university—would have an issue allowing me a couple days off for my mother's memorial ceremony at Arlington National Cemetery.

"I know I'm not as supportive as she was." He clears his throat. "But you have to understand how difficult it was to be the person left behind. She was gone for three missions, months at a time. Two six-month stints at the International Space Station—and one of them wound up being longer than that."

I remember. There was an issue with switching the crew, and her stay was extended by two months.

"Being an astronaut may be an amazing experience, but

it's anything but amazing for those of us left behind." Dad's eyes focus on the road ahead; he won't look at me. "I know you looked up to her—you still do. You've wanted to be an astronaut since you were little. With most kids, that's a phase, but I suppose most kids don't have an astronaut for a mother."

I release a quiet breath of laughter.

"Still, I'm not sure I could handle losing a son as well as a wife."

I bite my lip, unsure how to respond, what I could say. If I should say anything.

Dad doesn't wait. "I tried to protect you. I know it made things worse, but I don't know what else I was supposed to do. After the New England STEM Fair, after I learned what your project was, I didn't want to come here. Ethan was the one to convince me otherwise."

Finally, I find my voice: "Do you miss her?"

"Of course I do." His eyes dart toward me, then back to the road. "I loved your mother very much. I missed her every time she went on another mission, and I've missed her every minute since she left us. But she's always with us, you know."

"No, Dad. She's dead."

"She's with us in a way. And she would be proud of you."

I'm not convinced of that.

"If you want to attend Archer Collins, I'm happy to help fund your education. The funds are available, and I know you didn't win enough to cover tuition."

I turn to him, wide-eyed. "Even if I want to do what Mom did?"

"Even then."

"You hate the idea of me being an astronaut."

"I hate the idea of you being an astronaut on a deadly mission, Noah." Dad releases a shaky breath. "But your mother would've wanted you to follow your dreams. If you want to become an astronaut, I won't stand in your way."

Unease settles in my stomach. "Why do you never visit her memorial tree at the park?"

He swallows audibly. "It's easier to avoid the memories than admit she's gone. I can tell myself she's on an extended mission, that we'll see her soon. That doesn't mean I don't miss her. Just because I don't show how much I care doesn't mean I don't care." He stretches an arm across to squeeze my shoulder. "I care about both of you dearly. I miss your mom as much as you do."

I reach for his hand, but he pulls away before I can make contact.

"Perhaps it's time."

It has been nearly six months since the disastrous explosion.

"If I wanted to see her memorial at the park, would you consider going with me?" He glances toward me, but he has to focus on the road.

"Yeah." I swallow down the emotions, but tears leak from my eyes. "That would be nice."

CHAPTER 46

EDEN

PHOTOGRAPHS AND SKETCHES ARE PLASTERED OVER THE only wall devoid of furniture. Images from my childhood. Images of me growing up. My first chemistry set. Winning my NESEA award. Images of our family, though Papa isn't in many of them. The sketches, though, seem to be something he started to pass the time.

I rise from the chair for a closer look.

The photos are overwhelming on close inspection. There's easily twenty years of memories on the wall— images of Mama and Papa's wedding, photos from Vietnam while Papa was still the ambassador, baby pictures. So many things I wasn't born for or don't remember.

Yet, there's already several images of me winning the REGen Innovative Young Scientist Award only a week ago, even a photo of me with the four other grand prize winners—Noah right at my side.

I smile at the image.

We don't have any photos of us together. It's been a week since we returned to Tourmaline, and the only people who know are Tinsley and Noah's oldest brother—and Ethan left.

The summer before college should be our summer to relax and goof off without worrying about classwork yet, but the only time we have together is when Mama works. Her schedule varies; it's unreliable.

"Papa," I call over my shoulder. "Did Mama tell you about these when she put them up?"

Slowly, he joins me at the wall. His wall.

"This one," I say, pointing out the biggest photo of me with my Innovative Young Scientist plaque, grinning at the camera.

He leans forward, examining the image with pursed lips. "Hmm, no. Is that you, Linh?"

"No, Papa, it's me." My voice quietens. "It's Eden. Thien."

But he shakes his head. "Linh is the prettiest girl I ever met. Smart, persuasive, incredibly kind. But I don't think she likes me very much."

I frown. "Why not?"

He chuckles. "Look how lovely she is. Out of all her suitors, why would she choose me?"

"She loves you, Papa," I murmur, though according to her own words, the love came later—at least on her part.

Laughter bursts from his mouth then. "Why, I would move Heaven and Earth to make that true. You're very sweet…" He turns his hazel eyes on me and frowns. "What did you say your name was again?"

I take a shaky breath and force a smile. "I'm your daughter, Eden."

He nods, but there's no recognition in his eyes.

I avert my eyes, turning instead toward the small table, where his cup of peppermint tea remains untouched. I drank most of mine earlier. "Papa, are you going to drink your tea?"

Papa scoffs. "I don't know why they keep bringing me tea. Never liked the stuff. And they deny me coffee."

"You can't have that much caffeine anymore. Your blood pressure."

"My blood pressure's fine," he snaps, returning to his chair at the small table. He pushes the full mug away. "I've never had anything worse than one twenty over eighty."

I frown. That hasn't been true in years.

Instead of saying anything, I take my seat at the table again and slurp down the remaining droplets of my tea, and an unsettling silence fills the room again.

Mama sits in the waiting room when I walk out. She came with me, waited here to give us some privacy. I'm not sure whether it was better this way or if having her in the room would have been an improvement. Neither would have made his early-onset Alzheimer's better.

She rises from her seat and drops the magazine on the end table. "Ready?"

I nod.

Mama takes a moment to thank a couple staff members—their badges say Amy and Melissa—before we head out to the car.

"I thought we might have Bún bò Hué for dinner." She eyes me as she starts the car.

I frown. "What's the occasion, Mama?"

Not that Bún bò Hué is an uncommon meal, but it takes more prep time than she typically devotes to dinner.

Mama offers me a sad smile. "I thought you might want something special tonight."

The drive home is slow. The nursing home is on the outskirts of Tourmaline, and Mama drives at a leisurely pace five below the speed limit.

"What do you think of inviting Colton to stay for a week at the end of the month?" She casts a quick look in my direction before turning onto our road. "It's a shame to spend so much time together, then suddenly not see each other again, don't you think?"

Yes, but that has nothing to do with Colton.

"Maybe," I say, trying to stay noncommittal.

Mama frowns. "You are attending Archer Collins to be near him, Thien." She pauses. "Would you rather visit him there instead? He wouldn't have to worry about missing his internship while spending time with you."

It's the beginning of June now, and classes at Archer Collins begin the Tuesday after Labor Day. That's three months away, but every missed opportunity, every forgotten day, is wasted time I could have talked to her.

We pull into the driveway, and she turns to me expectantly.

But I can't give her the answer she wants.

"That's not why I'm attending Archer Collins, Mama." Her mouth falls open. "What?"

I push open my door, and she follows suit. "I'm not attending Archer Collins to be closer to Colton," I say as we head up the steps. "Archer Collins is the best science and engineering school on the East Coast. I don't even like Colton."

"What are you talking about, Thien?" She pushes past me, keys in hand, to unlock the front door, and we slip inside the house.

I hesitate, but now that I've started, I can't stop. "The Trustee Scholarship I received will help me pay for it as long as my GPA is above 3.5." I lean against the door, closing it all the way. "Financial aid and my REGen award scholarship will cover the rest. You don't have to worry about me."

Mama turns to me, creases at her eyes and forehead. "Who will provide for you?" She lays her hands on my shoulders, studying my face. "Someone has to take care of you."

I square my shoulders. "I'll take care of myself, Mama. I'm going to make the world a better place, help create a better future."

A wan smile spreads across her tight features. "You already make the world a better place, Thien. Just by existing."

"I want to do more."

"I know."

"And that's the thing." I take a shaky breath. "I know you want to make sure I'm okay, but I want more than that. I have so many plans for my future, and I'm not...ready for a serious relationship."

Mama's smile remains in place, but she swallows.

"That said"—here, I pause—"I do have a boyfriend."

She releases me slowly. "Who?" There's an edge to her voice.

"Noah. He's attending Archer Collins in the fall too." My eyes fall to the floor, but I have to defend him before she blames him for my choices, my decisions. "He's the kindest, most supportive person I know, and I will not yield on this."

Mama heaves a sigh. "Oh, Thien, you've become a remarkable young woman, so like your father. Why did you keep this from me?"

I wet my lips. "I didn't want to disappoint you again."

"I don't want you keeping secrets from me—ever." Her breath quivers. "I'm sorry I made you think you had to."

At last, I look up to meet her gaze again, and she pulls me into a tight embrace.

CHAPTER 47

NOAH

EDEN'S TREMBLING FINGERS ENTWINE WITH MINE AS WE meander the Tourmaline City Park. The area is quiet and calm—the weather hasn't turned particularly warm yet, but many of the trees and shrubs are covered in flowers and freshly sprouted leaves. It's springtime.

"Thanks for listening," she murmurs, squeezing my hand. "I don't mean to put all this on you."

I stop at the edge of the trail. "You're not. Don't worry about that." A smile tugs at my mouth when her brown eyes turn to me. "Besides, it's kind of important to know you told your mom about us, right?"

She smiles. "I guess."

I step close, and my fingers trace along her temple. "And I'm glad you visited your dad. I know how difficult that must've been."

Eden's eyes flutter shut, and she leans into the touch.

"Mama wants to meet you properly, get to know you."

"Should I be worried?"

"A little." She presses a kiss to my palm. "But we'll be able to meet openly." She closes the distances between us and covers my mouth with hers. "Not that I haven't enjoyed our secret rendezvous."

I chuckle and pull her into another kiss, mimicking many of those rendezvous, relishing her smooth lips and her wandering hands.

When we finally break apart, Eden's breathless. "Do you want me to stay? I don't mind."

"Nah." Not that I don't want her to. "It's Saturday. Didn't your mom want to do lunch?"

She pauses, taking a moment to catch her breath. "Yeah, but I want to stay."

I wrap an arm around her waist and press my nose to her cheek, but the embrace is short-lived.

"Maybe you can come over for dinner," I say, searching her eyes. "Watch a movie or something afterward?"

"Sounds like a plan." She presses another quick kiss to my lips and untangles herself from my grip. "I'll see you tonight then."

Eden heads for the parking lot, where her white Prius waits, and I walk in the opposite direction.

Toward the white ash sapling.

Dad isn't here yet, so I sit on the grass near the base of the small tree and examine the plaque. The metal is dirty now, but the words remain clear: *In memory of Dr. Genevieve Barton, National Hero.*

"Hey, Mom."

I still visit this memorial a couple times a week, but

between preparing for college and hanging out with Eden, there isn't enough time.

"Sorry I've been away." I chuckle. "I'm sure you understand, though. You were busy my entire childhood, no matter what was going on."

The ground crunches, and I turn to find Dad, carrying a bouquet of white lilies—Mom's favorite.

He crouches beside me and leans forward to lay the flowers between the plaque and the base of the sapling. "Sorry I'm late." He wraps an arm around my shoulders with a tight smile. "Six months late."

Six months already. Six months since the *Endurance* deteriorated upon reentry. Six months since you left us, Mom.

"What do you do when you come here?" Dad asks.

I shrug one shoulder. "Talk to her. Tell her what's going on in my life. Cry."

He nods. "And I imagine you already gave her an update?"

"Not really." I take a deep breath and try to relax. "I got my roommate assignment for the dorms. His name is Simon. We've exchanged a few messages, and he seems alright." I bite my lip, trying to think of something. "Talked to Ethan the other day. He's three weeks into his individual training, and he decided now is a good time to start a long-distance relationship. But that's a whole other thing."

It's strange to have an audience, but maybe it's time to invite Dad into my life as well.

"I, uh…I have a girlfriend."

Dad stiffens but doesn't speak.

"Eden. You met her a few times, mostly at the STEM

fairs. And you know, it's Tourmaline—everyone knows everyone. She's really smart, and she's funny, and we're both attending Archer Collins in the fall." I shrug to loosen my muscles, but it's not very effective. "We haven't been together long, so I don't know how serious it is, but I really like her."

Dad squeezes my shoulders, leaning closer. "Did he tell you he won a scholarship at the REGen Talent Search?"

I did, but I have no intention of interrupting him. Not when he's finally talking to her.

"That's the best he's ever done. You'd be so proud of him—as proud as I was. Ethan and Cliff came out to see the presentation, and we drove down to Portland and flew to New York together, as a family."

I lean into Dad's arm. "I, um, actually got a letter asking me to do a speech about my software at JPL for NASA."

"You did?"

I nod.

"That's amazing." Dad releases an uncomfortable laugh. "See how brilliant our son is, Ginny?"

And I smile.

When we rise from the ground a few minutes later, Dad leads the way to the car, his arm still slung around my shoulders. "When did you and Eden start dating?"

"At the Talent Search. I should've told you."

He shrugs. "Glad to hear she sorted things out," he murmurs, then continues in his regular voice: "I like her; she's smart enough to keep up with you—not many can."

I release a soft chuckle. "What are dinner plans? Can she come eat with us?"

"Sure." We reach the car, and he unlocks it with the key

fob. "I'd like to know her better if the two of you are going off to college together."

"We talked about watching a movie afterward. Hanging out, you know." I climb into my seat, closing the door behind me, and buckle up.

Dad sends me a sidelong glance. "Hmm, let's stop at the store."

I frown. "Why?"

He starts the engine with a blank face. "You need to be prepared. We're buying you those condoms."

"Dad, we're not…" My cheeks flush, and I avoid eye contact. "That's not necessary."

He shifts the car into reverse and checks his mirrors before backing up. "You don't want to be caught unawares, Noah. We'll stop on the way home."

I run a hand through my hair and heave a sigh. "You're going to embarrass me at dinner, aren't you?"

He shrugs instead of answering.

Yes, he will.

I wouldn't want it any other way.

ACKNOWLEDGMENTS

First, I must thank the intelligent, ambitious people who allowed this book to come to fruition without realizing how helpful they are. Noah's project was inspired by the brilliant Erika DeBenedictis, who won first prize at the Intel International Science and Engineering Fair for her computer science project in 2007. Eden's project was inspired by Daniel Burd, who isolated plastic-eating microorganisms for his paper *Plastic Not Fantastic* in 2008. Both Erika and Daniel made significant contributions to the scientific community as teenagers, and we can only hope they will do more with their talents and skills than help an author write a romance book.

Thank you to my family and loved ones for your eternal support and kindness. Thank you especially to my husband, who works long hours and then comes home to take care of our little boys to make sure I have time to work as well. Thank you to my critique partner Sam, who always listens to my story ideas, helps me brainstorm problems, and tells me what works and what doesn't. Thank you to my cover designer Sarah, who continually works her butt off to make the most amazing covers and who squees over them as much as I do. And of course, thank you to my readers for taking the time out of their busy schedules to read this emotional little book.

DISCUSSION QUESTIONS

1. How does this book make you feel?

2. What is your favorite aspect of the book? Why?

3. What is your least favorite aspect of the book? Why?

4. Which character stands out to you the most? What attribute or characteristic draws you to them?

5. Who in the book would you like to meet? What would you ask or say?

6. Where do you see the characters in six months? A year? Five years? Ten?

7. What are some of the major themes of the book? Are they well-developed?

8. What quotes, passages, or scenes did you find most compelling?

9. How did this book change you? Do you have a new perspective or learn something from reading this?

10. How does the book reflect the original Cinderella fairy tale?

11. Where does the book differ from the original tale?

12. What about the book makes it sex-positive? What does the sex-positivity add to the story?

A NOTE ON THE AUTHOR

D. L. Pitchford is a wife and mother of two, living in Springfield, Missouri. She graduated from Drury University with a Bachelor's in English, Writing, and Fine Arts in 2013.

Learn more at:
www.DLPitchford.com

A NOTE ON REVIEWS

If you enjoyed this book, please consider leaving a review on Amazon, Goodreads, or Bookbub. Reviews are like food for authors. This is not an instance where you shouldn't feed the wildlife. Please feed the starving artists with your reviews.